WHAT FOLLOWS

A Novel
by Antonio Michell

I want to thank four women in my life. First, I want to thank my beautiful wife, Knaee, and six-year-old daughter, Riley. Their understanding and patience as I hovered over the computer to write this novel was tremendous. Their support is unwavering. Secondly, I want to thank my mother, Karen, and sister, Ashlee. They were always available for feedback and copyedits. Their efforts have been invaluable.

PROLOGUE

Let me see your hands

The year is 2018. It is a typical summer night in Seat Pleasant, Maryland. The darkness is illuminated by streetlights, glowing store signs, passing car lights, and the occasional swirling of red and blue as police cars zoom by. The air has started to cool from the day but is still heavy, thick with humidity. A police car is parked on the side of a dark road. The officer inside is waiting. Eventually a car will speed by and he will give them a ticket. Until then, he will monitor the police radio. A call comes in. A robbery is in progress at a nearby gas station. The officer feels anxious. His body tenses. His muscles feel tight. Another unit is en route to the gas station, five minutes out; their backup should arrive moments later. His post tonight is traffic so he stands down and waits for the next update. Then he hears it from the dispatcher.

"Two suspects have fled the scene. They are headed east on Seat Pleasant Drive in a black SUV with tinted windows. Maryland tags. Tag number unknown. They are considered armed and dangerous. Approach with caution."

The officer's heart is punching through his chest. He feels as if adrenaline has replaced the blood in his body. They are headed right toward him. His car engine is on and ready. His gun is holstered on his hip and his clip is fully loaded; he checked.

Less than two minutes later, a black SUV with dark tinted windows passes the officer. He immediately turns on the lights and siren and begins pursuit. Moments later, the SUV pulls over. The police officer radios dispatch that he has the possible suspect vehicle pulled over and requests backup. Afraid the suspects will flee, the officer does not wait for the second unit to arrive before engaging the occupants. The entire encounter will not last three minutes. The officer scrambles for his bullhorn while keeping his eyes fixed on the vehicle. Using the bullhorn, the officer instructs the driver to turn off the engine and stick both hands out of the window while keeping them open and visible. He instructs the passenger to do the same. Inside the SUV is a young, black male driver accompanied by a young, black female passenger in the front and an infant in the back seat.

The passenger turns to the driver.

"Were we speeding?" she asks with a worried inflection in her voice.

"No, I don't think so. Don't worry. Everything will be fine. We haven't done anything wrong."

The driver and passenger roll down their windows to comply with the request. The police officer exits his patrol car with his gun drawn and pointed at the SUV. He leaves his taser on the passenger seat. The officer slowly approaches the SUV.

"Passenger, lift your hands in the air and keep them up and open so I can see them from this side of the vehicle," yells the officer.

The passenger complies.

"Driver, use your left hand to open the car door from the outside. Slowly."

The driver complies.

"Now, step out of the vehicle while keeping your hands visible at all times."

The passenger is frightened. Her internal panic is manifesting outwardly. She is shaking.

The driver's side door inches open and the driver steps out of the vehicle. The police officer orders him to step out slowly. As the young man emerges from the vehicle, an object falls from his lap to the ground. Instinctively, he bends down to pick it up. Even with the spotlight from the officer's vehicle illuminating the darkness, the officer cannot make out what the driver is reaching for.

"Hands! Let me see your hands!" shouts the officer. The young male is already on his way back up with the object. The officer sees a glare from what appears to him to be a metal object resembling a weapon in the driver's right hand. He focuses the aim of his gun.

"Wait! It's my phone!" shouts the now panicked driver.

At the very moment the driver shouts "phone," the sound of two gunshots ring out. Pop! Pop! A small fog of smoke hovers above the officer's gun and then, in an instant, dissipates into the night. The phone slides from the young man's hand as it goes limp. The passenger lets out an ear-piercing wail as she witnesses the driver's body fall and bounce off of the unforgiving ground. His body is lifeless.

"You shot him! Oh my God! You FUCKING SHOT HIM! For what? Dear God! No! Charles! Charles!" hollers the passenger through a sudden influx of tears submerging her face.

The infant is crying in the background.

Charles lies motionless. His body still warm. For a moment—a brief, *almost missable* moment—he looks peaceful. But the cement's red stain emerging from underneath his body tells a different story.

WHAT FOLLOWS

1

PG PROBLEMS

It is nighttime at a quaint boutique hotel in Orlando, Florida. The PG Problems, an AAU basketball team from Prince George's County, Maryland, are walking down the hotel hallway. The thick, regal, royal blue carpet, with a gold crisscross pattern resembling rows of three-tier crowns, leads the way to the last door at the end of the bare-walled, eggshell painted hallway. They knock on the door to their coach's suite.

Coach Craig Knight is expecting them. He opens the door without inquiring who is there. The first player through the door is Dink "Big Dink" Johnson. Big Dink is ranked fourth among the nation's high school centers and has verbally committed to play basketball at the University of North Carolina. He is tall. Exceptionally tall. But for a center, his six-foot, eleven-inch stature is average. That is the only thing average about him. He is a big guy. A big, powerful guy. He is built like

Shaquille O'Neal circa 1997. Every aspect of Big Dink looms large, from his personality to the magnetic smile that lights up his boyish face. He is the color of dark cherrywood.

Next to enter the room is Maximus "Mad Max" Miller. Mad Max holds the number five national ranking for high school point guards and is still undecided where he will play in college. Mad Max, with a head of large, dark brown curls tamed by a neat cut, has earned his sculpted shoulders through dedicated effort in the weight room. His thick dark eyebrows are a contrast to his coffee colored complexion. His six-foot, four-inch frame makes him smaller than most of his teammates.

Following Mad Max is Bobby "Bird" Banks. Bird is nationally ranked number seven for high school small forwards and has verbally committed to Gonzaga University. Bird, at six feet, nine inches, keeps his dirty blond hair in a crew cut and has piercing blue eyes that belie his easygoing nature.

The rest of the team files into Coach Knight's room. Just as the door is about to close, it stops, pushes back open, and one final player enters. It is Chance Knight, the number one ranked high school shooting guard in the nation. He is also the number one overall rated player and is projected to be the number one pick in the 2020 NBA draft. He has yet to commit to a school. Chance is six feet, seven inches tall. His skin is the color of caramel with a dark chocolate undertone. He has an air of confidence that is sometimes mistaken for arrogance.

The team is fresh off of their win at Georgia's NIKE EYBL Peach Jam Tournament, which hosts the best players in the nation.

The players take a seat joining the assistant coaches already in the room. Chance observes the coach's shirt and rolls his eyes in silent disapproval of its faded appearance and fabric worn down so much that its threads barely hold on to each other.

"Everyone listen up," says Coach Knight.

He reaches for the remote control to turn off the television. Before he can press the off button, a breaking news banner about an unarmed black male shot and killed by a police officer in front of his wife and newborn daughter appears on the screen. The entire basketball team and the coaches still their bodies.

"Not another one," says Chance as he shakes his head in disgust.

The newscaster begins to speak.

"We have breaking news coming in. There appears to have been another shooting of an unarmed black male. Let's cut to our affiliate network's on scene reporter, Angela Acosta."

"Thank you, Dan. Tonight an unarmed black male was shot and killed in front of his wife and infant by a police officer during a traffic stop. The shooting took place in Seat Pleasant, a city located in Maryland's Prince George's County. This is all the information we have that can be confirmed right now. This is a developing story and we will bring you updates as they become available."

The downcast facial expressions of the players and coaches mirror one another. Coach Knight turns the television off and addresses his players.

"How many times have we seen this shit over the past couple of months, even years? And this one happened not far from where we live. Basically in our backyard. In a blink of an eye everything can be taken away from you. It's bad enough that we're killing one another. Black men killing black men. Black boys killing black boys. On top of that, we're being killed by the police—law enforcement that's supposed to serve and protect citizens.

"If I don't teach y'all anything else, remember this: if you get pulled over by the cops, do whatever's necessary to stay alive," he says as he elevates his voice. "Your *only* job is to stay alive. I don't care if you didn't do a damn thing wrong. It's not the time to try and prove your innocence. You can do that later. I repeat, your *only* job is to stay alive. Don't talk back. I don't care if you were walking your mutha fuckin' puppy, or helping an old lady across the street. If the cops stop you, then I want you to be cooperative. It's life or death.

"Keep your hands where they can see them at all times, and never *ever* resist in any way. Unless you want to end up dead, it should be 'Yes, sir' or 'Yes, ma'am.' Y'all hear me?"

"Yes, sir," the players respond quietly in unison.

"I know it's hard after watching what we just saw, and it gets more disturbing with each instance we hear about, but let's get our focus back on tomorrow's game. I know we typically blow our opponents out of the gym, but this is the AAU National Championship. This ain't no cakewalk. This game ain't no gimme. The players you're about to face are among the best of the best. Remember, they were the prohibitive favorites to win the Peach Jam tournament. Unfortunately for them, but fortunately for us, they weren't able to make it. Because they missed that tournament, they're even more eager to try and claim their spot as AAU national champions tomorrow.

"Every big time college scout will be in attendance. I want y'all to clear your minds, get some rest, and focus on the task at hand. This game is yours, but only if you work for it. Two of the players we're facing have already committed to UNC and Duke. One of them, as you already know, is Chance's cousin Mike. They didn't come to lose. These guys mean business. Remember that. Don't get lazy. Don't get cocky.

"One last thing for tomorrow. I know the president continues his tweets about kneeling for the anthem being disrespectful to our country and that it shouldn't be tolerated. Colin Kaepernick started kneeling for the anthem to protest police brutality and social injustice; to protest incidents like what we just heard about tonight.

"The president changed the narrative and falsely made it about patriotism and the military. That couldn't be further from the truth. The reason we kneel is to bring awareness to injustices and to ultimately make our country better. Kneeling gives us a voice. It's a silent protest but still very much heard. Kneeling will continue until being heard leads to actions that preserve lives—black and brown lives."

Coach Knight pauses, first staring at Chance with intensity, then scanning the rest of the team as he goes on.

"So y'all know how I feel in regards to kneeling. If you want to kneel, stand, lock arms, put a fist up or whatever, it's totally up to you. I support you either way. These coward NFL owners are blackballing Kaep 'cause he took a knee. You have the president calling NFL players who take a knee *sons of bitches*. Yet he refers to the white nationalists at the Charlottesville rally as fine people. He bullies NFL owners into forcing their players to stand for the anthem. That's why it's so important for us as a people to be the decision makers, the owners, the presidents, the ones with the power.

"I want you guys to always think about that in life. No matter what you go on to do, be the owner or the decision maker. I'm the coach of this AAU team and I'm telling you that you can make your own decision and do whatever it is you want to do during the national anthem. Bird, even though you're white, we consider you one of us and I know you do too."

"Damn right, Coach," says Bird nodding in agreement.

"Now go get some rest. Curfew is in effect starting now. See you downstairs in the morning for breakfast. Eight thirty sharp."

The players and assistant coaches file out.

"Chance. Wait a sec. I want to talk to you."

"All right. But, Pops, why you always wearing that old ass Howard University shirt? I mean, damn. Look at it. Do you ever take it off? You wear it so much that it's literally about to disintegrate."

Amused, Coach Knight, "Pops" to Chance and his younger sister, Amaia, responds.

"I'll stop wearing it once you commit to being a Bison and play ball at Howard. Until then, I want you to see this shirt every day so that Howard's constantly on your mind during your decision process."

"Pops, I've told you Howard's facilities can't compete. They've got nothin' on big schools like Kentucky and Duke."

"How do you know? When have you seen Howard's facilities? And when have you seen Kentucky's or Duke's? Last I checked you haven't been on any college visits yet. And Howard facilities might not have everything you want, but they certainly have everything you need."

"When's the last time the basketball team won an NCAA tourney game? Oh wait, the answer's never. And I wasn't even alive the last time they made it to March Madness."

Chance pauses briefly before speaking again.

"And their games are rarely ever televised. Not to mention, when was the last time any Howard basketball player went pro? Man, please. Never gonna happen, Pops. Plus, you hold practically every basketball record at Howard. Why would you want me to go there and shatter all your four-year records in my one year there before I go pro? That'd be disrespectful."

Chance laughs.

"Yeah, yeah, whatever," Coach Knight says dismissively but light-heartedly.

His tone changes.

"One other thing before I let you go get some rest. This shit we heard on TV tonight is a major issue for people who look like us. The continued police killings of unarmed black people have to stop. But there's no support from our so-called president. There's a hateful MAGA mentality that exists where anything goes. You need to be very aware of your surroundings and the situations you put yourself in. Always remember what I just told you guys about interacting with the cops. Any injustices or mistreatment by the cops can be taken up after the fact. Remember, in that moment, your main concern is staying alive. You don't want to give that cop any excuse whatsoever. I'm not about to let you be their next victim, Son."

Chance assures his father that he understands. The love between the two men hovers in the air in the brief silence that follows. Chance gives his father dap and then they do their signature handshake with a quick pull-in one-armed hug.

"Good night, Son. Wreak havoc on them mutha fuckas tomorrow."

2

FUCK CANCER

An anxious crowd sits on the sidelines waiting for the tip off of the AAU National Championship game at the HP Field House in Kissimmee, Florida, near Orlando. ESPN's Field House is part of their multisports facilities that sit on 255 acres within the Walt Disney World Resort.

The PG Problems are facing off against The Wood from Inglewood, California. While the PG Problems are stacked with four- and five-star recruits, The Wood has two five-star recruits of their own. Their star player is Mike Jones. He is the number one rated high school power forward in the nation and has verbally committed to Duke University. Behind him is Jason "J.J." Jacks, the number three rated point guard in the nation. He has verbally committed to the University of North Carolina. Individually, they are remarkable players. Together, they are almost unstoppable. Mike, although a tall and solid specimen, moves his body with ease and an unusual quickness for someone of his stature—allowing him to outmaneuver his defender to get into position for the ball. And Jason has an impeccable knack of passing to Mike every time he is open and in position to score. Their dynamic is not lost on the PG Problems. They acknowledge this will be the toughest competition they have ever faced.

Coach Knight and his players are in the locker room reciting "The Lord's Prayer." As soon as the last "Amen" is uttered, he moves right into his pre-game speech.

"All right, fellas. As Vince Lombardi once said, 'Winning isn't everything, it's the only thing.' Go out there and win this championship. Claim what's yours. Let's go!"

The Spanish style arena, with its 5,500 seats completely filled, is both impressive and intimidating for the two teams as they warm up. The time on the scoreboard is counting down, nearing 00:00 on the pre-game clock. It is almost time for the PG Problems to solidify the legend they are building as the greatest AAU team in recent history and their title as the number one team in the nation.

Everyone in the stadium is asked to rise for the singing of the national anthem. The PG Problems, along with the coaching staff, lock arms and, together, drop down to one knee. Coach Knight's heart is full.

The game begins with Big Dink securing the jump ball and quickly passing it down court to Mad Max. Mad Max takes a few dribbles and sees Chance running down the left side toward the basket. As Chance approaches, Mad Max gently releases the ball into the air near the basket and Chance slams it down. The alley-oop sets the stage for the game. Although Mike and J.J. keep The Wood within reach, they are never able to stir a panic in their opponent. The game ends the same way it began, with Mad Max initiating an alley-oop to Chance. The crowd in the packed arena is in awe of the talent they just witnessed and the ease with which The PG Problems are able to decisively win the AAU National Championship. Chance is named tournament MVP. Coach Knight's already full heart nearly bursts.

The players and coaches raucously retreat to the locker room with the exception of Chance and his father. They remain on the court, savoring the moment.

"I'm so proud of you, Son," says Coach Knight.

"Thanks, Pops. I wouldn't be here if it weren't for the sacrifices you and Mom have made. I'll never forget it."

A reporter suddenly approaches.

"Chance, Coach, may I have a brief on-air interview?" she asks.

Coach Knight readily agrees.

"Chance, let's get right to what probably every college scout in this arena wants to know. Have you decided where you're going to play ball next year?"

"Actually, I've narrowed it down to three schools: Maryland, Duke, and Kentucky."

"I'm sure you've just made those schools extremely happy, and a lot of others very disappointed. As a Tar Heel alumni, I encourage you to reconsider."

Chance laughs. The reporter smiles and pivots to Coach Knight.

"As Coach and Dad, what's your preference?"

"H-UUUUUUUUUU," drawls Coach Knight in a deep cadence. "Howard University, my alma mater."

The reporter smiles again and redirects her attention to Chance.

"And what do you have to say about that?"

"First off, I would never play ball at Howard because it would crush me to have to break all my pops' records. Pops played all four years. It would really be embarrassing if I broke all of his records in my one and only year there before going pro."

They all share a good laugh, Coach Knight with a little less enthusiasm. Father and son make their way to find Mike and J.J.

The entire team and coaching staff are enjoying a boisterous post game celebration at Tony's Pizzeria.

"I've never seen so many pizzas consumed by one set of guests," their waiter jokes with the group. The players cheer and raise their slices of pizza in jest.

Chance sits across from his best friend since third grade, Walt Williams. Walt, through his dark-rimmed eyeglasses, looks at Chance.

"Bruh, you played a hell of a game tonight. Mr. Triple Double: forty-three points, twelve assists, and ten rebounds. You were doin' your thang, man."

"Thanks, bro, and you did a hell of a job clappin' and cheerin' for me on the bench. And the time you got me my water bottle was da shit," Chance says jokingly.

"Man, fuck you, bro. See, I try to give you a sincere compliment and all you can do is clown a brotha. I know I rode the bench, but that's okay, though. I just sat there while you did all the work and after the game I collected the same damn championship trophy as you. So thank you. I appreciate you, my brotha."

"Whateva dude."

Chance laughs.

Coach Knight stands up at the table.

"All right, fellas, listen up. I hope you enjoyed this celebration. I'm so proud of you guys."

As Coach Knight continues speaking, Walt's phone vibrates on the table. He grabs it, gets up, and motions to Coach Knight that he has to take the call. He heads outside.

Walt's mother's voice is anguished. His little brother's test results have come back. Leukemia. Chemotherapy in two weeks. Walt drops the phone and sits on the curb. He tries to wrap his head around what this could mean. Walt thinks, "Not my mini-me, not Teddy." Tears stream down the big guy's round face.

Back inside the pizzeria, Coach Knight is wrapping up his speech to the team.

"You all deserve this because you worked extremely hard for it. Hard work normally pays off in whatever you do in life. If it doesn't, then at least you can walk away knowing you did everything you possibly could. I couldn't be any prouder of you guys and I love each and every one of you. Looking forward to continuing the celebration tomorrow at Disney World!"

The players high-five and return the accolades. "We love you, too, Coach," shouts one of the players.

As Coach begins to take his seat he glances outside of the window and notices Walt sitting on the ground. He heads straight for the door and seconds later finds himself on the curb next to Walt.

Barely able to get his words out, Walt manages to tell Coach Knight what is wrong.

"Teddy's got cancer, Coach. He's got cancer and it's bad."

Coach Knight, a father figure to Walt ever since his dad passed away a few years ago, holds him tightly and offers a prayer. The day's celebration is over.

3   LICENSE AND REGISTRATION, PLEASE

The Knight family is comfortably settled into their 2016 black Chevy Tahoe heading home from Baltimore Washington International Airport after an uneventful flight. Traffic is unusually light on the Interstate 95 corridor. Coach Knight, mindful of the speed limit, is driving. Mrs. Knight, a five-foot, nine-inch slender figure with a slinkiness to her limbs, sits stiffly in the passenger seat. Chance maneuvers his long legs in the back seat as he listens to Amaia's rather startling loud snoring for such a petite thirteen-year old.

"I can't imagine what Walt's family is going through," Mrs. Knight says turning to her husband.

"Yeah, Walt was in really bad shape last night, understandably so."

"It's really hard on everyone," Chance says. "It kills me to see him like this. I remember the day Teddy was born. Walt was so excited. He finally had a little brother. He joked that he was going to mold Teddy in his image. For God's sake, Teddy just turned seven last month. It's just not right."

Silence envelops the car. There is nothing else to be said.

Chance takes a moment to appreciate his annoying little sister. The top of her chin-length, tightly-coiled hair slow dances in the air squeezing into the car through a barely cracked window. These are the moments that remind him to be grateful.

As they drive through Prince George's County heading to Capital Heights, one of the roughest sections of the county, Chance stares out of the window deep in thought. He imagines moving his family to Potomac, Maryland, where his father could spend his retirement playing golf at one of its exclusive country clubs, even if he has to relocate his father kicking and screaming. They live in the better part of Capital Heights, a tree-lined street with detached homes and manicured lawns. His father works for a non-profit organization in Northern Virginia and his mother is a kindergarten teacher. Chance knows that they could have moved to a better area in the county, Mitchellville or Upper Marlboro. But his father is committed to improving their neighborhood—the neighborhood he grew up in—by cultivating programs to help at-risk youth, and is an active member of the neighborhood watch group. Chance's eyes eventually begin to close as he drifts off to sleep to the sound of nighttime traffic.

A blaring police siren behind the Knight's vehicle abruptly interrupts the silence in the SUV. Chance and Amaia are startled out of their sleep. Through his rear view mirror, Coach Knight sees the flashing lights. He tells everyone to stay cool as he pulls the vehicle over.

"Craig, it sure didn't feel like we were speeding," says Mrs. Knight.

"We weren't. But don't panic, April."

A tall, chubby, red-headed police officer steps out of his vehicle and walks toward the Knight's SUV. Coach Knight rolls down the driver's side window as the officer approaches. Each mindful of the increasing occurrence of black lives being cut short at the hands of police officers, the Knights are gripped by fear.

"Good evening, sir. License and registration, please," the police officer says in a surprisingly reassuring, polite, and soft tone.

Coach Knight hands the officer his license and registration. The officer glances through the back window and notices a familiar face.

"Wait just a second. I know that's not Chance Knight?"

"Yes. Yes, sir. He's my son. Is there a problem?"

The police officer beams.

"No problem at all, sir. My son plays for Eleanor Roosevelt High School. Last year Capital Heights destroyed them. Chance dropped thirty-five points and had fifteen rebounds in that game. I've followed him ever since. You have an amazingly talented son there, sir. Look, I'm not going to hold you fine folks up any longer. I only stopped you because your back left taillight is out. Please get that fixed as soon as you can. I apologize for the inconvenience."

The officer hands Coach Knight back his license and registration.

"You all have a wonderful evening and get home safely. Good luck, Chance. Except, of course, when playing against my son."

The officer laughs at his own joke and offers a wink.

"Keep doing your thing, son," he adds.

The officer heads back to his car and drives away.

Mrs. Knight exhales. "Thank you, Jesus," she says.

"Amen to that," says Coach Knight. "Let's get home, fam."

4

HOUSE PARTY

The night before the first day of school, Chance is in bed reading *Sports Illustrated*. The cover features him palming a basketball in each hand with his arms extended sideways. The caption above his picture poses the question, "Chance Knight, the Next LeBron?" He finishes reading the accompanying article, which argues his potential to be the greatest player of all time. He smiles, tosses the magazine aside, and turns off the light—ready to start his senior year.

The next morning Chance is walking down the hallway with two of his teammates, Walt and Big Dink. They pass a group of girls who flirtatiously eye them. Chance cracks a smile, revealing the bottom of his perfectly aligned white upper teeth. He adds a wink and the girls giggle with excitement befitting a popular celebrity. Walt stops, turns back, and approaches them with a wide grin on his face. They dismissively walk away.

"But you just smiled at me a second ago," Walt shouts out to them.

The oldest of the girls turns around.

"That was for Chance, not you, sweetie," she shouts back.

Big Dink looks at Walt in disbelief. "Fool, you know damn well she wasn't smiling at you."

"Besides, even if she was, you wouldn't have the slightest idea what to do with her," adds Chance. "You know, considering you're still a virgin and all."

He and Big Dink laugh.

"Whatever. This is senior year and I'm definitely leaving this school with a bang! Literally! Maybe even two or three bangs. Just watch!"

Walt starts to walk away. Chance and Big Dink look at each other and laugh again. Walt holds up his middle finger and continues walking.

"All right, Big Dink. I'll catch you later in study hall. I'm 'bout to holla at Walt."

Chance runs and catches up to Walt and puts his arm around him.

"Man, I believe you. I believe this is the year you finally lose your virginity," says Chance, louder than he should have.

"Man, shhhhh. Keep your damn voice down, dammit."

"Please. Everyone up in here knows yo' ass still a virgin."

"Whateva," says Walt, while removing Chance's arm from around his shoulders.

The two friends hurry to their first class before the late bell rings.

The Knight residence is small but cozy and tastefully decorated, and serves as a haven for the neighborhood youngsters. There is always a pleasing aroma of food wafting through the air. Tonight is no exception, with macaroni and cheese, pork chops, collard greens, and freshly made rolls spread before the Knight clan.

"Chance, how was your first week of school?" asks Mrs. Knight.

"It was cool. You know, school is school. I'm excited to be a senior now so I can hurry up and go to college."

"Well, don't rush it, baby. Live in the moment and enjoy being a high school senior for now. You'll have plenty of time to enjoy your college years."

"Years? April, you do know that our son is going to the NBA after his freshman year of college, right?"

"That's right, Mom! Chance will be what you call a one and done. He's gonna be rich. He'll be able to buy me all types of sneakers and awesome outfits. Ya girl gonna be fly!"

Chance backs Amaia and gives her a high five. Everyone laughs.

Mrs. Knight cuts through the laughter.

"Well until then, we have to continue living in the real world. That real world requires us all to be up and outta here bright and early tomorrow morning. So I don't want you staying out too late at that house party tonight, Chance."

"Your mother's right. We have your University of Maryland visit tomorrow and I want you well-rested and attentive."

"Don't worry. We aren't staying too long. We'll be back home by midnight. I'll get in my eight hours of sleep before we leave out in the morning. We don't have to be there until nine thirty."

A few hours later, Chance hears a loud knock on the door and opens it to greet Big Dink, Mad Max, and Walt. The Knight family warmly welcomes them.

"Hey, fellas. Y'all have fun tonight and be safe. Have Chance back home by midnight because he has a college visit tomorrow," says Coach Knight.

"Yes, sir. We'll make sure to have him back by eleven forty-five," replies Walt.

"Man, you trying to kiss up to Coach. All that kissin' up you do and you still rode the bench in AAU," says Big Dink.

"Man, forget you. Coach knows I'm the furthest thing from a kiss ass. Ain't that right, Coach?

"Coach?"

There is dead silence as Coach Knight covers his face to avoid answering the question. Everyone except Walt laughs.

"Come on, let's bounce," says Chance.

Even though it is a tight fit, the teenagers pack into Big Dink's black Ford Explorer that is almost as old as he is.

"Yo, Chance. Tasha been sweatin' you hard this week at school. What up with that?" asks Walt.

"Yeah, bro, she been on me super hard this first week. When I see her at this party I'm gonna have to go ahead and give her what she wants. A brotha gonna have to go ahead and give her some of this vitamin D!"

Everyone laughs.

"Yeah man, she fine as hell. But you betta make sure you strap up. Word on the street is she's received quite a few DNA samples from multiple niggas, my brotha," says Big Dink.

"Thot alert," shouts Mad Max.

"Man, why she gotta be a thot just 'cause she been with a couple, okay, maybe several, dudes? We each been with multiple chicks. Are we thots?"

Big Dink is eager to respond. "Well first off, when you said *we*, I know yo' ass wasn't including Walt. We all know Walt's virgin ass ain't fuck shit. And to answer your question, hell yeah we thots."

"I'm definitely a thot," adds Mad Max.

"Well, damn. I'm tryin' to be a thot," says Walt.

His friends laugh uncontrollably.

The house party is in McLean, Virginia, a forty-minute drive in the evening. They pull up to the house, an impressively large contemporary craftsman-style home in a newer development.

"Yo, Chance," says Big Dink. "This house is dope. You said this Tasha's friend's crib? I wonder what her parents do."

"Yeah. She said they go way back. Tasha's mom used to work for the real estate company her friend's parents own. The girl invited Tash to the party and asked her to bring some of the basketball team. I get the impression she and her girls are some freaks and thirsty for some *big* black athletes."

"Well I can certainly help them out with that."

They laugh as they approach the door. They make their way inside the home and are excited to see that the party is in full throttle with pretty girls in abundance. Chance, with amusement, notices his friends practically drooling at one in particular. Tasha's movements on the dance floor are drawing attention from the crowd. Getting hot, Tasha, with both hands moving in rhythm with her seductive hips, pulls her long black hair back and up in one fell swoop, revealing her soft, inviting neck and glossy voluptuous lips. She then shakes her hair free once again.

Walt thinks she is the most beautiful shade of brown he has ever seen.

"Man, I wish I was you, Chance," says Walt. "I'm so in love with Tasha's fine ass."

Big Dink strolls in another direction, drawn to a group of well-endowed blonde-haired girls he wants to get to know better. And one in particular clearly wants to get to know him as well. Chance observes Mad Max being sandwiched on the dance floor by two tall, brown-skinned girls. Chance is encouraged that they have only been there a short while and the fun has already begun.

Tasha spots Chance and makes her way over to where he and Walt are standing.

"What up, Walt?"

"Hi, beautiful. Um, I mean, Tasha," a nervous Walt says awkwardly.

Tasha smiles at him.

"Thank you, Walt. You're such a sweetheart. And cute."

She pinches Walt's cheek. He appears a bit unsteady as a result.

"Walt! Just sit your ass down for a little while and chill out," orders Chance.

Tasha smiles at Walt and then takes Chance by the hand, guiding him to a corner of the room.

"Is Walt gonna be okay?"

"Yeah, he's fine. He's just crazy in love with you. Pinching him on the cheek was obviously too much for him to handle."

The recollection amuses them.

Tasha stares seductively at Chance and licks her lips. "Enough about Walt," she says.

She pushes Chance against the wall as she leans in toward his ear and slowly whispers.

"Well, well, well. Finally, some one-on-one time with none other than Mr. Chance Knight himself. What's goin' on, champ?"

"Just been chillin'. I *have* been thinkin' 'bout you lately."

"Oh really now. Thinkin' 'bout what? Things you wanna do to me?" asks Tasha in a singsong cadence.

Chance chuckles.

"Yup."

"Well, what you waitin' for? I want you to show me how you shoot."

Chance bites down on his lower lip and appreciatively looks Tasha up and then down. Her full lips and full hips are calling out to him. He leans in closer.

"Okay, but you need to know something, though," he whispers into her ear.

"Oh yeah, what's that?"

Chance finds Tasha's voice tantalizing.

"When I shoot, I don't miss," he says in his best Rico Suave voice.

"You better not," Tasha says smiling while walking toward the steps.

Chance admires her from behind and is mesmerized by her every sway. When Tasha reaches the fourth step, she turns back to look at him and gives him a knowing nod. Chance eagerly follows her up the stairs. She guides him to a finished attic then draws him close with a long, tender, arousing kiss. Burning with anticipation, they quickly throw their clothes in every direction. Their youthful energy creates a heart-pounding, explosive encounter. After sex, they lie there, on their backs, for a few minutes with only the sound of their panting as each catches their breath.

"OMG, that was fucking amazing," says Tasha. She lets out a satisfied giggle.

Chance turns his head to Tasha and gives her a playful smile.

"Told ya I don't miss," he whispers.

"Mm-hmm. You sure don't," Tasha sensuously whispers back.

On the way home, Chance, unable to stop smiling, is sitting in the passenger seat of Big Dink's SUV.

"Man, Tasha got dat bomb! I'm afraid I might be addicted, bro."

"Nigga, I hope you strapped up," says Big Dink.

"Absolutely."

"Damn you lucky," Walt says enviously. "I would do anything to get some of that pussy."

"Bro, you would do anything to get *any* pussy."

Chance, Big Dink, and Mad Max burst out laughing. Even Walt smiles.

"Thank God you're a minute-man 'cause we right on pace to get you home by midnight as promised," Mad Max teases.

"Man, whateva. I was in that wetty-wet for a good long while. You right, though, 'bout us being right on schedule. I don't need any problems from Mom and Pops tonight."

"Yeah and we don't want any problems with Coach," adds Big Dink.

Mad Max and Walt both agree.

"But, bro, what was up with you and that big-titty Becky that was all up on you?" asks Chance. "Don't think I didn't see it."

Big Dink grins. "Man, low-key, dem girls were some freaks. She gave me some head in one of the bathrooms. Bruh, it was some professional head. I would pay for that head. And one of her girls was tryin' get me to go upstairs with her. But I just wasn't feelin' that whole situation. She was drunk and they was all poppin' mollies. Dem rich white kids is wild."

"Man, for real? That's crazy."

"Yeah, for real, Big Dink?" asks Mad Max. "You couldn't come tap a brotha in if you didn't want to hit it? You selfish. You could've at least tried to put one on to Walt's virgin ass."

They all laugh.

Without warning, they hear a police siren and see flashing lights behind them.

"Man, fuck!" exclaims Big Dink.

"Yo, just be cool," says Chance. "We ain't been drinkin' or smokin' weed so we good."

"Yeah but our asses is black, though," retorts Walt.

Big Dink pulls his SUV over on the shoulder of Interstate 495. A Virginia State Police Trooper pulls up behind them. The ruddy-faced, sandy-haired trooper, his hands poised on his gun holster, exits his vehicle and approaches the SUV.

"License and registration, please," he orders.

Big Dink reaches for the glove box to get his license and registration.

"Slowly!"

The trooper keeps his right hand on his holster. With his left, he shines the flashlight on the glove compartment. Big Dink, in slow motion, opens the glove box and removes the license and registration. He carefully hands it to the trooper. The trooper tells them to sit tight.

"All right, be chill, remember what Coach always preaches. Be cool and compliant," cautions Chance.

He looks out of the back window and sees the trooper returning to their SUV. The trooper hands the license and registration back to Big Dink as a second trooper pulls up. While the trooper explains to the young men why they were pulled over, the second trooper approaches.

"What seems to be the problem here?" he asks.

"I pulled them over because their SUV matches the description of a stolen vehicle, but I ran their info and everything checks out clean. I'm about to send them on their way."

The friends breathe a sigh of relief.

The second trooper, dark-haired, grim-faced, and physically imposing to most people, looks at the teenagers and then spits on the ground. He shines his flashlight in each of their faces and then shines the flashlight throughout the SUV.

"Everyone out the truck," he orders.

"But he just told you we're clean," objects Big Dink.

"Boy, don't fuckin' question me. Get the fuck out the truck. Now!"

Thoughts racing to premature deaths, they nervously comply.

"Get up against the vehicle with your hands behind your backs."

He tells the ruddy-faced trooper to cuff them and sit them on the curb. The trooper looks puzzled, briefly hesitates but acquiesces. To Chance's surprise, he appears almost as intimidated as they are. He cuffs all four.

"All right watch dem bitches as I check the vehicle."

Big Dink again objects, tempting fate. "Man, that's an illegal fuckin' search and you know it."

The grim-faced trooper shines the light at Big Dink's face.

"What, you a fuckin' lawyer, boy? Shut the fuck up! You hear me? Shut-the-fuck-up!"

"Not another fuckin' word y'all. Remember what Coach always preaches," Chance says again as he looks over at Big Dink. He is clearly agitated.

"Man, fuck that shit. I know my rights. I just wanna know what da fuck we did exactly. Besides driving while black. Why da fuck is that pig searching our shit?"

The grim-faced trooper comes over and snatches Big Dink up by the collar.

"Because I fuckin' can, boy. And don't you ever forget that! Know your fuckin' place."

An intense face-to-face stare down between the trooper and Big Dink ensues. Despite his efforts to control them, tears of anger and humiliation start to trickle from Big Dink's eyes.

The trooper, triumphant, lets go of Big Dink's collar and proceeds to roughly uncuff the boys.

"Now get da fuck outta Virginia and take your asses back to whatever hood you came from."

As much as they want to say something back, Big Dink is too shaken up and the others hold firm to what has been instilled into them by Coach Knight.

On the way home in Big Dink's Ford, Walt's eyes are watery. Mad Max, struggling to process what just happened, remains silent.

"Racist ass mutha fucka!" screams Big Dink.

"See that's that bullshit right there," says Chance. "That right there is precisely why Kaep took a knee. The sad part is taking a knee is a bigger issue for people than what just happened. Something's gotta change." A tear from each eye slowly trickles down his face.

The teenagers, black and male, feel marginalized and defeated. Their tears do not lie.

5 COLLEGE VISITS

The Knight family piles into their SUV and traverses the Baltimore-Washington Parkway, heading to the University of Maryland in College Park.

Coach Knight can't hide his annoyance any longer.

"So how did last night go, Son? I'm assuming it went well considering I heard you come in almost a half-hour late."

"Yeah, sorry about that, Pops. It was a great night until we got pulled over on the way home by a state trooper, and then a second one, who was definitely racist, showed up."

Mrs. Knight's reaction is swift.

"What! Why didn't you call us or say anything about it until now? What happened?"

"To be honest with you, I didn't want to talk about it. I was so angry and didn't want to upset you guys, too.

"But long story short, we got pulled over 'cause Big Dink's truck matched the description of a stolen vehicle. The state trooper who pulled us over ran the plates and registration and was about to let us go.

"That's when the second one showed up and made us all get out of the truck, cuffed us, and talked crap to us. You know, same ole same ole."

"Did you get the trooper's badge number or anything identifiable so we can file a complaint?" asks Coach Knight.

"No. In the heat of the moment I didn't even think about it. I just wanted to get out of there alive. If he had a body cam, based on how racist he was acting, it was probably turned off."

"I'm so sorry, Son. It's a shame that even in 2018 you kids still have to deal with some of the same nonsense that your father and I had to deal with back in the day."

"Thanks to our current president, we're living in a make America great again society," says Coach Knight. "He thinks America was great back when blacks were always second-class citizens, and he's trying to get things back to how they were. The man is dangerous—especially to us.

"Lord knows I'm grateful that no shots were fired and that none of you became the latest headline.

Think about all the years we've been complaining about police brutality and no one believed us. There were no phones to record it—no police dash cams or body cams. The saddest part, though, is that even now with the video evidence, these cops are still getting away with these murders—no matter how blatant. There seems to be a notion out there that this type of behavior is okay.

"It's been six years since the killing of Trayvon Martin by a wannabe cop.

"Four years since Eric Garner, Michael Brown, and Tamir Rice were killed by cops.

"Three years since Walter Scott and Freddie Gray were killed.

"And two years since the horrific killing of Philando Castile in front of his girlfriend and her four-year-old daughter.

"These are not one offs or anomalies but rather a pattern. Yes, police have a scary, tough job and they put their lives on the line every day. But murder by cop is not okay."

Coach Knight's voice rises. "The bully in the White House refuses to come out against police brutality or hate. As a matter of fact, he tells police to be rougher with people during arrests. This is 2018 for crying out loud. When President Barack Obama was elected, I thought everything was changing for the good. I knew it would take time, but I truly believed our trajectory was positive. Despite Republican plots to make him a one-term president, Obama was able to kick butt. He ended the recession, saved the automobile industry, stimulated the economy, created jobs, helped millions of Americans have access to affordable health care, helped clean the environment, led the way on climate change—don't get me started.

"He was all about unity and tried so hard for bipartisanship—to his detriment. He wanted inclusiveness. This current president is obsessed with erasing every Obama policy one by one. He's trying to wipe out Obama's legacy. He thrives on divisiveness.

"How the hell did we get here? What *is* clear is that now's the time we have to stick together as a people. We need to realize the power that we have to effect change. It's time that we use it.

"Now, Son, you know your mother and I met and fell in love while we were at Howard. She basically stalked me once she found out that I was a star basketball player." He winks at Chance.

"Honey chile, please. You know dag on well that you were the one doing the stalking. You and basketball were the furthest things from my mind. Besides, I preferred big, strong, muscular football types over the scrawny, bowlegged basketball types,"

43

Mrs. Knight balks but is betrayed by the sparkle in her eyes.

Chance and Amaia enjoy their parents playful banter, particularly because it lightens the mood.

Coach Knight laughs and resumes his monologue.

"Whatever. My point is I really wish you would consider going to Howard or another HBCU. I know the schools recruiting you are the crème of the crop. They've got top notch facilities and they play nationally televised games. I understand that the top rated star athletes are ecstatic to play sports at big time schools. But I didn't raise you to be like the norm. I didn't raise you to follow the crowd. I raised you to be a trendsetter. I raised you to lead and create your own path.

"The reason these big, predominantly white schools have all that *stuff* is because talented black athletes such as yourself go there and generate millions of dollars for them."

Coach Knight glances at Chance through the rearview mirror before returning his gaze to the road, then continues speaking.

"What if we as a people change it up? What if these four- and five-star black athletes started going to HBCUs instead? What if you, the number one high school basketball player in the nation, committed to play at an HBCU?

"Can you just imagine for a second if the Fab Five had gone to Howard, or Kevin Durant or Anthony Davis had gone to Hampton or Florida A&M? Do you understand that these HBCUs would then be the ones generating millions and would be the ones with top notch facilities, playing nationally televised games attended by NBA scouts? It would change the entire landscape of college basketball as we know it.

"This obviously would take time to develop and the initial athletes that made that leap would be making the sacrifice for what follows. But it takes one super star, the right super star—like you—to take that first step and lead the way for others."

Chance has remained quiet throughout his father's speech but can no longer remain silent.

"I hear ya, Pops. But I've always dreamed about playing for Maryland or Kentucky and I want to win an NCAA championship in my one year before I go pro. Let's face it. I'm not winning a championship at Howard."

"Actually, you can do anything you set your mind to, Son. With hard work and a little bit of luck, anything's possible."

"Howard winning the national championship, that wouldn't be luck, that would be a damn miracle or even an act of God."

His parents have to suppress a smile. On that statement, he has a point. At least for now.

As they pull into the parking lot at the University of Maryland for Chance's official visit, Coach Knight hopes he did not put a damper on his son's enthusiasm. He earned his place in the sun and no matter how well intended his lecture was, this is Chance's moment.

He soon realizes he need not have worried. Excitement is in the air for each Knight as the Maryland coaches, a marching band, cheerleaders, and current Maryland star basketball players greet them. Part of the visit includes a tour of the state-of-the-art weight room, the Maryland Basketball Xfinity Center, and the athletic dormitories.

Chance leans over to his father.

"And you want me to turn all this down to go to Howard? I don't think so, Pops," he says in a quiet voice.

One week later, Chance and his father arrive at the University of Kentucky. They are greeted by the head coach who personally conducts the tour of the campus and facilities. Chance cannot stop staring at the national championship ring on the coach's finger. The coach notices.

"I see you looking at this ring, Chance. You want one of these, correct?"

Chance smiles and nods.

"Well, this is where you come for the best chance to win one. We're practically the favorite to win the national title every single year because of five-star recruits like you. You also want to play in the NBA, correct?"

Chance again smiles and nods.

"Then this is where you want to be."

As if on cue, in walk four former Kentucky Wildcats and current star NBA players.

Chance's heart is beating so rapidly he's afraid he will have a heart attack on the spot. He cannot believe that these players are standing right in front of him. Coach Knight smiles broadly. The four NBA stars walk up to greet them.

"Each one of these guys was a one and done player. Now they're all in the NBA living their dream and making millions for their families. This can be you, too, if you decide to come to the University of Kentucky. I see you as a one and done and then a sure fire number one overall pick in the draft."

Chance and his father look at each other, sporting huge grins.

The next day, Chance is lying in bed engaged in a three-way phone conversation with Walt and Big Dink. Chance decides to share his news.

"Yo. I think I'm gonna sign with Kentucky. But don't tell anyone before I officially announce it after the season at the signing ceremony."

"Oh snap! Man, that's what's up, Chance," says Walt. "You can't go wrong wit' that choice, my brotha."

"Hell yeah. Congrats, bro," Big Dink adds.

"Thanks y'all."

"Speaking of colleges, I have no intention of actually playing for Howard, but I'm still going on my official visit next month," says Big Dink. "My cousin Logan said they got baddies galore and the parties be off the chain.

"And he said that since my visit is on a Friday, I should get wit' some of the HU players and roll to one of the campus parties. He said there's a good chance I could get some college pussy outta the trip. I figure, shit, it's worth a try. Y'all tryin' to roll with me?"

"Oh you know damn well I'm tryin' to roll," says Walt. "I've heard that Howard has the best parties and the chicks are bad as hell."

"Shit, count me all the way in," Chance says. "Pops gonna love me going to check out Howard, for sure. He's been tryin' to get me to play for them ever since I picked up a basketball. It's not gonna happen, but the visit will still make him happy. And you know I'm definitely gonna get up on some Howard ass. And maybe Walt will actually lose his virginity. Man, this could be a win-win for all of us. Let's do this."

Walt ignores the tease. "What about Tasha? Will she even let you go?" he asks.

"That ain't my girlfriend, shit. We just hooked up once. But I ain't gonna lie. I definitely want to get up in that again. For real, for real."

"I bet you do, my brotha. Man, I would do anything to get me some of Tasha. Anything!" exclaims Walt.

Big Dink and Chance laugh.

6 THE MAGIC

It is a clear autumn day, unseasonably warm, when Big Dink, Walt, and Chance arrive at Howard. The sun is bright. The trees branches are exploding with orange, yellow, red, and brown leaves. The air still has a little bite but is warm enough for coeds to wear short skirts with bare legs.

Big Dink is scheduled to meet Coach Miles MacIntyre, Howard's head basketball coach, in his office. But since he is early, they decide to find The Yard, familiar to the three of them because of the homecoming stories they have heard. Howard University homecomings are legendary in the black community and attract guests from all over the country and from all walks of life—poor to rich, ordinary worker to world-wide celebrity. The Yardfest that takes place during Homecoming weekend includes concert performances by stars like Drake, P. Diddy, Wale, and Rick Ross.

When the Yard isn't obscured by students, alumni, and visitors, the aesthetic beauty is inescapable. The strategically centered grassy quadrangle has crisscross pathways leading to the bordering campus buildings, including Andrew Rankin Memorial Chapel, Frederick Douglas Memorial Hall, and Founders Library.

The Yard is also often the center of campus activity, much of which is captivating the three visitors. They notice, with keen interest, the different fraternities and sororities congregating in various sectors of the quadrangle, and the sorority and fraternity members practicing the step movements popular at most HBCUs.

The high school seniors are also in awe of the young ladies casually walking along the pathways or in grassy areas sprawled out on blankets, books laid out in front of them.

"Man, there are fine ass chicks everywhere on this campus," says Big Dink as they stop and stare.

Coach MacIntyre is returning from a late lunch in the faculty dining room at the Blackburn Center. As he crosses The Yard heading toward his office, he spots Big Dink and Chance and approaches them from behind.

"What's up Big Dink? How you feelin' young brotha?"

They turn around.

"Oh hey, Coach Mac. I'm well, sir, thank you."

"Glad to hear that. I see you brought Chance Knight with you. It's good to see you again, Chance."

"You as well, Coach Mac."

"Oh y'all know each other?" asks Big Dink.

"Yeah. I go way back with Chance's father. We both played here together. Now, I don't think I've met this other fella with you all. Do you play ball?"

"My name is Walt Williams, sir. Yes. I play on the team with them."

"Oh okay, great. And that's an iconic name you got.

"Well, all of you, welcome to Howard University. This is the finest HBCU around. I'm so glad that you're taking the opportunity to see our beautiful campus and learn what our athletic program has to offer.

"Big Dink, I know your basketball abilities and athleticism would help turn this program around. And our coaching staff and athletic trainers would help elevate your game and help you showcase all your strengths on the court. We would love to have you play here and I truly believe you would love attending Howard University. And just in case you plan on visiting

Hampton, I want to let it be known, you're standing on the campus of the *real* HU."

Amused with himself, Coach Mac widens his smile. He redirects his attention to Chance.

"How's my main man Craig doing? And April and Amaia? We haven't spoken in about a month."

"They're good, sir. I'll tell them you asked about them."

Chance is impressed that Coach Mac never seems to age. He seems younger than his father, maybe because of the absence of gray hair. He reminds him of Denzel Washington in the movie *He Got Game*, only taller.

"Yes, please do. Man, let me tell y'all about Coach Knight. Back in our day we called him 'Night-Night" 'cause he would knock opponents out early. He'd take them out of their game scoring wise; defensively he'd shut their offense down, block shots, out rebound, basically take their heart. And when he did, he would say 'night-night' and wave goodbye to the opposing player or team. That meant game over! Goodnight, folks."

They all laugh.

"Chance, you know how much of a legend your father is at Howard? Your dad has every possible school record. The man was a beast!"

"I've heard all the stories a million times. Pops desperately wants me to follow in his footsteps and play for y'all. But I told him it would devastate me to come here and break all of his four-year records in my one and only year before going pro."

The coach smiles.

"Oh, he won't mind. Trust me. So what the hell are you waiting for? I can have the letter of intent drawn up and ready for you to sign along with Big Dink before you leave.

"I'll tell you what, Walt. If you can convince them both to sign, then I have a scholarship waiting for you, too."

"Oh snap. Thank you, Coach. Fellas! We need to sign on the dotted line!" exclaims Walt.

"Chance, Big Dink, I know both of you are looking to sign with a major Division I school," says Coach Mac. "But this is a rare year for us here at Howard. We had six seniors graduate and we had three players transfer out. That leaves us with only four returning scholarship players. This has never happened since I've been coaching here.

"One of our returning scholarship players is our three guard, Deon Diggs, from Brooklyn, New York. He was MEAC Freshman of the Year last season. He averaged twenty-three points and eleven rebounds a game, a double-double. The boy got skills! He's six feet, five inches and can jump out the gym. So, with that said, I have nine scholarships available for next season. I would love for three of them to go to you all.

"Big Dink, I know you're verbally committed to UNC. Chance, I know you've narrowed your school choices down to either Maryland or Kentucky. But man oh man, can you just imagine the type of super power we would have if the two of y'all joined Deon here?

"Again, I'm excited you're all here to see everything Howard has to offer. Initially, it might not seem like much compared to what those big schools entice you with, but HBCUs, especially Howard, offer an experience those schools will never be able to provide. There's a magic here that can't be duplicated there.

"Walt, don't forget what I promised. If you get these two gentlemen to come to Howard, I have a full ride waiting for you."

"I would love that, Coach Mac. Thank you, sir. Come on, fellas, let's sign right this fuckin' second!" exclaims Walt as he unsuccessfully tries to stop staring at a passing young lady.

They are all amused and enjoying their camaraderie as they start their tour. Chance reflects on how much he values his friends, and is reminded of Walt's burden. He and Walt trail behind as Coach Mac and Big Dink talk up ahead.

"How's Teddy doing?"

Walt pauses before answering.

"He's still going through his treatments but fighting cancer like a little warrior. We won't know anything until after he's finished with chemo. At that point the doctors can determine if they got it all and what his prognosis is."

"Well, just know that I'm praying hard and so is my family. Teddy is strong. Remember that."

"I appreciate that."

"You know I always got your back. I love you, bro."

"Back at you."

Coach Mac leads the recruits into Burr Gymnasium. The young men observe the mediocre basketball court, the worn blue spectator seats, and the tightness of the overall space. As they take in the scene and try to reconcile what they are seeing with what they expected, Chance, Walt, and Big Dink exchange looks. Without a word, they all know. They all know they are thinking as one brain. Coach Mac excuses himself to respond to an assistant coach trying to get his attention.

Big Dink uses this opportunity to mouth "WTF?" to Chance and Walt. They knew the gym would be lacking, but they didn't realize Burr would be only slightly bigger than their high school gym.

The coach returns and walks them downstairs to the weight room, another disappointment.

Coach Mac takes a cue from their facial expressions.

"Okay, okay. I know these facilities aren't on par with the big schools that you've visited."

He tries not to sound defensive.

"Those schools have multimillion dollar facilities. Winning seasons generate millions of dollars for their programs. When they sell players' jerseys, the schools get that money. Rich alumni boosters can't donate fast enough. TV contracts guarantee a windfall. And how do you think they earn the winning season? The multimillion dollar facilities? The TV exposure? Can anybody tell me that?"

"From us, the star black athletes," answers Chance.

"Bingo! There it is. Imagine if you guys, along with other star black athletes, stopped going to the big power schools and started going to HBCUs instead."

"Man, you sound just like my pops."

"There's a reason for that, Chance."

Coach Mac motions the guys to sit down.

"When your father and I played here at Howard, we were the best of friends. We weren't considered top recruits by any means when we were coming out of high school.

"But years after we graduated college, we were at a sports bar watching the Fab Five at Michigan play on TV. To my knowledge, the Fab Five was the first grouping of star athletes/friends to go to the same school as part of the same recruiting class. It reminded us of the 'what if' conversations we shared in college.

"We sat at the bar wondering what would have happened had the Fab Five chosen to go to Howard. It had us thinking about all the possibilities.

"In case you haven't noticed, many HBCUs are struggling financially and some might have to close their doors forever. Black lives matter. Black education matters—HBCUs Matter. What better time could there be for a movement like this? We have to bond together.

"There was a time when black people didn't even have the option to go to those big schools. That's why we have HBCUs. We didn't have choices then. Eventually, more and more athletes like yourselves could not only go to these schools, they were heavily recruited by them. You don't think they realized how letting young black guys like you play for their school increased their revenue? And young guys like you not going to black schools is taking money out of black hands. Yes, money is green in white hands or black hands, but what's done with the green isn't the same. Ya hear me?

"We have to depend on one another. We have choices now, but we're not choosing *us*. That's the shame of it.

"The reality, though, is that this won't happen overnight. So, yes, the athletes who start this movement will be the sacrificial lambs. Hypothetically, say, the three of you, along with five other five-star recruits, came to play here next fall. Certainly for the one and doners, but probably for the four-year players as well, you would never reap the same benefits that you would have gotten had you gone to a Kentucky or UNC.

"Howard must first get the wins, play the top teams, enjoy consecutive years of super stars. Only then will we see wide exposure, TV deals, money flowing for inner-city scholarships, enhanced academics. The athletes who start this movement will be sacrificing themselves for all the other athletes to follow. They will be the trailblazers who go down in history. They will have a different kind of legacy."

Chance is thinking he just can't escape his father's speeches.

"It's important to note that whoever they would be, they probably wouldn't be sacrificing the NBA. There was a time when players could enter the draft right after high school. Those type of players' biggest sacrifice would be not winning the NCAA championship. They would already be top five-star recruits. The NBA would already have them on their radar. Come on, if you're that talented, it doesn't necessarily matter where you go because they'll find you.

"Anyway, I want what's best for you guys and you have to make that decision. Let me stop preaching, for now."

"Thank God," Big Dink mumbles to Chance and Walt, who are also relieved the tension is broken.

"One day you guys are going to understand what I'm trying to school y'all on."

Coach Mac tries to lighten the mood.

"There's a party on campus tonight over in the Blackburn Center. You should stick around for a while after dinner and go over there and experience black college social life. You'll have a better understanding of 'the magic' I was talking about." He winks. "Here are three meal tickets for y'all. I'll have someone from the coaching staff point you in the direction of the cafeteria so you can get some dinner."

Chance, Big Dink, and Walt stroll across The Yard, feeling like big men on campus.

Walt breaks the mood.

"Coach Mac and your dad do have a point, though."

"Oh no, not you, too. Look, Walt, I can't take anymore preachin' today, bro," moans Chance.

"Amen to that," Big Dink says loudly.

"I'm just sayin' they got a point. These racist ass cops out here shooting us black folk down like target practice. We got this white nationalist up in the White House who clearly doesn't give a fuck about equality.

"Man, just think, it would be amazing if black athletes of your caliber came together and started a movement of going to HBCUs. Not to mention the fact that some of these white schools are allowing these hate rallies to take place on their campuses. Look at the Charlottesville Unite the Right Rally. That shit took place on Virginia's campus. And that one racist ass white nationalist dude gave a speech at the University of Florida. And Ole Miss allowed the people celebrating the confederacy to do it on campus.

"The fact that those schools allow that type of hate to happen on their campuses is reason enough to not go there. Even after that we still have elite athletes going to play for those schools and making those schools millions and winners. Man, I'm feelin' what Coach Knight and Coach Mac are preachin'. It would be special if we start this movement y'all."

"Man, you ain't slick. Yo ass just wants that full ride Coach Mac offered you if you get me and Chance to sign."

They all start laughing.

"But, I do agree with you, Walt, that if that ever happened it would be special. You want to know what else is really special, though?" asks Chance.

"What?"

"Her right there! Now that's what I call special."

Big Dink and Walt follow his gaze to a young woman lying face down on a blanket in the grass reading a book. She is wearing nude color leggings and a navy blue Howard University cropped sweatshirt.

"Lawd have mercy," says Walt.

"Damn!" exclaims Big Dink.

"I'll be right back," says Chance.

With a brisk and confident stroll, he approaches her.

"Excuse me, sweetheart, how you doin' today?"

"Fine, but I'm not your sweetheart."

"I'm sorry. I hope I didn't offend you. I'm Chance. What's your name?"

She looks up at him with large brown eyes that reveal a hint of hazel in the sunlight, deep set in a coffee with cream colored heart shaped face, with dimples the size of twenty-five karat diamonds.

"Kia."

Just the sound of her voice does something to him.

"I don't mean any disrespect, but honestly, I couldn't help but notice how bad you are."

Kia smiles politely.

"Are you studying for a test or something?"

"Nope. Just reading a book to kill time while I wait on some of the volleyball players to take me to the cafeteria for dinner."

"Oh, word. That's where my boys and I are headed. So you play volleyball here? What year are you?"

"Nah. I'm still a senior in high school. I'm being recruited to play here. They don't know it yet, but I've already decided to commit."

"That's what's up. So you from around here?"

"Silver Spring, Maryland."

"Oh, so you one of those privileged Montgomery County girls I see."

Kia chuckles.

"Oh, it's like that, huh? So where are you from, big man?"

"P.G. County. Capital Heights."

Kia rolls her eyes.

"Oh, you one of those P.G. dudes."

"Damn, it's like that?" Chance laughs.

"I'm just sayin'. I heard about y'all P.G. dudes."

"You shouldn't believe everything you hear."

"Maybe you're right." Kia shrugs.

"It's all good. My boys and I are going to a campus party tonight at the Blackburn Center. Have you heard about it?"

"Yep. The volleyball team was tellin' me it's gonna be lit. We'll definitely be coming through. So what's your deal? Are you a student here?"

"Nope. I'm just here with my man, Big Dink, over there while he's on his official basketball visit. And the other guy is my best friend, Walt."

"Oh, that's awesome. You play, too? You're tall enough!"

"I dabble a little in the sport." Chance is uncharacteristically modest. "This is my last year of high school, too. I haven't decided which college I want to attend yet."

"Is Howard one of your options?"

"It wasn't until I found out that you're coming here. So now it is," he says in his well-practiced Rico Suave voice.

Kia blushes and pauses before responding.

"That's sweet and all, but my man, Deon, already goes here. He's the star of the basketball team.

He was MEAC Freshman of the Year last year! He'll be at the party tonight."

Chance wasn't expecting that response, and it shows.

"Well, it was a pleasure meeting you, Mr. Chance. Feel free to say hi at the party if you see me. I'll introduce you to Deon and he can probably give you some basketball pointers."

Chance gives her a funny look.

"Okay, well it was a pleasure meeting you, too. Take care, beautiful."

Chance walks back over to his boys.

"Yo, son, what happened? Was she feelin' you?" asks Big Dink.

"Yeah, she seemed like she could be feelin' a brotha. But yo, check this shit out. She's a senior in high school, too, and comin' here next year on a volley-ball scholarship. And you remember Coach Mac telling us about that dude on the team who won MEAC Fresh-man of the Year last season?"

"Yeah. So?"

"Well, that's her fuckin' man, bruh."

"Aw damn, cuz. Well shit, what the hell do you care? You ain't coming here and you don't know her man. There ain't nuffin' stopping you from tryin' to push up on shawty tonight at the party."

"True dat, Big Dink got a point," says Walt.

"Oh y'all know how I go. It's on. Now let's go get us some grub 'cause I'm starvin'!"

As Chance, Big Dink, and Walt wait in line for their food, they resemble bobble-heads as their heads bounce from admiration of one attractive young woman to the next. The cafeteria is filled with pretty faces or curvaceous bodies, with many of the ladies endowed with both attributes. The three basketball players have never experienced so much sex appeal in one place. Chance wonders if this is the "magic" Coach Mac was talking about.

Conjuring up courage, Walt addresses three young women with voluminous curly-kinky hair standing directly in front of them. Walt does not know they are seniors.

"Hello, ladies. Can my homeboys and I sit with you?"

They turn and the most outspoken one responds.

"Boy, bye. Are you even old enough to be here? You look young and I've never seen any of you before."

"We're seniors."

The young woman, head tilted and eyebrows raised, gives him a questioning stare.

"In high school," adds Walt, reluctantly.

A round of laughter erupts among the young ladies as they turn to face the front. Determined, Walt tries one more time.

"So you not gonna let us sit with y'all or nuthin?"

The outspoken one turns back to Walt and addresses him.

"If you don't know how to add a 'g' to the end of 'ing' words, then no. You all can't sit with us or *'nuthin'*."

The other two young ladies snicker. Walt relents and backs away.

Big Dink taps Chance on his shoulder. "Yo, look. There goes your girl right there," he says.

"That must be the dude Deon she's with."

Kia and Deon are holding hands and smiling as they walk with some of the volleyball players to a table in the far corner of the cafeteria.

"Damn, he blockin'. How you gonna get close to her now?"

Chance has an idea. With their dinner trays filled with a spread of food looking far better than any other cafeteria food they have seen, Chance leads his friends over to the table where Kia and Deon are sitting.

"What up, Miss Kia?"

"Oh, what's up, Chance?"

Chance introduces Big Dink and Walt to Kia. Deon is watching this interaction with increasing interest.

"Hey, y'all," Kia says. "This is Deon."

"Yeah, her boyfriend," Deon adds. "What's good?"

"Nice to meet you, my brotha," says Chance. "I meant no disrespect. Kia was tellin' me you're the star basketball player here and might give us youngsters a few tips to help us play at college level next year."

Big Dink and Walt give Chance a curious look.

"We're goin' to dat party tonight. Maybe at the party we could holla at you a bit. My man Big Dink here is on an official visit. We're hoping you can talk to him about the basketball program."

Deon turns to Big Dink. "Oh shit, my bad man. I didn't know you were the recruit on the visit here. Hell yeah we can talk at the party." He returns his attention to Chance. "We can all talk at the party."

"Bet. We'll see you tonight then," says Chance.

"Okay, cool. And nice to meet you Big Dink."

Chance makes eye contact with Kia as he walks away and elicits a slight smile before she puts her head down.

Chance, Big Dink, and Walt finally find a table in the crowded cafeteria.

"Yo, I can't believe he didn't know who you were," says Big Dink. "I guess he doesn't read *Sports Illustrated*."

"Not everyone knows who I am, bro. And I'm glad he doesn't. It'll be easier to get at Kia —less of a threat."

"So if you do still want to get with Kia, then what the fuck was all that about? You all up in his face fuckin' tryin' to bond with cuz and shit."

"Have faith in your boy. While you two occupy Deon, I'm gonna make my move on Kia."

"Ohhhh snap. I feel ya, playa. The art of distraction is genius."

"Well wait just a damn minute here," objects Walt. "Did y'all forget that we're partly here for me to lose my damn virginity? I ain't hardly tryin-g to be talkin-g to no dude all night long 'bout hoopin-g when I should be up on some college ass."

"Yeah, good point," adds Big Dink.

"Don't worry. I just need y'all to occupy him for twenty minutes or so. That's plenty of time for me to get a sense of what's up."

"All right, fine. Twenty-minutes tops and then I'm goin-g to be doin-g my thang," says Walt.

"Man, your no pussy gettin' virgin ass ain't gonna do shit! Stop fakin'," Big Dink says teasingly.

"Keep sleepin-g on me, bro. Keep sleepin-g."

"And why the hell do you keep talkin-ggggg like that?" asks Chance. "What the hell is wrong with you?"

"I'm practicing adding 'g' to the end of 'ing' words.

Chance and Big Dink roar with laughter.

"That's why yo ass still a virgin!" exclaims Big Dink through his laughter.

Chance puts his arm around Walt and offers encouragement.

"I have faith in you, bro. I think tonight's the night. If you lose your virginity to a college chick, then you'll really be the fuckin' man. Ain't none of us been with a college honey yet."

"Oh hell yeah. I would be the fuckin' man."

A huge smile brightens Walt's face.

7

MO COUNTY

The party in the Blackburn Center promises to be everything they had hoped. Women with varying skin tones of chocolate brown, ebony, yellow, and caramel are everywhere—all shapes and sizes. Some of them stand shyly on the sidelines hoping for male attention; others are popping and gyrating to the reggae song thumping the room. Chance, Big Dink, and Walt are on the dance floor, rhythmically making their "I am here" statement. As a young woman is enticing Chance with her sexually seductive moves on the dance floor, Kia and Deon's entrance catches his attention. He is surprised when Deon is afforded celebrity status. Guys are high-fiving him and girls are greeting him in their most tempting voices. Kia shows no sign of insecurity.

They stroll to the dance floor and start moving slowly in sync, with a familiarity that gives Chance pause. He is riveted by Kia who is wearing tight fitting blue jeans with cutouts, one under her buttocks that exposes just a hint of her cheek. Her red tee-shirt is tied under her plump, perfectly rounded, standing at attention breasts, leaving her hard, yet soft looking, flat belly exposed. Beyoncé and Jay-Z's "Apeshit" starts to play. Kia looks over at Chance as Deon holds her closely from behind, their bodies pulsating with each booming beat. Locking eyes, she smiles bewitchingly.

When the song ends, Deon, sweating profusely, heads to the restroom. Kia lucks up on finding a recently vacated seat in the crowded room. Chance pounces.

"Girl, you was workin' it on the dance floor. I didn't know Mo County girls could get it poppin' like that."

"If you don't know, you betta ask somebody."

They laugh.

Deon exits the restroom and spots Chance and Kia clearly enjoying each other's company. He storms over.

"Yo, out of all these women in here, how is it that you found your way over to laugh it up with mine?"

"Take it easy my dude. We were just people watching and clowning folks up in here."

"My bad, man. I can get really possessive when it comes to my baby girl." He leans in and kisses Kia on the lips.

Big Dink and Walt approach.

"What's up, Deon? Is now a good time for you to talk to me about Howard and give me some playing tips?" asks Big Dink.

"Yeah, man, I want to hear, too," adds Walt.

Deon looks at Kia to make sure she doesn't mind. Kia nods and then struts over to where some of her friends are standing. Chance can't take his eyes off of her.

"Hey guys. Go ahead and get started without me. I gotta hit the head and then I'll be back."

He emerges from the restroom, searches the crowd, and spots Deon, Big Dink, and Walt engaged in conversation on one side of the room. He then notices Kia conveniently on the opposite side talking with two girlfriends from the volleyball team. Chance makes a beeline in their direction and approaches a surprised Kia.

"Umm, I thought you were supposed to be getting some basketball tips from Deon?"

"Girl, please. I should be giving tips to him. I would destroy that brotha on the court."

Kia's two girlfriends let out loud, deep belly laughs.

"Oh, would you now? You already know my man was MEAC Freshman of the Year last season. And now he's this season's favorite to win MEAC Player of the Year. I don't know what you think you're gonna teach him. His game is fire!"

"Oh shit. My bad. I didn't know he was nice like that. I guess I can't mess with him then. But I'm tryin' to mess with you, though."

The girls all look at each other wide-eyed.

"Excuse me?"

"I'm just being honest, Kia. You're beyond fine and I just want to get to know you better."

"Well thank you, but that ain't happenin'. Deon would kill us both. Besides, I love him. That's why I'm coming to Howard—so we can be together. I'm extremely flattered, but I just want you to understand that it ain't happenin', bruh. Not an option."

"You might just force me to come to Howard to take over Deon's spot as the star player *and* as your man. And trust me, I know I can do both!"

Kia's two girlfriends, enjoying his boasts, high-five each other.

"I like youngin's swag. He definitely believes in himself," says the taller of the two girlfriends.

"Well, put an end to all that swag because here comes Deon," warns the other girlfriend.

"Aw shit. You betta bounce, champ," urges Kia.

"Never that."

Deon approaches. "Yo, my man, why do I get the feelin' you tryin' to step to my girl?"

"Probably 'cause I am, cuz."

Deon aggressively steps up to Chance's face and looks the short distance up at him.

"Yo, I think you need to step off before you get stomped out."

"Man, please. You ain't gonna do shit. Come on, fellas. Let's bounce."

"Come on, Kia. Let's go," says Chance as he grabs her hand.

Walt, Big Dink, and both of Kia's friends stare in dismay. Kia snatches her hand away quickly.

"Mutha fucka!" Deon shouts in anger.

Deon charges at Chance, taking a powerful swing. Chance ducks to avoid it catching. Deon then tackles Chance. They wrestle, each trying to pin the other so their fists can find an unobstructed path to inflict maximum pain. Big Dink pulls Deon off as Walt does the same to Chance.

"You don't want this, son. I'm not gonna tell you again. Stay the fuck away from Kia."

Chance laughs.

"Whateva, cuz. Come on y'all, we out. Sorry, Kia."

Chance, Walt, and Big Dink walk toward the exit.

"Yeah, go back to high school you lil bitches. Fuck outta here."

Deon grabs Kia by her hand and leads her away. Kia looks over her shoulder and glances at Chance as he is leaving. He stops, and turns back for one more look at her. They lock eyes once again and Kia saddens at the thought that it might be the last time. She thought he was amusing and they could have had a friendship. Chance nods and she quickly turns back around.

Chance, Walt, and Big Dink get into Big Dink's Ford Explorer to head home. The first five minutes are quiet until Chance cannot contain himself any longer.

"Man, that shit was crazy! I should sign wit' Howard just so I can take that fool's basketball shine *and* his girl."

Walt readily endorses that plan.

"Hell yeah, man. We all need to go ahead and sign with Howard. Let's do it."

Chance and Big Dink laugh.

"Quit playin'. You know I'm not serious. I got more important things to focus on like winning the NCAA Championship and being the first pick in the draft. Howard ain't the place for me if I want to accomplish either."

8

DARK SUNDAY

Chance and his parents relax in their living room watching CNN. Amaia is spending the evening with her best friend, Joy. Holding the remote, Chance mutes the television panelists who are animatedly dissecting the latest presidential tweet. His parents look expectantly over at him.

"I've made my decision," he says.

They instinctively know what he means. Coach Knight jumps up from his weathered, chestnut brown leather recliner and pumps his fists.

"I knew it! I knew when you visited Howard yesterday you'd be sold. I'm so excited, Son."

Chance looks incredulously at his father and shakes his head.

"In your dreams, Pops."

"Well if it's not Howard, then where is it?" asks Mrs. Knight. "Spit it out, Son. I can't take the suspense anymore."

"I've decided to play for the University of Kentucky."

His mother stands and embraces her son.

"I'm so happy for you, Chance. I know that's where you've really wanted to go for a while now."

Coach Knight, back to reality, congratulates him.

"That's awesome, Son. You can't go wrong with Kentucky. You'll be among the best of the best and have a legit shot at winning the NCAA championship next year. This is a dream come true—for all of us."

"Couldn't have done it without you. I really am excited. Pops, I'm gonna verbally commit to the coach on Monday but wait till the signing deadline after the season to make it official. But I'm gonna ask him to keep it quiet until after I sign."

"Son, I'm just so proud. Look at my baby, going to University of Kentucky. I don't know what I'm gonna do without you here."

"It'll just be for a while, Ma. You know I can't live without you and your homemade biscuits and gravy, woman."

Mrs. Knight laughs.

"Boy, please."

Chance picks his mom up in a bear hug and she begs him, giggling like a schoolgirl, to let her go.

The next few months are a blur of newspaper headlines highlighting Chance's senior year accomplishments.

"Knight's 45 Points Carry Capital Heights HS in Rout Over Rival DeMatha Catholic HS"

"Undefeated Capital Heights HS Still Ranked Number 1 Entering Playoffs"

"Knight Named MVP as Capital Heights High Wins State Title 4th Straight Year"

"Number 1 HS Basketball Player Chance Knight, 4.0 GPA in National Honor Society"

"Capital Heights High Invited to GEICO Nationals Tournament as Number 1 Seed"

"Capital Heights High School Wins GEICO Nationals Invitational Championship"

With Chance's senior season behind him, two weeks remain before the college signing deadline. It is "Sports Sunday" in the Knight house. Almost every Sunday during a sports season, Chance and his father spend the day watching whichever sports are televised. This afternoon, baseball is the entertainment until the NBA playoff game starts later. Chance and his father assume their usual seats in the living room. Chance sprawls out on the couch, with his long legs dangling over the end, while his father relaxes in his recliner. Bowls of potato chips and Cheetos are set out in front of them on the coffee table. They are poised to watch the Washington Nationals versus Baltimore Orioles. For this game they are rivals, Chance rooting for the Nationals and his father for the Orioles—which he considers to be the real hometown team. A pretty, petite young blonde woman begins singing the national anthem. None of the players stand with locked arms, kneel, or hold their fists in the air. All stand, most with their hands over their hearts.

"Can you believe that shit?" asks Coach Knight. "Not one of these athletes looking like us, and in a position to make a public statement, takes a knee to stand up for the total disregard for the lives of our people. Major League Baseball doesn't have a ban on kneeling. Why do none of them take a stand, or rather a knee, over all these unarmed black men getting shot dead by cops?"

"Exactly!" exclaims an irritated Chance. "Oh but wait, there was one player last year. He was a catcher, I think. I can't remember what team he played for, but he took a knee."

"Well find out what team he plays for so I can watch and support him."

"I don't think he was re-signed anywhere."

"Oh, so probably another Kaep situation? That's that bullshit. Here we are a little over a year and a half later and Kaep still doesn't have a job in the NFL. The players are still being harassed about these protests.

"What's so sad, though, is that everyone is talking about the anthem protests, but no one is talking about the reason they are protesting. The actual cause itself has been lost in all this mess. Son, I don't want to start preachin' again, but . . . "

"Oh Lawd, here we go," Chance says while rolling his eyes.

Coach Knight ignores him.

"Look at Kaep. The NFL owners blackballed his ass. That's why we need black owners in pro sports. If there was a black owner in the NFL, Kaep would most likely have a job right now.

"All I'm saying, Son, is don't be afraid to speak out for what you believe in. Don't be afraid to stand up for what is right. I want you to be able to look hate right in the face and fight it. That's something I admire about LeBron James. He's not afraid to call the president out on his foolishness. LeBron isn't afraid to take a political stand. No owner is going to cut LeBron or any athlete of his caliber. He generates too much money for them.

"If Kaep had knelt during the year he led San Francisco to the Super Bowl, he would still have a job. Even though we know it's bullshit, owners can still make the argument that they don't want Kaep because he's just not good enough anymore. They can't say that about LeBron. Bottom line is we have to start thinking about ownership, building our communities up, and bringing our HBCUs back to glory."

Chance closes his eyes and starts making a fake snoring sound.

"Oh that's how you gonna play me as I try to kick some knowledge?" His father teasingly asks. "Whatever, Son."

Chance stops snoring and then starts laughing.

"Look, Pops. I hear ya on everything you said, but right now I'm just trying to watch Nats whoop dat Orioles' ass. Let's go, Nats!"

"Oh no, my boy. This is the Orioles' year, I'm tellin' ya."

"There is one thing that I will admit, though, Pops. Walt said something to me when we were on our Howard visit that has really stuck with me. He was defending the argument that both you and Coach Mac have been trying to make about top recruits going to HBCUs.

"Walt reminded us that the University of Virginia and the University of Florida each allowed white nationalists to come and preach hate on their campus. Ole Miss allowed folks to have a confederacy celebration on their campus. So, as a black athlete, why would you choose to go to a university that would allow that?

"Not only are you going there to play for them, but you're potentially generating millions of dollars for their school, their program. We need to wake up."

"Exactly! It all ties in to what I've been trying to tell you."

"Yeah, I feel ya, but that particularly struck a nerve with me the more and more I thought about it. But, hey, I ain't goin' to Virginia, Florida, or Ole Miss. I'm going to Kentucky. So as long as Kentucky doesn't hold any white nationalist rallies, I'm solid."

Couch Knight doesn't respond. They watch the game. Hours later, Chance's hunger pangs begin.

"Pops, I'm starving for some real food. Let's order a pizza."

"I could eat some pizza, but delivery will probably take too long since the playoff game's about to start. Everyone's probably ordering. Let's call it in, DVR the start of the game, and just run and pick it up."

"Okay bet, I'll call Joe's Pizza and Wings."

About forty-five minutes later, Chance is leaving the pizza shop and climbing into his father's vehicle.

"Man oh man that pizza smells good," says Coach Knight.

"Sure does and I'm smashin' it when we get home."

Coach Knight turns to look at his son and chokes up.

"I preach a lot, Son. Maybe I don't tell you enough how proud I am of you. I just want you to know that. Not only do you have brains, but also you have a gift that people would kill for.

"I want you to maximize that talent at the next level and show the world what you can do. Great things are in store for you. I just know it. And I'm going to be on the front row for everything."

"Pops, I've never ever doubted your love. You show me every day."

Their conversation is interrupted as they notice police activity. Two police cars have pulled over a vehicle occupied by a group of guys. Coach Knight leans over for a better look. The sky hasn't fully transitioned to night, but the natural light has greatly dimmed.

"Isn't that Big Dink's truck?"

"Yup, sure is," says Chance. "Fuck!"

Coach Knight pulls his car over to the side.

"Chance, stay in the car. Whatever you do, don't get out; you got too much on the line. I'll be right back."

He jumps out of the car and walks quickly toward the policemen who now have all four vehicle occupants lying on the pavement with their hands behind their heads. An officer looks up, sees the six-foot, three-inch brawny and broad-shouldered black man walking purposely toward them and instinctively draws his weapon.

"Freeze right there! Not another step."

"Wait, Officer. I'm their coach. What seems to be the problem?"

"This is none of your fuckin' business. Now get back in your vehicle and get the fuck outta here."

"None of my business?" The anger is rising in Coach Knight, who momentarily forgets what he has always preached. "These players *are* my business. I'm their basketball coach. Look, here's my ID if it helps."

Coach Knight reaches for his license.

"Hands! Let me see your fuckin' hands."

Coach Knight, his hand inside his jacket, realizes too late the danger this action might put him in.

A second police officer, who has been out of earshot while cuffing the four occupants from Big Dink's SUV and sitting them on the curb, observes Coach Knight's movements. He quickly aims his Taser. He does not miss. Coach Knight drops to the ground and writhes. Both officers jump on top of him. One of the officers places Coach Knight in a tight chokehold while the other handcuffs him. During the brief struggle, the forty-five-year-old Coach Knight faintly utters a few words.

"I can't breathe."

The officer, high on adrenaline, does not loosen his grip. The players, still in cuffs, use their feet to push themselves up to standing position while yelling.

"He can't breathe!" Big Dink cries out. "Let him go! Get off his fuckin' neck! He can't fuckin' breathe, yo! What's *wrong* with you?"

As the officer finally loosens his grip, Coach Knight's head slips from the officer's arms and lowers facedown onto the pavement. Coach Knight convulses. More officers arrive on the scene.

Back in the Chevy Tahoe, Chance's view of his father is blocked by Dink's SUV, but he senses something is wrong. With fear rising and ignoring his father's earlier orders, he throws open the truck door and starts sprinting. Two officers tackle Chance and he lands about five feet from his convulsing dad. Held down, the side of his face pushed into the pavement, he looks directly at his father. Chance feels the bile rise and fall in his throat. The convulsions stop and Coach Knight is still, head turned toward Chance. Eyes void.

"Pops! What did you guys do to him? Pops! Help him! Call an ambulance!"

Chance's tear-filled eyes are staring helplessly into his father's—searching for life but finding none.

"Nooooooooooo! Pops! Get up! Pops! Please get up! Pops!"

The other players watch silently in utter disbelief. The officer, who had performed the chokehold, searches for a weapon and then for a pulse. Both efforts are fruitless. He shakes and then lowers his head. Another officer runs over and quickly starts to perform CPR. Officers and players absorb the excruciating pain in Chance's mournful screams. The players are full of sadness for what just happened. The officers are full of fear of what is to come.

"God why? They killed my Pops! They killed my fuckin' Pops!"

Chance wails.

The story makes headlines all over the country.

"Father and AAU Coach of Nation's Number One High School Basketball Player Dies at the Hands of Police."

9 | "SWEET LOW, SWEET CHARIOT"

Coach Knight's funeral is standing room only even in the large Baptist church. The cream colored, gold trimmed casket is open. The mortician has done his job well. Coach Knight looks remarkably like himself. The air is filled with a pungent scent wafting from the many floral arrangements. Chance, trying to be stoic, is sitting in the front row with his family. His sunglasses can't mask the tears streaming down his face. Mrs. Knight and Amaia are both weeping uncontrollably. The PG Problems and Capital Heights High School basketball teams and coaching staffs sit protectively behind them.

The casket closes as the service begins. Chance, a broken soul, only hears snippets of the accolades offered by the parade of speakers as they describe his father: "hero," "man's man with a big heart," "role model," "inspirational," "hard worker," "devoted to his family and community."

The Baptist minister is ending the service with an affirmation of faith.

"We don't know why he was taken from his wife and children, taken from all of us who loved him. I don't have an answer. But we have to believe God has a plan. Rest in peace, my dear friend," he says with his booming voice.

A chorus of Amens can be heard.

As the recession begins, Chance finds a measure of comfort in the choir's hauntingly beautiful acapella rendition of "Swing Low, Sweet Chariot." The refrain, "Coming for to Carry Me Home," fills his heart. He reaches to hold his mother up as she falters.

It appears as though nearly everyone at the service is attending the burial. The procession is one of the longest the city has seen for a private citizen. After the minister's final blessing, friends and extended family gently rest roses on the casket. Mrs. Knight's sister, Linda Jones, and nephew, Mike, linger a moment before stepping away. Coach Mac is last and lays down a replica of Coach Knight's old Howard University basketball jersey. Pinned to the shirt is a picture of Coach Mac with his friend, both wearing Howard jerseys, grinning broadly with their arms around each other's shoulders. Coach Mac steps toward Chance. As he approaches, Chance notices that today he is showing his age.

"Your father was a hell of a man, son. He will never be forgotten. God bless you and your family."

Coach Mac puts his hand on Chance's shoulder before leaning in to kiss Mrs. Knight and Amaia.

Friends and family return to their cars and head for the repast, lovingly prepared by the churchwomen, and served in the basement of the Baptist church. In order to privately say their final farewell, Chance, his mother, and sister remain seated in the unsteady chairs provided at the cemetery. Mrs. Knight is relieved that the casket will not be lowered until sometime later that afternoon. The scene is still too much for Amaia. She bursts into tears and runs to their limousine. Her mother hurries to join her. Chance is still, transfixed by the picture of Coach Mac and his father. Enveloped in his grief—his enormous loss, he falls to his knees. Walt and Big Dink, who had been standing in front of Big Dink's SUV watching, hurry to Chance and help lift him up until he is standing once more.

10 BLUEPRINT

Chance is on the outdoor basketball court by himself shooting around. His mind flashes back to playing one-on-one with his father; to his father embracing him after big wins; to laughing together as they tease one another. Feeling cheated, Chance angrily throws the basketball as far as he can into the nearby woods. He cries. Again.

Later that night, Chance is lying in his bed throwing a basketball up toward the ceiling and catching it as gravity pulls it back down. Thoughts of his father are still swirling in his head. He longs for a distraction. The thoughts are too depressing. He puts the basketball down on the bed beside him, grabs the remote control, and switches on the television. *Sports Highlight Center* is on and the sportscasters are focusing on Colin Kaepernick remaining unsigned and his lawsuit against the league last year for collusion to keep it that way. They ponder whether Kaepernick will have enough evidence for the case to move forward after initial arbitration. They then move on to "Black Lives Matter" and the police shootings that have taken place over the past few years—the key reason Kaepernick began taking a knee. As Chance stares at the TV, he suddenly finds the peace that has eluded him since his father was killed a week ago. And for the first time since that fateful night, he smiles.

A few days later at the Prince George's County Recreation Center, Chance and several other AAU allstars are playing a scheduled pick-up basketball game in the gymnasium. Chance has the ball on the final play and dazzles his audience. A tall, boney middle school aged boy, sitting on the sidelines with his friends, pumps his fists.

"Wow, that crossover was nasty," he says.

"No, that vicious one-handed dunk to win the game was nasty!" says his friend.

They look at Chance in awe as the players high-five one another.

The players begin walking off the court ahead of Chance.

"Fellas, hold up," Chance calls out to them. "I want y'all to hear something."

Coach Mac, waiting on the sidelines, walks over and shakes Chance's hand. Chance and the other players sit on the bleachers as Coach Mac addresses them.

11

SEVEN YESSES

It is National Signing Day. Capital Heights High School has opened its assembly hall to the media. Students and coaches are settling into their seats. The media fills the orchestra section of the room. They are eagerly waiting for Chance to step up to the podium and make his official announcement as to where he will play basketball next season. The orchestra section is buzzing. Reporters are battling back and forth with their predictions and defending their stance. Kentucky and Maryland are echoing the most, but Kentucky is the clear stand out.

The time has come. Chance enters the assembly hall and makes his way down the aisle. Instantly the melody of clicking cameras fills the auditorium. Following Chance are his mother, little sister, and his closest friends, Walt and Big Dink. He climbs the small set of stairs and takes his place behind the podium. His family, teammates, and coaches stand behind him for support. A table on the stage is lined with three hats: University of Maryland, University of Kentucky, and Duke University.

Chance adjusts the microphone attached to the podium and begins.

"I'd like to thank everyone for coming out today. I want to start off by paying respects to my pops. We dreamed about this day ever since it looked like I might have a little skill. We both worked extremely hard to get me to this very moment. It's ironic that on the day he died, he promised me he would always be front and center watching. To not have him physically here with me today…"

Chance pauses, puts his head down, and takes a deep breath. He steels himself and continues.

"I watched my pops die at the hands of the police. *In front of my eyes!* I play that moment in my head every single day. It's like a video in my mind on a constant loop. I can't stop it, no matter how hard I try. Police violence against unarmed black men has to stop. Black lives matter! My father's life mattered!"

Chance levels his voice and continues.

"My father preached endlessly about taking care of one another and standing up for what's right; especially when it comes to social injustice affecting the black community. I didn't really understand because I was only thinking about myself and couldn't see beyond me. No more. I'm going to honor my pops who fell victim to the same injustice that Colin Kaepernick is protesting. I'm going to do what my father wanted all along."

Chance pauses.

The room momentarily falls silent. The clicking melody has come to a full stop. The expression on the reporters' faces reveals that they are moved by Chance's words but equally puzzled by where he is going with his speech.

Chance looks toward the ceiling and points his index finger in the same direction; he softly speaks to his father.

"This is for you, Pops."

Chance makes the announcement everyone is waiting to hear.

"I am going to follow in his giant footsteps and attend his alma mater, Howard University."

As Chance is making the announcement, he pulls a Howard University basketball cap from behind the podium and proudly places it on his head. There is an audible collective gasp in the room. Everyone appears to be in shock. The clicking melody returns with a quickening tempo.

Chance stands a bit more erect.

"Rightfully, my father's basketball number has been retired. But I'm thankful to have found another way to honor him on the court. In honor of my father's support for Kaep's cause and admiration for his peaceful activism, I'm pleased to announce that I will be wearing Kaep's number, number seven. I'm extremely determined and motivated to take my talents to Howard University and to see what follows.

"Starting today and moving forward, I'm challenging other top rated black athletes to attend HBCUs. My father had a vision that HBCUs could capitalize on the talent that we have in our community and change the HBCU landscape from struggling to thriving. One day, maybe, HBCUs can have the donors, television contracts, exposure, and revenue that can strengthen our colleges and universities, as they do for Duke, Kentucky, Maryland, UNC, to name a few. Not only in state-of-the-art facilities but in our academics and ability to provide scholarships to kids like us looking for access to the means necessary to build a better life."

He pauses for a moment and then continues.

"Everyone won't be happy with my decision here today. Particularly Big Blue Nation. I understand that. I accept that. However, I'd like to thank the Kentucky coaching staff. They were amazing during this entire recruitment process, especially after I verbally committed to them last fall."

Unaware of the prior verbal commitment, the room gasps again.

"And I appreciate their support after my pops was taken from us. I hope that the coaches and players, along with Big Blue Nation, can forgive me. I hope they can understand that this is bigger than basketball. I have a greater mission now. In honor of what my father always preached to me, I want to show young athletes of color that we have the power to create change. The president and the NFL owners can try to stop players from kneeling all they want and they can blackball Kaep all they want. But they can't stop top rated black athletes from choosing which colleges to attend, now can they?"

The entire stage and a large portion of the audience burst into a thunderous applause. The rest, confused, applaud slowly—almost in that awkward, obligated to clap because everyone else is kind of way.

"That's right," shouts a young man with well-maintained dreadlocks.

"Preach, young brotha!" exclaims an older, light-skinned balding man.

"What the fuck is happening right, now?" a middle-aged Caucasian reporter, turning to his cameraman, asks rhetorically.

Chance has found his stride.

"I want to thank all of you for coming out today. I also want to thank God for making all things possible. I want to thank my father. Rest in peace, Pops. We did it!

"My father's voice will forever guide me through darkness, his spirit will guide me through light, and it's the memory of my father that will continue to drive my inner fight.

"Mom, Amaia, thank you. You both are my everything.

"Lastly, I also want to thank my coaches and teammates. Your support has been invaluable."

Chance grins—a wide, knowing grin.

"Speaking of my teammates, my AAU teammates, when they found out what I was doing, some of them decided to join me in honoring my pops, also their coach. My father wasn't just Coach Knight to them. He was like a father, too. He was always a father figure to any youngin' who would allow it. And now, it's with great pleasure I get to tell everyone that it will not just be me attending Howard University in the fall. The fourth ranked center in the country, Dink Johnson, will be joining me. The fifth ranked point guard in the nation, Maximus Miller, will be joining us. The seventh ranked small forward in the nation, Bobby Banks, will be joining us. Yes, white people can attend HBCUs, too."

Laughter and applause reverberate through most sections of the assembly hall.

"And our teammate, who happens to be my best friend since we were kids, Walt Williams, will also be joining us at Howard."

Applause is heard again.

"Big Dink, Mad Max, Bird, Walt, come on up to the podium and get your shine!"

All four approach, accept a Howard University hat from Coach Mac, who has now joined the young men on stage, and individually make their announcement. Their cheering families can barely be heard over the applause each one receives.

Chance finds his way back to the podium. He grins again, only this time his grin suggests he is about to reveal an even greater secret.

"Come on, we're not done yet. I know y'all didn't think those *little* announcements were the only ones?"

The room falls silent once more. Everyone's eyes are fixed on Chance in anticipation of what he will say next.

"The love and support shown to me and my family, and the desire to honor my pops, and his legend as a basketball coach and mentor—and all he stood for and believed in—has spread beyond the players who played on our AAU team. It has transcended across enemy lines.

"Two of our AAU arch rivals—my cousin and friend—have decided to change coasts from West to East and join our revolution at Howard. I would like to introduce the nation's number one power forward and number three point guard. Mike Jones, Jason Jacks, the floor is yours."

Wide eyes, blank stares, and open mouths fill the room. Heads turn from right to left searching for the faces of Jones and Jacks. Reporters don't believe the announcement. There is no way this can be happening.

Mike and J.J. emerge from the side of the stage and make their way to the podium on the opposite side. Those on stage explode with excitement. The cheers and sounds from fast clapping hands carry to every corner of the Assembly Hall. Their high school coaches are concerned about their choice, but their parents are proud of the maturity of their decision. As the honored granddaughter of a prominent southern civil rights leader, and with a family lineage of activists, Mrs. Jones is particularly moved. Although she is not an activist herself, she knows now that the family tradition is being carried on through her son and nephew. Through long talks with J.J.'s family, she was able to convince them to allow J.J. to embark on this unprecedented journey. So maybe in her own right she is an activist, too.

Mike and J.J. accept their hats from Coach Mac, and Chance steps back as each makes their official announcement and gives a short speech. Chance watches and is so overwhelmed he feels as if he is having an out-of-body experience. Before he realizes it, Mike and J.J. have called him back to the podium to speak. He is unsure of what just happened, of what was said, but it is clear people cannot believe what they are witnessing. There is a buzz in the auditorium that he has to quiet before speaking.

"The fact that these guys, who were on their way to play ball at major powerhouse programs, have quickly and thoughtfully decided to throw that all away to instead attend Howard with me in honor of my pops, in honor of what he stood for…"

Chance pauses and lowers his head. Choked up, he tries again.

"It just truly means the world to me. These guys are forever my brothers. I will never forget or take for granted the sacrifice that they all are making for our black institutions today—for this movement.

"I want everyone to hear about what we did here today. I want everyone to witness what we are about to do. I'm excited for us all to see what follows. Thank you everyone and God bless.

"As my pops would say, H-UUUUU!" he calls out.

"You Know!" respond the other six Howard University recruits.

"And guess what? He kept his promise. He's still with me *front* and *center*."

Chance electrifies the audience. They give him a standing ovation. They know they are witnessing history, even if everyone might not like it.

Media immediately tries to swarm the podium to ask Chance and the other players questions. Coach Mac, who is standing off to the side, comes over and addresses the reporters.

"Please let the players have a moment to take in this experience. I'll take a few questions regarding today's announcement and then we're all off to celebrate—especially me." He winks.

"Coach, how long have you known that these players, arguably the top in the nation, were coming to Howard?" a reporter asks.

"Believe it or not I only found out this past week."

"How did you have enough scholarships to accommodate all these new players?" asks another reporter.

"It was a very rare situation. We had six seniors last year and three players who transferred to bigger schools in the summer. That left us with only four returning scholarship players for next season. I'm excited that one of these players is Deon Diggs. He was MEAC Freshman of the Year two seasons ago and just made First Team All MEAC this year. As a sophomore, his contribution to the team has been remarkable. His freshman year, he averaged a double-double in scoring and rebounding. As a sophomore, he averaged twenty-five points, nine rebounds, and three assists."

"Coach, Deon Diggs was the sophomore sensation and stand out star on your team," says another reporter, slightly more familiar with black school athletes. "Although he didn't win it this past season, he's anticipated, at least he *was*, to be MEAC Player of the Year this upcoming season. How is he going to feel about these top recruits coming in and possibly stealing his spotlight?"

"That's a question you would have to ask Deon. I can only speculate. But Deon is a fine young man and is developing into a leader. The team is the priority, not one individual person. I anticipate that his two years of seasoning will add a little flavor to the soup we're getting ready to serve up."

After frantic fact gathering, another reporter yells out.

"Coach, how many games will you guys win next season and can this team make it to the NCAA tournament? Howard men have not been to the NCAA tournament in over seventeen years."

Coach Mac smiles.

"Well I'm no psychic, so I have no idea how good we'll be. I can promise you that we're going to give it our all. But if we can come together as a cohesive team, then I think we have a very good shot of winning the MEAC."

"With this announcement today, you essentially have a Fab Seven, or should I brand them the Super Seven, going to Howard to play for you. How does it feel?"

Coach Mac smiles again.

"It feels great, but don't forget these are freshmen jumping to a totally new level of basketball. College ball is a lot different from high school. Yes, I'm very excited for the possibilities, but let's not get ahead of ourselves.

"That's all for now folks. Thank you and have a great day," he says quickly and dismissively to prevent another question.

The coach and his players step down from the podium and walk away.

Following this announcement, the media latches on to the story and runs with it.

The cover of *Sports Illustrated* reads, "Kentucky? Nope. Duke? Nope. Maryland? Nope. Howard? Seven Yesses!"

USA Today's sports cover page reads, "Super 7 Reject Big Schools. Choose Howard University."

The front page of the *Washington Post* reads, "National HS Basketball Player of the Year Honors Slain Father/Coach. Will Attend His Alma Mater."

Street and Smith cover page reads, "Black Colleges Matter, Basketball Star Chance Knight and Other Top Athletes Choose Howard. Big Schools Caught Off Guard."

12   TWENTY-FIVE GRAND

The Knight family pulls up to Chance's dormitory. The dormitory sits on the 600 block of Fairmont Street in Washington, District of Columbia. The building is unassuming but one of the nicer dormitories offered by the campus. It is suited in red-orange brick, with spots of brown that reveal its age. Undoubtedly, stories from many generations have been made within those walls.

College move in day comes much too fast for Mrs. Knight. She was quiet for most of the car ride, reflecting on the loss of her husband and now, for all practical purposes, losing her first-born. She has not brought herself to give the "parent" speech but knows she cannot put it off any longer. Before unloading the car, Mrs. Knight turns to Chance.

"I am so proud of you, Son," she says quietly. "Your father would be beside himself. I know that academics have always been easy for you, but understand that college academics are going to be much more challenging.

"And college level basketball programs are much more demanding than high school. You'll have less time to dedicate to schoolwork, so you need to maximize your study time. Apply the same discipline in studying as you do in basketball.

"Don't get me wrong, I want you to still have fun and make stories that you can tell ten years from now; Lord knows your father and I made plenty. But promise me, don't be distracted by these thirsty girls. Stay away from the drugs, and yes, weed is a drug. And don't get caught up in drinking alcohol. You're not old enough to drink anyway so don't let me catch you with a fake ID. I'll know what it's for."

Mrs. Knight gives Chance "the eye." She rights her face and addresses him in a sincere tone.

"Always remember. You're a hero to a lot of people in our community. You're a hero to me. You're a hero to your sister. You're a hero to all of these young men that followed you to this school. And most importantly, I know you're a hero to your father. Make us all proud, baby. And any time you need us, your sister and I are only twenty minutes away."

Mrs. Knight's voice cracks as she fights back tears. In an effort to prevent the tears from winning, she ends the conversation quickly.

"Now let's get out of this car and start unloading."

Chance puts his arms around his mother and the hold lingers. For a moment Mrs. Knight thinks he will never let go, and she is fine with that.

"I got you, Mom," Chance whispers in her ear.

He beckons his sister. "Get up here and get in on this hug, girl."

From the back of the car, Amaia, with a huge smile, climbs halfway over the seats and eagerly joins the embrace.

The trio exits the Chevy Tahoe and walks around to the trunk.

Chance turns to his mother. "Mom?"

"Yes, Son?"

With a hint of mischief in his eyes, Chance questions her.

"Going back to what you said, about girls being thirsty. Thirsty, though, Mom? Really? Where did you even learn that word? Were you *thirsty* for Pops?"

"Boy, please. I already told you your father was the pursuer. But I did make sure to keep the thirsty ones away from him. Mmm hmm."

They both laugh.

As Chance and his family are unloading the truck, Walt and his mom have finished unpacking in his dorm room and are exchanging their goodbyes.

"Son, you're the most caring, considerate young man I've ever known. Nobody has a bigger, more genuine, or more generous heart than you. You're a shining example for Teddy. We both love you so much. Just so proud.

"Your father and I have always wanted the best for you. Going to college was on the top of the list. We were going to make it happen no matter what. But instead, you made it happen.

"There's something you don't know. Your father and I were saving for your college fund. It isn't as much as I would have liked, though. After your father passed, I didn't have as much money to contribute. But what I do have is all yours . . ."

"Mom. No way. That's your money. I can't take it. I won't," Walt says, interrupting his mother.

"Baby, I want this money to go to you. Your father wanted this money to be used on you. This is your money and you will take it. This isn't a debate. There is no democracy in my household. You know this. What I say goes. I said it and that is that. We have $25,000 saved for you."

Walt, in shock, feels his way to the bed and slowly sits down.

"You'll get $2,500 a semester. I expect that you'll spend wisely and make it last. I hope you'll save some of it. I do expect that you'll get a job during summers, or an internship. The remaining $5,000 will be given to you once you graduate. I think that's fair."

Walt processes what he has just been told. For him, this is like winning the lottery. He stands up, walks over to his mother, and plants a wet, forceful kiss on her check. He wraps his arms around her, squeezing so tightly she almost loses her breath.

On the other side of campus, Deon soaks up the adulation as he strolls across The Yard. Women call out his name and the guys high-five and dap him up; confirmation he is still the man.

Smoke, a Howard football player, walks toward him.

"What up, Deon? What's good witcha?"

"What up, Smoke? I can't call it, man. Just out here enjoying the sights of all this fresh ass on campus."

"Hell, yeah. Some of my teammates and I just met a group of dope freshmen chicks 'bout an hour ago. They were from ATL. Fine as hell and body for days, ya heard me?"

"Yeah, it's hard for me 'cause I gotta watch my back for Kia, you know? I ain't tryin' to mess that up."

"Yeah, I don't blame you, cuz. Kia's wifey material. Play that one safe, my brotha."

"Indeed."

"Oh, but yooooo, what's up with these freshmen your squad got coming in? I hear their game's supposed to be legit!"

"Man, I hope so. You already know I was supposed to play for Virginia Tech. But Coach was recruiting me hard. He said if I played here, then I'd be *the man*. He made sense. I might not have gotten any real playin' time at Tech until junior or senior year. But with the team they had, I might not have gotten to play at all."

"That's what's up."

"Yeah, and he said coming here wouldn't take away my chance of going to an NCAA tournament. He'd build a team around me with enough talent to win the MEAC tournament. And you know that's an automatic bid to the NCAA tournament."

"Yeah, that'd be sick."

"Not only would I be going to the Big Dance, I'd definitely be playing in it. That's how he got me to commit."

"Well, you're definitely *the man*."

"But we ain't winning shit. No disrespect to my team, but I haven't been surrounded by legit talent.

I'm already two years in. I only have two more seasons. I ain't tryin' to leave Howard without winning the MEAC tournament. I've got to play in the Big Dance at least once.

"I didn't pass on Virginia Tech for the team I've had so far. So these freshmen better be as good as I hear. They need to be able to come right in, follow my lead, and help us reach our goal."

"Well, I think y'all got what you need. I hear these brothas' game is tight. Especially that dude Chance Knight."

Just the sound of that name boils up resentment inside of Deon, but he will not expose himself to Smoke. He will play it cool, for now. Although he did not know who Chance was during their encounters last year, he knows now. He is a threat. He is a threat to his stardom and his position as Kia's boyfriend.

"Yeah, well, college ball is different from high school. Hype doesn't always equal performance. I just need their performance to live up to their hype. I met that kid, Chance, sophomore year but didn't realize who he was. We had some words, but I let him know what's up so we shouldn't have no problems." Deon lies. He knows they will have problems.

"Well, he's on your team now so I'm sure he'll follow your lead and fall in line, my brotha."

"Right, right. All right, well I'll get up with you later. I'm headed to meet up with Coach to talk 'bout everything." Almost everything.

Smoke nods.

"Oh okay, that's what's up. Holla at you later."

Arriving at the basketball office, Deon sees Morgan Seymour, Coach Mac's Administrative Assistant.

"Hey, Morgan."

She looks up from her tidy desk. "Hi, baby, how you feelin'? You ready for the new season?"

"Yes ma'am. Let's get it." Deon gives Morgan a respectful smile. "Is Coach Mac in his office?"

"Yup, go on back. He's expecting you."

"Thank you, Morgan."

Deon heads back. He courtesy knocks on Coach Mac's door as he enters his office. Coach Mac looks up from his desk and grins.

"D! My main man! How are you, buddy?"

"I'm great!" He lies again. "Just super excited to get this season underway. Thanks for keeping your word and bringing in some real talent, finally. If these freshmen come in ready to play and follow my lead, then I think we can win the MEAC this year."

Deon manages to suppress his thoughts of Chance, and excitement builds in his voice.

"We can go to the Big Dance!"

Coach Mac smiles.

"D, with the type of talent we have coming in, we not only can win the MEAC, but we can, potentially, be the NCAA Cinderella story—maybe make it to the Sweet Sixteen."

"That's what I'm talkin' 'bout, Coach. I met Chance, Big Dink, and Walt on Big Dink's visit last year but haven't met the others. When do I get to meet them? I've seen some good clips online but haven't had an opportunity to see them play. I want to get us in the gym ASAP and start working on our chemistry." He already knows what kind of chemistry he has with Chance.

"And don't you worry, Coach, I'm gonna take these youngins under my wing and be their leader from day one."

"That's what I like to hear, son. I'm setting up a meeting tomorrow for three o'clock to discuss team business. I'm heading out right after, but the gym will be open for y'all to play. You can take the lead on setting that up. I suggest you show up prepared to ball!"

While trying to keep the dread of seeing Chance bottled up, Deon claps his hands in excitement. "Let's get it baby! Let's go!"

The Super Seven are enjoying The Yard. Chance, Big Dink, and Walt are sitting on a bench while Mad

Max, J.J., Mike, and Bird stand beside them. They are watching the scenery, scenery not to be confused with the first glimpse of fall colors adorning the tall trees or the manicured emerald grass. They are watching the coeds sprinkling the lawn as they sit in groups, or solo, while reading a book or people watching. The teammates are joking with, and hollering at, young women walking across The Yard.

Bird sees a trio walk by. He focuses on the tall, slender one. She has silky, shoulder-length curly hair. Her features suggest mixed heritage.

"Excuse me, beautiful. You're the baddest joint I've seen since I've been here. What's your name?" he asks with his pale blue eyes fixed on her.

"My name is Shannon, and first of all, I ain't a joint," she responds with a sassy tone. "And secondly, I'm not interested but thank you."

"Okay. It's all good.

"Let me ask you a question, though. Do you have any white in you?"

"Nope."

"Well, would you like some?"

The fellas double over with laughter. Even Shannon's two girlfriends laugh. Shannon is less amused. The look she flashes Bird leaves no need for her to respond with a verbal "no."

One of Shannon's friends looks at Bird and sizes him up as ruggedly good-looking. "What's your name?" she asks.

"Bobby, but my friends call me Bird."

"Well, Bird, *I* might want some white in me."

The teammates collectively say, "Ooooohhh shit!"

"Word?" asks Bird.

"I said *might*. I'll be seeing you around I'm sure."

"Yes, you will my dear. You absolutely will."

She winks at Bird as the trio moves on. As that exchange concludes, Chance spies his prize a short distance away.

"Excuse me, Mo County," hollers Chance.

With two girlfriends, a surprised Kia walks over.

"Oh, snap. What are you doing here?"

"Once I found out you were coming to Howard, I made up my mind right then and there that I was coming here to get you."

"I see he still got that confident swag thing goin' on," says one of Kia's girlfriends.

"Yup. That's that same swag that almost got you fucked up by my boyfriend, Deon, too."

"Yup, 'cause we all know Deon's crazy ass is even crazier when it comes to Kia," adds another friend.

116

Sitting on the porch of the library overlooking The Yard, Deon notices Kia and her friends talking with Chance and his crew. His lips tighten. His eyebrows furrow. He feels his boiling resentment about to spill over.

Kia's girlfriend spots him walking toward them. "Well speak of the devil. Here comes Deon."

"Fuck me," Kia says.

Deon makes his way over and is now face to face with Chance.

"Man I thought I told you never to be around my girl again. What part of that didn't you understand?"

"Look, cuz. I'm just doing what college kids do. Meeting new people and having fun. What the fuck are you so uptight about?"

"I don't care what the fuck you do as long as it doesn't involve Kia! *My* girl!"

"Deon, baby, it's cool."

"Nah, fuck that. This dude is real disrespectful and I'm 'bout to put him in his place."

"Yo, Deon. Chill, cuz. We're all teammates, bro," Big Dink interjects.

Deon pauses and knows he needs to play the game. He feels disdain for what he is about to do.

"I apologize for coming off the way I did. Big Dink is right. We're teammates now. We gotta be able to coexist and work together. As the veteran, I need to be an example. Welcome to HU. I overreacted," he says as he daps up Chance.

"It's all good, bro."

"I just want to win games," Deon says as he addresses the larger group. "If y'all are as good as the hype that surrounds you, all y'all are welcome. I'm setting up an open gym for tomorrow after our meeting with Coach. I hope each of y'all shows up. I can't wait to see what y'all got. Until then, continue enjoying your view. As you can see, HU is known for its beautiful women. And since there are double the number of women here as men, take your pick."

Deon's true feelings snap back. He takes a step closer to Chance's face and gives him a warning in a low, stern whisper.

"Stay the fuck away from my girl, though, for real. Are we clear?"

"Crystal," Chance says with a cocky smile.

The next day does not come soon enough for Chance, but his teammates are tense and anxious entering the gym. As Chance laces his shoes, he feels Deon's eyes boring into him.

Deon steps forward to the group. "Let's get ready to ball, fellas. We're going freshmen versus upperclassmen."

Deon notices a few spectators trickling into the gymnasium. Their presence fuels his energy. He smacks the ball with both hands really hard.

"Let's go!" Deon shouts enthusiastically. He cannot wait to be physical with Chance.

The freshmen briefly huddle. "All right, fellas, this is our chance to make our mark," Chance says taking the lead. "Let's let these upperclassmen know right from the jump whose mutha fuckin' team this is now."

"Hell yeah," says Big Dink. "Let's bust they ass. Chance, go at Deon every opportunity you get. Put him in his place and show him what a *real* star looks like."

Their huddle breaks and they all high-five. Play begins with back and forth basketball action. The freshmen make an indisputable statement on the court. They look like they are playing a middle school team, leaving the upperclassmen embarrassed and ashamed.

Chance has his way with Deon, controlling Deon's game as if he were a marionette puppet. On the very last play, Chance dunks on him with authority to win. As the dunk happens, Deon falls to the ground and a spectator lets out an "ohhhhh shit." Deon knows open gym is over.

Walt walks over and reaches down to help Deon up. Deon ignores Walt's gesture and walks angrily away.

"C'mon fellas. Let's shower and go to the cafeteria for dinner," he barks at the upperclassmen.

He ignores the freshmen.

Chance, Big Dink, Bird, Walt, J.J, Mike, and Mad Max stand in the dinner line.

"Yo, Chance. You was givin' Deon the business," boasts Walt.

"Hell yeah. Low-key, you looked like you were the upperclassman and he looked like the freshman. You flipped that shit on him," adds Bird.

"Man, y'all know I do what I gotta do. Fool had to be put in his place for talkin' all that shit."

At that very moment Deon walks into the cafeteria with his arm around Kia.

Big Dink elbows Chance and motions his head in Deon's direction. "Yeah, you busted his ass on the court, but he still bustin' dat Kia ass off the court, though," ribs Big Dink.

Everyone starts laughing except Chance.

Chance stares intently at Kia as she and Deon go to another dinner line.

"Damn she bad! Yeah, you right, ha ha. He might have taken that 'L' today on the court but he definitely winnin' off the court."

"You ain't lyin'," agrees Mad Max.

The next day Chance walks into his first college class, freshman English. He glances around the room for a seat and, to his surprise and delight, sees Kia. Chance nearly knocks classmates down in his rush to grab the open seat next to her.

"Hey, Mo County."

Kia smiles. "Oh gosh. I can't get rid of you. What's up P.G.?"

"Is it all right if I sit next to you or is Deon's crazy ass gonna pop up outta nowhere and press me out?" Chance asks playfully.

"Ha ha. Let me find out Deon got you shook."

"Picture that, girl."

They exchange smiles.

The professor begins class by reviewing material that Chance already knows. The room is insufferably warm and the windows are closed. Thirty minutes later, Chance has his head in his arms snoring. Kia reaches out and grabs his hand. Chance lifts his head, sees Kia, squeezes her hand, and smiles. Kia returns a slight smile and then pulls her hand away, concerned that his touch feels inappropriately familiar.

Chance writes on a piece of paper, folds it, and hands it to Kia. She takes the note and silently reads, *"I appreciate you waking me up, but I was in the middle of a very good dream about the two of us."* Kia shakes her head with an unintentional flirtatious grin. Without reply, she folds the note back up and hands it to Chance. Class is dismissed.

At the next day's open gym, the freshmen once again dominate the upperclassmen. Chance delivers a crossover move on Deon. He goes in for a ferocious dunk and accidentally busts Deon's lip. He immediately apologizes. He really didn't mean to draw blood—at least not here. A frustrated Deon swings at Chance, who instinctively ducks to avoid the punch. This is the second time Deon has swung at him and missed. Chance tackles Deon and they begin to wrestle. Some of the other players—freshmen and upperclassmen—rush over to pull them apart.

As the scuffle begins, Morgan is walking by.

"Hey! Hey! Hey! Break it up, break it up NOW! Dammit," a shocked Morgan says. "Look, Coach Mac is all for competitiveness. He even likes feisty play. But he absolutely won't tolerate fighting and swinging on each other. Deon, if Coach ever catches you pulling something like that . . . "

Morgan doesn't need to finish the warning.

"You can talk trash, argue, and even get mad at each other, but never swing on one of your teammates. Ever! Y'all are on the same team and you have the same goal. You're in this thing together. Don't y'all ever forget that, babies. Y'all better hope your coach doesn't find out about this. Now wrap this up and get out of the gym."

As the players start to walk away, Deon stops the upperclassmen.

"Yo, y'all should be fuckin' ashamed of yourselves. We just let a group of freshmen make us look like garbage. They embarrassed us, again. This is the second straight time. Get your shit together. Everyone's position is up for grabs. At all times. Coach is gonna play the best player at each position no matter freshman or senior. This shit can't happen again."

Twenty feet away, the freshmen are high-fiving each other and laughing. Deon frowns and catches Chance's gaze. Chance smiles and walks away. Deon's glare is full of rage.

13
MAKE AMERICA GREAT AGAIN

Chance and his crew are inside the Shaw-Howard University metro station.

"Yo, Deon's still actin' like a little bitch from when Chance busted his lip a few days ago," Big Dink says to the group.

"Yeah, he needs to get over it. It was an accident," says Chance.

"He'll get over it," assures Walt. "Anyway, Teddy's gonna be so excited to see you guys with me. Thanks so much for coming."

"Man, you don't have to thank us, bro. We're family. Teddy is like our little brother, too," says Chance.

"Exactly," says Big Dink as he slaps Walt on the shoulder.

The metro train pulls up to the platform. They take seats once the doors open. Something catches Mad Max's attention.

"Look at this mutha fucka in the MAGA hat over there."

"Oh, no, this mutha fucka is not out here in Chocolate City with that shit on," adds Big Dink.

"With all this DC gentrification, you can't even call it Chocolate City anymore, for real for real," says Chance.

"True dat. Man, I should go snatch that shit right off that mutha fucka's head," says Big Dink.

"Yo, chill," orders Walt. "That man has his right to wear whatever hat he wants. You remember after President Obama won there were folks all over the place wearing Obama hats, tee shirts, sweatshirts, pins, and all that. It wouldn't have been okay if people snatched Obama hats off folks. So it's not right for you to go snatching off MAGA hats."

"Sorry, Walt, but this is different. An Obama hat didn't represent the hate and blatant racism that the MAGA hat stands for," responds Big Dink, not backing down. "Man, come on. Make America great again. Really? Are they talkin' 'bout back when there was slavery? Are they talkin' 'bout back when black folks were being hanged? Are they talkin' 'bout back when black folks couldn't even drink out of the same damn water fountain as whites, or sit at the front of the bus? Are they talkin' 'bout back when Martin Luther King, Jr.

was assassinated? Is that when America was great? Is that what the MAGA hat is referring to?"

"Preach!" Chance shouts.

"Yo, don't even let that man and his red hat get to you," Walt says firmly. The train enters the next metro station and comes to a screeching halt. "Come on, this is our stop."

"Yeah, you're right, Walt. Let's go," says Big Dink as he seems to give in.

The metro doors' chime signals that the doors are opening and they stand up to step off. As they are exiting, Big Dink approaches the guy in the MAGA hat. Without warning, he snatches the hat off of his head. Fearing attack, the guy defensively balls up in a fetal position. Several onlookers laugh, a few cheer, but most are startled and shocked. One passenger attempts to record the incident's aftermath but is unable to locate her phone in her purse fast enough to capture anything worthwhile.

The players run off of the metro car and Big Dink throws the hat at Walt. Walt catches it and the other players laugh. The doors close. As the metro car begins to move, the man who was wearing the MAGA hat unfolds, rises, and looks out of the window just in time to get a good look at Walt holding the hat. Walt looks up and they make eye contact. Walt senses his fury and feels sorry for the poor guy.

"Man, what da fuck, Big Dink? That ain't cool," says an angry Walt.

"Man, that racist mutha fucka got exactly what he deserved," says Bird.

Walt is now exasperated. "Haven't any of y'all heard of freedom of speech? That man is entitled to wear any hat he wants."

"And haven't you heard of freedom of fuckin' a racist mutha fucka up?" retorts Big Dink. Their friends laugh.

"Man, that shit ain't right. That's all I'm sayin'."

"Chill out, Nelson Mandela. We ain't never gonna see that dude again. It's all good. Just chill the fuck out, bro."

"Yeah, whateva."

Walt takes the MAGA hat and throws it in the trash. He walks off ahead of his friends. Chance catches up to him. He puts his arm around Walt's shoulders.

"Don't even trip, bro. It's all good. You know Big Dink is a ruthless, angry mutha fucka. Big Dink is always gonna be Big Dink."

"Fuck you, Chance. I heard that."

They head out of the metro station, everyone in a good mood except Walt. The hospital looms larger and the mood sobers for everyone.

The guys crowd around little Teddy's hospital bed. Chance has his arm around Mrs. Williams. Teddy is overjoyed to see Walt and his friends.

"What's up big guy?" asks Walt.

"Hi, Walt," responds Teddy in his high-pitched voice. His eyes brighten.

"You see who I brought with me? They wanted to come to see you."

Teddy's smile widens to capacity.

"What's up, Teddy Ted? I brought you something," says Chance.

"What is it?" an excited Teddy asks.

"Guess!"

"A thousand dollars?"

Everyone laughs.

"A thousand dollars? Boy, I wish. Naw, I got you this."

Chance pulls off his book bag and pulls out seven tee shirts. He gives a shirt to Teddy and everyone in the room. The shirts are all black with white lettering that reads, "*TeddyStrong*." Below the words is an all-white screen print of the profile of Teddy's face.

"I've created an online page telling Teddy's story. Pop up shops will be announced on the page so folks will know when and where to buy the shirts. My mom and Amaia are gonna set them up every chance they get.

The profits are going to Teddy once he beats this. He can use the money to do whatever he wants to celebrate."

Chance directs his attention back to Teddy. "I just want you to know how strong you are, Teddy, and that everyone is supporting you and fighting with you. I love you, little man."

"Thanks, Chance! I love you, too. I want to go to Disney World and take all y'all with me!"

The big guys all smile. Mrs. Williams is visibly moved as her eyes swell with tears, her right hand clutches her shirt, and her shoulders sink toward her hips. She is thankful that he may have another opportunity to visit Disney World. She ponders the irony. Instead of traveling to Disney World when the PG Problems played in the AAU championship, he was learning he has cancer.

Chance gives Teddy a long and tender hug. The players stay until Teddy is clearly getting tired.

"Man, thanks again so much for coming," says Walt. "You have no idea how much it means to Teddy. He gets so excited when he knows you guys are coming to see him."

"Anything he needs. You just let us know," offers Chance.

"Can't thank you enough man. Imma stay here overnight with my mom and Teddy. I'll see y'all tomorrow."

"All right, bro. Love you. Be safe."

Chance glances back at Teddy and gives him a nod as he closes the door behind him. An emotional Mrs. Williams tightly squeezes Walt's hand. They both stare at Teddy as he starts to doze off. Through the hospital room window, Chance stops to look at Walt standing beside his mother. That quickly, the joy in Mrs. Williams' face has dissipated. They both look beaten down, caught in the cruel limbo of cancer— not knowing whether Teddy will live or die.

Across town in a forgotten blip of Alexandria, Virginia, several men are playing pool in an old neighborhood dive bar. A man with thinning dirty-blond hair walks in. Greeted by his friends, he sits down at a table and they join him.

"Dude, where's your MAGA hat?" Aaron, one of the pool players, asks. "You're never without that friggin' hat."

Billy, another pool player, never misses an opportunity to rib Charlie. "Yeah, Charlie, where *is* that dirty shit, at the cleaners?"

Everyone in the group laughs, but Charlie is furious.

"These damn niggers snatched it off my head on the metro and then ran off. I was gonna fuck them up, but they timed that shit perfectly. I couldn't get to them before the doors closed."

The third man, Bryce, who has listened with increasing interest says, "Man, you let a fucking spook take your damn MAGA hat and get away with it? Uh, hell no. We should whup your ass right here for that shit."

"Man, fuck you. I saw the guy who took it. We made eye contact. I won't ever forget that nigger's face. If I ever see him again I swear I am going to pay that four-eyed ugly nigger back."

"Man, how the hell would you ever see him again? Those mother fuckers are long gone. And your dumb ass let them take your MAGA hat—the one you got from that big Trump rally. They totally disrespected you. That shit can't ever happen again. I tell you what. If you do ever see that mother fucker again then let us know. We'll handle that nigger with you," says Billy.

"I appreciate it, brothers, but this one is personal. I want to handle it on my own. It's the principle. They think they own this country now. They don't. We do. And always will. I wish we could ship them all back to the shithole countries they came from."

14
CALLING 911

Walt's clothes are ripe after staying overnight in the hospital with Teddy. He can't wait to take a long hot shower and change. Walt hugs Teddy goodbye and gives him a fist bump. He offers a few encouraging words to his tired mother and leans down to kiss her. She has always been strong, but he worries. She is losing more weight than Teddy.

Walt emerges from the metro and walks up Georgia Avenue toward Howard's campus. He passes a homeless lady, opens his wallet, and shuffles through the cash, slightly exposing a thick layer of crisp bills. He finds a ten-dollar bill and freely offers it. He continues walking. He sees a group of women he senses are freshmen a little ways ahead. He reaches them and stops.

"Good morning my beautiful black sistas."

"What's up my handsome king?" asks a pretty petite young lady with smooth ebony skin as her companions giggle.

Walt adjusts his black-rimmed glasses and tries to suck in his belly.

"Y'all need me to come with y'all and be y'all's security for the day?" he asks teasingly.

"Thank you, sweetie, but we good," responds a very tall light-skinned young woman.

"You want my number in case you change your mind?"

They laugh good-naturedly.

"Have a good day, love," says the tall one.

"Bye," a third one says sweetly.

Walt smiles. "All right, y'all. Be safe."

He continues to walk and passes another homeless person, this time a man. He opens his wallet and shuffles through the cash, again slightly exposing a thick layer of crisp bills. Other than one single dollar, now his lowest bill is a twenty. With no hesitation, he takes out the twenty-dollar bill and places it in the man's coffee cup that is occupied by only a few coins. He walks the few steps to the corner and turns onto the street that leads to his dormitory.

Walt is suddenly struck by a powerful blow to the back of his head. He falls to the ground. Someone starts punching him as he, weak from the blow, tries to shield himself. Two more attackers start kicking him. An attacker reaches in Walt's pocket and snatches his wallet while another quickly removes his size thirteen newly released retro Jordans. Then the men run off. Walt is left bloodied and in pain.

After what seems like an eternity but was only a few minutes, Walt manages to pull himself up. The street is eerily deserted. Slow and unsteady on his feet, he wills himself to make it back to the dorm. Chance and Big Dink are in the lobby flirting with the security guard who is flattered but still attentive to the door. Over their shoulders she sees Walt clearly in distress. She brushes quickly past Chance and Big Dink. They turn and rush to their friend just as he starts to collapse.

"Yo, what the fuck happened, bro? Who did this?" asks Chance. He is frantic.

"What da fuck," screams Big Dink.

"I got jumped and robbed," a weary Walt manages to say.

"Jumped? Jumped by who?" asks Chance.

"Man I couldn't see shit. They came out of nowhere. They all had on hoodies."

"Yo, Big Dink. Go get the fellas."

"Bet."

Big Dink runs down the hallway.

"I'm calling 911," says the security guard.

Walt is coming out of his fog. "No, please! Please don't call 911. I'm fine. Really, I'm fine."

The security guard reluctantly acquiesces.

"Chance, the school doesn't need any negative press, especially if they want to bring in more recruits."

Chance stares at Walt for a moment. "Man, fuck that, you might need to go to the hospital."

Big Dink comes running out with his friends following.

Walt gets a rush of adrenaline.

"Let's go find these dudes who did this. They have my wallet."

Chance helps Walt get up and walk. They pile into Big Dink's truck. Walt is in obvious pain, but fights through it. They drive around campus and a few surrounding blocks searching in vain for the attackers. Disappointed, they decide to call it and head back to the dormitory.

Over the next few weeks, Walt fully recovers from his injuries. The conditioning and open gym play increase in intensity. Deon and Chance continue to spar and too often stop just short of fighting.

Kia and Deon also start arguing frequently. The more possessive he becomes, the more resentful she feels. Kia and Chance continue to sit next to each other in class. Chance continues to flirt. Kia continues to bashfully rebuke his advances. But a genuine friendship is steadily growing.

A month has now passed since Walt was robbed. Chance is at his desk trying to decipher a physics equation when he hears his roommate enter the room. Grateful for the interruption, Chance turns around and glances up at Walt.

"What up, cuz?"

Without responding, Walt collapses face down on the bed.

"What's wrong with you? You sick?"

More silence.

Chance takes the few steps to Walt's bed and notices something red on his sheets. He turns Walt over and is taken aback by his bloody face. Walt moans.

"Mutha fuckas! Were these the same dudes again?"

"Yeah, I think so. I'm pretty sure one of them had on my Jordans."

Chance walks over to his closet and grabs a baseball bat. He runs down the hallway and bangs on Big Dink's door.

"Dink! Dink! Open up!"

Big Dink swings the door open.

"What da fuck is wrong?"

"Yo, get ya shit. Dem mutha fuckas just jumped Walt again. They gotta still be around here somewhere."

Big Dink pounds on Mad Max and Bird's door to enlist more muscle.

"Yo fellas, c'mon! Walt got jumped again. We gotta go handle this now."

They drop their video console controllers, throw on sweats, and with shoes untied, race out of the door. They follow Big Dink to get Walt, who is being helped by Chance. Determined to have more success this time, they jump in Big Dink's SUV. The tires screech loudly as Big Dink presses hard on the gas. Having barely driven a few hundred feet from the dormitory, Walt, embarrassed, points out where the robbery occurred. Big Dink lightens the pressure on the gas pedal and slowly drives around a four block radius hoping that Walt will spot his assailants. He does.

"There they go right there!"

Three locals, who appear to be in their late teens, are sitting on the steps of a row house. Big Dink quietly pulls up about ten houses down. Everyone except Walt exits the SUV.

The leader of the three locals notices them eying the house as they move purposefully in his direction. He perceives trouble. He stands, pauses briefly taking their massive sizes into account, but then feels his 45 semi-automatic handgun and smirks. He knows these guys are not from his DC hood, assumes they go to Howard, and surmises why they are here. Feeling untouchable, the leader asserts himself.

"Yo, y'all college boys know where da fuck you at?"

Before the leader realizes what is happening, Chance rushes over to him and swings the bat at his head. He manages to duck. He lunges at Chance's long legs. They both fall down. As the leader gets up, Big Dink sees the gun in his waistband. He uses his enormous fist to flatten him. Big Dink reaches down for the gun and throws it into the sewer. The now normally docile Mad Max—who earned his nickname from his fighting days when he really seemed to "go mad"—and Bird quickly overpower the two larger men. One of them is wearing Walt's shoes. Bird roughly yanks them off. The locals are on the ground feeling a mixture of pain and humiliation.

Chance, holding up the unused bat, looks down at all of them.

"Imma tell you mutha fuckas this once and once only! That dude you jumped and robbed tonight— and it took three of you—is our boy! If you fuck with him then you fuck with all of us! So let this be your first and last warning! If y'all ever come close to Walt again, we will fuckin' beat the living daylights out of y'all punk ass bitches!"

Chance reaches down in the leader's pockets and finds Walt's new wallet.

"All right, let's be out fellas," he says.

He looks back once more at the locals and spits in their direction.

That night, Walt lies in bed and looks over at Chance.

"Can you believe this shit keeps happening to me? I think they targeted me. They got $500 from me and my Jordans the first time."

"Man, it may just be a classic case of wrong place wrong time. Those guys are a bunch of low-life losers doing nothing positive with their lives and want to take from someone who's trying to accomplish things the right way.

"From what I hear there've always been issues between some of the locals and the college students. You were kinda trippin', though. You're getting a little too flashy. You need to be more aware of your surroundings especially if you walkin' around by yourself in $240 fresh kicks all the time. With an ATM in your wallet. But, man, I can't help but wonder if we would be having any of these safety concerns at any of the powerhouse schools. But who knows."

"Man, I just want to let you know that I'm so grateful to have you. You're like the older brother I never had."

"Dude, I'm literally like three months older than you."

Walt laughs, and it hurts.

"I know, man. I'm just sayin' I really appreciate having you by my side. I look at you as a brother, for real."

"As far as I'm concerned, we *are* brothers. I always got your back, bro."

A video call from Teddy is coming in on Walt's phone.

"What up, Teddy?"

"Hi, big bro."

Chance runs over to the phone.

"What's up, Tedster? How you feelin', buddy, now that you've been home for a while?"

Teddy has a huge smile on his face.

"Hi, Chance, I'm good. Thank you."

"You're coming to see us at Midnight Madness if you're well enough, right? Is your mom gonna let you stay up late so you can see us?"

Teddy looks over at his mother.

"Mom, can I go to Howard's Midnight Madness so I can see the Super Seven?" he implores.

"Sure you can, honey. We're going to have a blast."

"Yup, my mom said I can go. So we'll be there."

"Well, then I will see you there, buddy."

"How has your energy been?" Walt asks.

Teddy sighs and answers more honestly. "It's been up and down. Mainly down." Teddy drops his head.

Walt moves the phone directly in front of his face leaving Chance out of camera range.

"Teddy, look at me. You're going to beat this cancer. You hear me? We're going to fight this thing together. You're strong."

"What happened to your face?"

"Ummm." Walt is caught off guard.

"It looks bad, Walt. It looks like you got beat up! Did you get beat up?"

Mrs. Williams immediately turns her head to Teddy and gently takes the phone from his small hands. She gasps at Walt's bruises and swollen features.

"Oh my God, boy. What the hell happened to your face?"

Unsure of the response, she rushes into another room outside of Teddy's hearing. She wants to shield Teddy from anything that might add worry to his already worrisome existence.

"I'm good, Ma. It's okay."

"Okay my ass. Who the hell did this to you, boy?"

"I got jumped and robbed by some DC locals."

"What? Oh my gosh, did you go to the hospital? Did you contact the police?"

"No, Mom. It's really not that serious. Chance and the fellas tracked down the boys and got my stuff back for me."

"I'm on my way down there to take you to the hospital. And we're calling the police," she adds sternly.

"C'mon, Mom. I'm good. I promise. The situation is resolved. You're embarrassing me."

Chance grabs the phone.

"Hi, Mrs. Williams. We're taking care of Walt. He's been using ice on his face and doesn't have any broken bones or anything bad. I'm monitoring him and making sure he's okay. We didn't want to get the police involved. We were able to locate the boys and get Walt's stuff back. I can assure you they won't be messing with Walt anymore."

Knowing the answer, Mrs. Williams still inquires.

"You didn't kill them did you?"

Chance laughs while Walt puts his face in his hands and shakes his head.

"Of course not, Mrs. Williams. Walt's fine. I always have his back. You have enough to worry about with Teddy."

Mrs. Williams is not completely reassured, but she knows she can only handle so much. Chance is right about that. She considers Chance for a moment, smart, confident, and kind. Still, he tries to be the tough guy a little too much for her liking—especially since his Dad died. Bottled anger, no doubt.

He can move from street talk one minute to college boy talk the next. Smooth.

"Thank you, Chance. But if this happens again I want to know immediately. The authorities *will* be involved."

"Yes, ma'am. Absolutely. Here's Walt." He hands the phone back.

"Son, please take care of yourself."

"Sure, Mom. How's Teddy been?"

"It's been a real struggle for him. He's been weak and tired. The chemo treatments are going to start back up in three weeks."

Walt refuses to think the worse.

"We already lost Dad to cancer. We ain't about to lose Teddy to it, too. We're going to fight this and we're going to fight it with all we got."

"Amen to that, sweetie."

"Can I speak to Teddy again?"

"Sure, baby. I'll get him."

Walt's mom walks back into the room where her young son is. She positions the phone to show Walt a sleeping Teddy.

"Okay, Mom. Love you. Can't wait to see y'all for Midnight Madness."

"Yup, we'll be there if Teddy's up to it—though we won't stay too long. Love you, too."

15 MIDNIGHT MADNESS

The air is electric as the crowd filters into Burr Gymnasium. The band is playing loudly. Each instrument section is in step with captivating dance choreography. Both students and parents are dancing on their way to their seats.

Not too far away, those rousing beats echo lightly but distinctively onto the front steps of a row house crying out for repair. The local teenagers slouching on the porch are still stewing about the big men who humiliated them in their own neighborhood. Red, a lanky, freckle-faced teenager with a curlyish red high-top fade, looks at the others.

"Man, it's time to talk about it. I'm tired of it not gettin' addressed. When y'all tryin' to get some mutha fuckin' payback on them college boy bitches?" he asks.

"Hell yeah, man, we ain't lettin' that shit ride," Tyrone, the tallest and bulkiest of the three, says eagerly.

"In due time y'all," cautions Tarik, the thinker and leader of the group. "Right now we just gonna chill. We want them to get comfortable. We want things to get back to normal for them, be routine. And then, boom! We'll get they ass when they ain't expecting it.

"'Cause right now, they expecting and probably preparing for it. Now, while it's hot, we just gonna chill out. We know who they hang wit'. All we gotta do is find him when the time is right. But in the meantime, let's go check out this Midnight Madness and holla at some college honies."

"What if dem college boy bitches up in there and they recognize us?" asks Red.

"Then we fuck dem bitches up right there on the spot," says Tyrone, raring to go.

"Man, I doubt we'll run into them," says Tarik. "But we not gettin' into any nonsense up in there. Too many cops and campus security up that joint."

Tyrone laughs derisively. "Campus security? You scared of campus security? Man, fuck dem flashlight cops. They ain't shit. Get the fuck outta here. We gonna fuck those bitches up if we see 'em."

"You do some shit, then you on your own. I said we simply gonna hang and book some college shawties. And that's that."

Inside Burr Gymnasium, young and old are filled with anticipation for the Midnight Madness showcasing of the Howard Bison new recruits.

In the locker room, Coach Mac tries to disguise his own anxiety.

"All right, fellas. Tonight marks the official start of what's going to be a truly amazing season. Look at one another. We have some of the best talent out there. Chance, for crying out loud, was rated the number one player coming out of high school—not in the state but in the entire country. The nation. That's a powerful statement right there.

"A whole new spotlight will be shining on our program. Everyone is watching. And we're gonna give them a show. Do you realize, truly, what we have the opportunity to do this season? If we can win big, we'll show other players that their basketball goals can be achieved at an HBCU. If some of you can come here, win, and then go on to get drafted by the NBA, then you'll have changed the landscape of college ball. You'll have changed the face of HBCUs. Hell, before this is over, other sports like football may follow suit."

He pauses. The team is hanging on his every word. He knows the very green freshmen have never played on this level. He knows this will not be the cakewalk he makes it seem, but he has seen them in action, and knows

146

their potential. He is going to push them as hard as he can. It is more than about just them. It is about the survival of HBCUs and valuing one another. The white man's ice is not colder and he is determined to prove it.

"You want to be the best, right?"

"Yes! Hell yeah!" the players respond in kind.

"Remember this," says the coach, pointing his finger at no one in particular. "Know this. None of that will be possible if we are not together as a team. Don't think I don't know about these inner team beefs and clicks. I have eyes everywhere. The beefs have to stop now! Too much is at stake for foolishness.

"We have to be totally united and on the same page if we're going to accomplish our goal—winning it all and bringing it home to HU. And I ain't talkin' 'bout the fuckin' conference championship. I'm talkin' about an NCAA championship trophy!"

The players and assistant coaches clap and chant. Coach Knight quiets and bows his head.

"Now bring it in for the Lord's Prayer."

In perfect unison, they recite the prayer. Chance is reminded of his father.

"Now give them the show they've been waiting for."

The atmosphere inside the gymnasium is electric as Midnight Madness is about to begin. The locals make their way through the crowd and to their seats just in time.

"Man, this shit is off da hook. It's all types of shawties up in this joint," says Red.

"Hell yeah," agrees Tyrone as he takes in the view.

The gym darkens and recorded music blares.

"HU, are you r-e-a-d-y?" asks the public announcer in a crescendo. "Introducing your 2019 Howard University men's basketball team."

A huge burst of smoke blows and the HU basketball team comes running out to rumbling applause. Midnight Madness is always a crowd pleaser, but this night is pure magic.

Chance leads the team out and immediately goes up for a LeBron James-style thunderous one handed dunk in the layup line. Big Dink accentuates that action with his own signature dunk. The crowd is on their feet. They settle down as the team goes through their layup line routine. Following warm-ups, the players sit on the bench awaiting introductions and their individual time in the spotlight—figuratively and literally.

As the players are being introduced, Red leans forward.

"Hold up, I know that's not dem niggas right there."

"Who?" asks Tyrone.

"Oh snap, shit, that *is* dem niggas we was fightin'. They was all tall—that shoulda been a fuckin' clue," says Tarik.

"Ain't that about a . . . ," adds Red.

The announcer introduces Walt and the locals exchange glances. Two rows in front of them, Walt's mother and little brother are sitting in the stands clapping and cheering. Teddy has summoned every bit of energy his little body has to give.

Chance's name is called and the entire place erupts!

"Look on the bright side, fellas. Now we know where to find these mutha fuckas anytime we like," says Red. He smirks.

"Yup, they're sitting ducks whenever we want get back," Tyrone adds.

Red smirks again. "Bingo."

The students, faculty, and alumni cannot believe their eyes. The crowd is witnessing a spectacular display of basketball talent. Chance's mother, sitting with Amaia, revels in the excitement, and is reminded of the sweet college days she shared with her husband in this very gymnasium. She marvels at how she never could have predicted a night like tonight. She chuckles to herself thinking the number of high-fives in the stands could probably earn a spot in the Guinness Book of World Records.

To close out the night, taking off from the free throw line with the basketball palmed in one hand, Chance delivers a classic Jordan-style dunk—a crowd pleaser.

The after-party is full of young, sweaty, hormonal bodies swept up in the intoxicating freedom college offers. There is a separate room entrance called the slow dance room. Chance finds himself in that room leaning up against the wall with a glass of Hennessy mixed with coke. No less than four brave young women try to entice the basketball star, but he politely shrugs them off. He just wants to sip his drink and focus on someone across the room.

Chance cannot take his eyes off of Kia as she dances with Deon. There is nothing separating them as he holds her close. While in Deon's embrace, sensing someone staring at her, Kia looks up. She locks eyes with Chance. He nods. They both smile. He mimics Deon's grasp and Kia can't contain her laughter.

Deon smiles. "What's so funny, babe?"

"Oh, I was just thinking about something that made me laugh. It's nuffin'."

"Oh. Okay." Deon lets it go but is left wondering.

Kia and Deon continue to dance and Chance continues to mock Deon with funny imitations. Kia lets out another big laugh. This time Deon pulls away and catches Kia glancing across the room. He notices Chance and realizes that he is the reason Kia is laughing.

"Oh, so that clown is what was so fuckin' funny?"

Scowling, he storms across the room and stops inches from Chance's face. Alarmed, Kia follows.

"Man, I thought I told you to chill with Kia."

"Man, I can't help it if I make your girl laugh from all the way over here, bro."

Deon gives Chance a death stare. He grabs Kia's hand and pulls her toward the exit. She glances back. Chance is still looking.

A stunningly striking young woman puts her arm around Chance and moves her body close. He stands there drinking his drink, still staring at the exit.

Outside the party, Deon confronts Kia. "Yo, why the fuck you even entertaining this freshman clown? You my girl and I don't want you associating with him!"

"Relax, baby. It's nothing. You're trippin' for no reason. Chance and I are acquaintances. Nothing more." She pulls him toward her and kisses him long and hard.

Chance exits the party with the stunning young woman who can't keep her hands off of him. Kia and Deon, locked in each other's arms, are right in front of them. Deon sees Chance and, feeling victorious, smiles and winks. Chance's gaze turns to Kia and he walks off with Miss Stunning. Kia notices. She quiets the unexpected tinge of jealously.

16

CAUGHT SLIPPIN'

The Howard Bison are in the thick of practice and running plays in preparation for their upcoming public scrimmage during Homecoming week.

"All right fellas, run ISO 1000 for Chance," directs Coach Mac.

"But Coach, that's my play," objects Deon.

"Just run the damn play as I called it," says Coach Mac in a raised voice.

Deon rolls his eyes and mumbles his dissatisfaction under his breath. The team runs the play and Chance gets the ball and shoots a jump shot. Nothing but net. Deon glowers and then looks over at Chance. Chance smiles and winks at him, mimicking Deon's wink from the other night.

"Deon," says Coach Mac, pulling him aside. "This is still your play and you'll be able to run it on your team during the scrimmage Wednesday night.

Since you and Chance want to see whose nuts are bigger, we're gonna put you two head to head, maño y maño. Center stage. In front of everybody. It's going to be Deon and the upperclassmen versus Chance and the freshmen. This is your chance to claim what's yours.

"Regardless of who wins or shines, what I'm trying to get y'all to realize is that together we can be unstoppable. If the two of you would just take the energy that you're expending against each other and use it to unite, man oh man, the sky's the limit. But I understand what's going on right now. It's alpha dog versus alpha dog.

"So, for now, I'll let you two play this little game. But once we start playing for real, we're all one. We all have the same goal. Don't ever forget that."

Later on that night, Deon stares into his dorm room's full length mirror affixed to the wall next to his bed. Taped to the top of his mirror is a newspaper clipping from last year. It reads, "Howard's Deon Diggs, MEAC's Next Great Star."

His eyes move left and hone in on a more recent article thrown on his dresser. The article is headlined, "Basketball Superstar Chance Knight Chooses Howard." Deon grabs the paper with the article and, consumed by frustration, jealousy, anger, and fear, he rips it up before tossing. As the ripped paper lands in the trashcan, Deon sees the condoms from his time with Kia last night. This time when he thinks of Chance, he smirks.

Howard's first public scrimmage is minutes away. Anticipation is high as students and alumni pack Burr Gymnasium to take in the greatest talent their team has ever boasted. Deon and his squad, wearing white Howard practice uniforms, are putting on a show with synchronized passing and layups, three-point jump shots, and perfectly executed crowd-pleasing dunks. Chance and his squad, sporting blue Howard practice uniforms, are equally impressive warming up. As the game is about to begin, the players fist bump one another. Chance walks up to Deon to do the same, but Deon pretends not to notice. Chance is left with his hand hovering in the air. He and Deon stare at one another as the whistle sounds and play begins.

The action is nonstop. Deon answers every bucket and three-pointer Chance makes. Each one makes the other work for every point. The upperclassmen hold their own during the first half, earning Coach Mac's nod of approval. The second half is a different story. The freshmen defeat the upperclassman fifty-eight to forty-two. Chance finishes with the game high, twenty-five points and eleven rebounds. Deon finishes with a respectable seventeen points and seven rebounds but not quite Chance's double-double status. They both know Chance won this round between them.

The next night, Chance, Walt, J.J., Mike, Big Dink, Bird, and Mad Max take their seats in Crampton Auditorium to watch the homecoming fashion show. Shortly after, Deon and several of the upperclassmen basketball players walk in with Kia and a couple of her friends. The stage curtains pull back. The lights dim. The models sashay and strut up the stage well enough to be mistaken for professional runway models with a little extra flavor. The male models, with their muscles and swagger, also command respect and more than a few catcalls. The DJ's music complements their movements. The women take in the fashion and the men take in the models.

"I have to run to the bathroom y'all," says Tonya, Kia's girlfriend.

"I'll go with you," says Kia. "Be right back, babe."

Deon, eyes fixed on the models, nods. As Kia and Tonya near the ladies' room, Chance is exiting the men's room.

"There she go! You know you badder than any of these models, right?"

Kia flashes a coyish smile. She is slightly embarrassed by the loud display of adoration.

Chance looks at her friend. He is familiar with her friends now and careful to remember their names.

"What up, Tonya?"

"What up, Chance?"

"Look, Chance. You know I think you're really cool peoples, but we both know how Deon feels about us conversing. I'm here with him tonight. I'm not trying to have another incident with y'all. I don't want any more problems."

"Yeah, you know Deon be trippin'," agrees Tonya.

"Man, I ain't worried about that fool. But I do respect you, Kia. And your situation. So I'll respect your wishes. I just have a super crush on you and it gets worse every time I see you." He winks and flashes his smile. "I can't help it. But I'll let y'all go. I'll see you in class, if not before."

Chance starts walking away.

"Chance," Kia calls out.

He quickly turns around.

She looks up at him with her big brown eyes. They never fail to captivate him.

"Sorry about this. You're my friend. But Deon is my boyfriend. I just don't want the drama."

Chance smiles. "I get it." There is a pause. "Beautiful," he adds.

Kia returns his smile and playfully rolls her eyes. She is beginning to believe he is incorrigible. She turns and walks into the restroom with Tonya. Chance heads to the concession stand to get a drink for him and Walt. He is discouraged by the long line, but promised Walt he would bring him back a bottled water. After waiting in line for what seemed to him to be forever, Chance heads back to his seat.

Movement in a dark secluded area beyond the stairwell catches his attention while he walks down the corridor. He is surprised when he notices Deon up close and personal with another woman. Deon is unabashedly kissing her, his tongue deep in her throat, while palming her buttocks. Still holding his waist, she steps away slightly. She smiles provocatively, drops to her knees, and starts to unbutton his pants.

Chance contemplates pulling out his phone and snapping a picture. He chooses not to. He does not want to be *that* guy. But he does not want Kia to get hurt either. Deon stops the girl to peek into a nearby room to see if it is empty. It is. He pulls her in and closes the door. Chance shakes his head and walks back into the auditorium, wondering if he made the right decision by not taking the picture.

Back in his seat, Chance hands Walt his water.

"Man, you've been missin' these baddies. What took you so long?"

Chance looks over at a seated Kia. He observes her looking in every direction. He is certain she is wondering where Deon is.

Walt is surprised by Chance's silence.

"Chance, you hear me, bro? What's wrong?"

"Man, I want Kia bad. I got it bad for that girl. I just don't know why she's so stuck on this fool Deon. I mean, her faithfulness is very attractive but Deon is a clown."

"Bro, that's our teammate's girl. It's like Coach said. In order for us to come together as a team and win this year, you and Deon have to squash this beef."

"Man, I know, but I can't stand by and watch such a good girl be with such a scumbag."

"Bruh, we're star athletes in college. We're all scumbags when it comes to these chicks. Well maybe not me because I don't get any play. But I would be if I could, I think. Anyway, you're one of the main scumbags outta all us so what da fuck you talkin' 'bout?"

"Well yeah, you right about you. Your virgin ass." Chance laughs.

"But for real, this chick is different, man," he says, his tone serious. "She's truly special. I just saw Deon with some other chick in the cut tonguing her down, 'bout to get some head. He must have planned to meet that chick as soon as Kia was out of his sight. He's lucky she didn't pass him going back to her seat. And he's lucky I didn't record it, for real."

"Damn, that fool go hard doin' that while Kia's in the same damn building."

Just then, they observe Deon returning to his seat next to Kia. He kisses her and they continue to watch the show.

"Damn, that's cold-blooded. Dude just fucked around on ole girl and then came back and kissed her and carried on as normal. Straight savage," says Walt.

"He doesn't deserve her. I'm gonna take her from him and show her what she's missing. He ain't no real man."

Walt sighs. "Aww shit. Here we fuckin' go."

Chance looks over at Kia sitting there holding hands with Deon and enjoying the show. He then scans the crowd and makes eye contact with a honey-colored young woman who is smiling and giving him all the right signals.

"Yo, she's all up on you, bro," Walt says noticing.

Chance nods in agreement.

"That's sexy ass Tiffany, bro. She's a senior *and* an Ooh La La dancer for the football team. Damn she sexy as shit! Oooh-wee," says Walt.

"Yeah, I know all 'bout her. I just been so focused on Kia that I never really gave Tiffany no mind. Maybe I should get to know her if you know what I mean."

Tiffany rises from her seat and heads toward them. She slows down as she passes and head motions to Chance to follow her outside.

"What are you waiting for? She wants you to follow her."

Chance glances over at Kia and sees Deon with his arm wrapped around her as he whispers in her ear. He shakes his head and then gets up to oblige Tiffany.

"Take pics!" shouts Walt.

Chance steps outside but does not immediately spot Tiffany. He looks around and then sees her on a corner. Tiffany, eyes lasered on Chance, once again motions her head for him to follow. Chance smiles and obeys. She is about fifty yards ahead of Chance and turns the corner. He walks quickly. He turns the corner and does not see her. He fears he has lost the chase. But then he eyes her sliding into a two door blazing red Audi. She gives him what he hopes is the final head nod; at this point he knows for sure she is thirsty. She is what his mom warned him about. But he cannot resist.

Chance casually approaches the passenger side. Just as he is about to open the door, Tiffany pushes the gas pedal and stops about fifteen feet ahead. Chance thinks to himself that this is a very different kind of foreplay, but he walks up to the car again. Just as he is about to open the door, she once more peels off, stopping about ten feet ahead.

"Come on, yo," Chance says, now slightly more annoyed than amused.

In what is becoming a familiar motion, he walks up to the car for the third time, and opens the door.

"Are you done playing now?"

Tiffany grins. "Get in."

Chance struggles to get his tall frame into the two door sports car. Tiffany immediately puts her hand on his thigh and whispers in his ear.

"Do you think you can handle a senior?"

He cannot believe that the question actually unnerves him. He doesn't show it.

"Yeah, of course. The real question is can you handle this freshman?"

Tiffany fully presses down on the gas pedal. Chance, startled, jerks back in his seat.

"Well damn."

Tiffany smiles, knowing Chance will be given quite the ride that night.

The next day, Kia walks into her 9:30 a.m. English class and places her book bag in the seat next to her. Several minutes go by and the professor begins. Kia anxiously looks out of the window to see if she can spot Chance coming. When she does not see him, she guiltily realizes her disappointment. About twenty seconds later, Chance walks in and apologizes to the professor. Kia tries to hide her relief as she quickly moves her book bag. He takes his place beside her.

"Well it's about time, buddy."

"You were actually missin' me weren't you?" asks Chance teasingly.

"Umm, no! I just didn't want you to have an excuse to track me down, alone, to find out what you missed! C'mon, P.G. You know betta."

Chance writes a note and passes it to Kia. Kia smiles at the scribbled, *"Hi, Beautiful."*

She writes, *"Boy, Bye"* on the back of the note and returns it.

They laugh spontaneously and loudly, momentarily forgetting where they are. The professor stops and, along with the other students, looks questioningly at them.

"Sorry, Professor," says Kia.

The professor continues speaking. Kia studies Chance's profile as he turns his attention to the lecture and, at first, assuages her guilt by acknowledging that any woman would find his extraordinarily handsome looks hard to resist. She then convinces herself that her gaze is more about trying to figure out this new friend of hers. When class ends, they stroll out of the building together walking toward a main campus road.

"There's something that I've been wanting to tell you," says Chance.

"Oh yeah? What's that?"

Out of nowhere, Tiffany swoops in and grabs Chance by the arm and pulls him with her, ending the inquiry. Kia is stunned.

Tiffany looks back at Kia.

"He'll chat with you some other time, sweetie."

Tiffany puts her arm around Chance and leads him to her parked car. When he is once again squeezed into the front seat, Tiffany rolls down the window and glances back at Kia, who still has a surprised look on her face. Tiffany gives a dismissive wave to her as they speed off.

"Um, you do know that I was in the middle of a conversation over there, right?"

"Sorry, but when I'm in need I don't like to wait."

"In need of what?" asks Chance as if he does not know.

She pulls the car off of the road into an isolated empty parking lot. She puts the car in park and, despite the tight fit, nimbly manages to climb onto Chance's lap.

163

"In need of this!"

Tiffany starts kissing Chance's neck while taking off her clothes. Chance, remembering last night, chuckles.

"Well hello, hi, how you doin'? Nice to see you, too."

"Shut the fuck up and fuck me."

Tiffany pulls Chance's sweatpants down and all conversation stops.

17

HOMECOMING

People from all areas of the country descend upon Howard for Homecoming week. As they converge in the football stands and surrounding area in advance of the big game, the atmosphere is highly charged. Cheerleaders and the curvaceous Ooh La La dancers are moving rhythmically to a dynamic band that steps, spins, and sways to the rousing beats belting from their instruments. The stadium is filled to capacity as Howard and Morgan State run onto the field.

The action begins as Howard kicks the ball off. Morgan returns the kick to the twenty-yard line. On the first play from scrimmage, Morgan throws the ball to their wide receiver who catches it and runs for ten yards before getting hit extremely hard by the Howard safety. The receiver fumbles the ball. The Howard safety picks it up and returns it for a thirty yard touchdown. The home crowd goes wild.

Chance and Walt are relaxed in the stands enjoying the eye candy.

"So what's up with Tiffany? She's been *extra* all over you lately."

"Man, let me tell you. That girl is an absolute freak. She be workin' the shit out of it. On top of all that, she's mad cool. She ain't even pressed to hang out or take up my time, or nothin' like that. Tiffany just wants to fuck around and then she goes ghost. She's like a dude in that respect."

"Damn. You lucky as hell."

"I know, right? It's simply just sex with her. But even though she's mad cool, there's just no true connection. Strictly physical. Whereas with Kia, I'm truly into her and want to be her man. I have an all-around connection with her. There's nothing I dislike about her except her boyfriend. And she's so loyal to him.

"I've been giving it a lot of thought. I'm gonna tell her what I saw at the fashion show. Hopefully she'll leave that bum and give me a chance."

"Man, I know you and Deon ain't cool, but you can't snitch. That's guy code right there. And he's our teammate."

"Man, fuck all that. I really care about Kia and I don't want her getting hurt. Especially by that lame."

Walt nods. "That's a tough one right there, bro. She'll be hurt either way. Just think about if you want to be the one who exposes that hurt to her. You don't know how she'll take it or if she'll even believe you.

"But speaking of Kia and Deon, there they are right there by the concession stand."

Having barely digested Walt's advice, Chance strides in their direction.

"C'mon, Walt."

Walt sighs. "Ah shit man, here we go. Don't go startin' no shit, bro."

"Man just bring your scared ass on."

Chance and Walt are making their way over to the concession area when four young ladies interrupt them with flirtatious chatter. In an effort to make Kia jealous, Chance takes advantage of the situation and puts his arms around the two best looking young ladies, walking with one on each side. Walt converses with the remaining two.

They approach Kia and Deon.

"What up, Deon? Kia?" Walt says, cutting through the tension.

"Hi guys," responds Kia.

Deon gives Kia a salty look.

"What up, Kia? D," says Chance.

"Ain't shit. Come on, Kia, we out."

"Damn, Deon, I'm not ready to go yet. What's with your attitude all of a sudden? Everything was cool just a minute ago. Anytime Chance comes around you start actin' all weird. I'm sick of it. We're just friends, barely. And he's on your freaking basketball team. Y'all are teammates!"

"Man, come on. I ain't gonna tell you again," he orders, grabbing Kia by the arm. He pulls her away with him.

"Don't put your hands on her like that," Chance says sternly.

Deon stops and looks at him. "Dog, this is my girl. Mind your business. You don't tell me what da fuck to do wit' my girl."

"Are you sure she's your girl, or is your girl the chick that I saw you kissin' on the other day at the fashion show while Kia was in the bathroom?"

Walt groans and puts his hands over his face.

"What the fuck is Chance talkin' 'bout, Deon? Is that true?"

"Hell naw that ain't true." Deon is fuming.

"Chance, why didn't you tell me about this before? If it's true?"

Chance is caught off guard. "Well I…"

"You know what, the hell with all y'all. I'm out," says Kia, interrupting Chance. She races off.

"Kia, wait," Chance calls out.

"You snitch ass mutha fucka," says Deon as he charges at Chance.

Walt jumps in and stops him before he is able to connect with Chance.

"Man, remember what Coach said, y'all. This shit has to stop. If y'all ain't gonna like each other, then keep it in-house. We can't be out here, especially at a big event like Homecoming, airing our dirty laundry. It's a bad look for the team."

"Man, whateva," Deon says dismissively. He storms off.

"You cool, bro?" Walt asks Chance.

"Yeah, I'm good. Thanks, man. You're right."

Chance, Walt, and the four girls go stand in the concession line for food. Chance's mind stays on Kia.

Later that night, those attending the official after-party are jubilant after Howard's victory. Walt claims a corner in the party room.

"Man, I'm getting fucked up tonight," vows Walt in between chugs of his Corona.

"If I can't lose my virginity during Homecoming, then I give up. I'm making it a priority to get on some bad ass pussy tonight."

"Bad, huh?" asks Chance.

"Man, I ain't stutter. She gonna be on Beyoncé status. I ain't playin' around tonight." Chance, Bird, and Mad Max laugh.

Chance acknowledges Walt's resolve. "You're feelin' it tonight, bro."

Walt puts down the empty bottle of Corona. Not by any means a seasoned drinker—but not quite a virgin on this front—he cracks open a new one and immediately starts chugging it down.

"Yo, chill out, cuz. I can't be babysittin' you all night if you get fucked up. I got plans of my own, ya feel me?"

Walt finishes the second Corona and slams the bottle down.

"Watch me work, fellas."

Walt ventures out to find his prey. He trips and almost falls down. His friends holler with laughter.

Over the next hour, Walt dances with different women and continues to throw back Coronas. Chance and his friends mingle and dance with multiple girls. Kia, looking stunning in a tight fitting red dress and matching red heels, makes quite an entrance at the party. Heads turn.

Deon approaches Kia.

"I need to talk to you," he says commandingly.

Kia lifts her head.

"I have nothing to say to you, Deon."

"What the hell, Kia? That punk Chance was lyin' to mess wit' your head."

"Naw, it all makes sense now. I was wondering where you were when I came out of the restroom."

"I already told you I ended up going to the restroom, too."

"Well, you must have been takin' a shit 'cause yo ass was gone for a nice minute. Look, it's been a long day and I just need some time to think. I'm going to hang with my girls tonight. I guess I can meet up with you tomorrow for lunch and talk about everything."

Deon is somewhat relieved.

"Okay, babe. I'm sorry for everything. I just want my baby girl to know I would never do any fucked up shit like that. You know how I feel about you."

"Okay."

Deon leans in to kiss Kia. She turns her head to the side and lets the kiss find her cheek.

"All right, babe, I'm going back to my room."

Chance notices Walt dancing with an extremely robust freshman. From Walt's inebriated perspective, she looks like a proportionately thick music video vixen.

Chance taps Big Dink on the shoulder.

"Yo. Do you see your boy grindin' up on Two Ton Tina over there?"

Big Dink and the others look over and are entertained.

"Watch this," says Mad Max. He saunters over to Walt.

"Yo, Walt, she's the baddest youngin' up in this joint," he whispers in his ear.

Walt grins.

"Duh, why do you think I'm with her right now?"

"Man you gotta take her back and smash. This is the chick you're gonna lose your virginity to. If you lose it tonight to her fine ass, you'll forever be the fuckin' man on campus."

"Consider it done, young fella. Now fall back and watch me work."

Mad Max returns to the guys.

"Yo, what did you tell him?" asks Bird.

"I simply told him that she's the baddest chick up in here and that he'll be the man on campus if he loses his virginity to her tonight."

They can't control their laughter.

Walt whispers into the young lady's ear. She smiles. He takes her hand and leads her in front of him and then guides her toward the exit. He looks at her and, in his alcohol induced haze, observes a beauty with a very large, perfect derriere for what he has planned.

Meanwhile, Kia and her girlfriends, buoyed by the popular tunes the DJ is playing and the magic of Homecoming, dance with each other without restraint.

Big Dink taps Chance on the shoulder and points to their uninhibited movements. Chance is transfixed by Kia's pulsating curves, hugged by the red dress. He imagines devouring her at that very moment.

Chance and his crew walk up to Kia and her friends and start dancing with them. Chance and Kia are in sync as the beat dictates their movements. Within a few minutes, the DJ slows down the mood. Kia and her friends start to walk off the dance floor, but Chance grabs Kia's hand and pulls her close.

"I can't," says Kia as she pulls back.

Chance cajoles her with his smile.

"Just one dance. Deon's gone and it's just a dance."

Kia acquiesces. "Just one dance."

Chance pulls Kia next to him and the whiff of her tantalizing perfume makes his body ache for her even more. The music is a throwback. Maxwell croons "This Woman's Work."

"I could get use to this," Chance whispers.

"Chance, don't start. Let's just dance," responds Kia with slight annoyance.

"I'm sorry, Kia. You know how I feel about you. Deon's no good for you. I know I can treat you way better than he ever could. I wasn't lying about what I saw the other day. Deon's a no good cheater. And he did it while you were in the same building with him while y'all were out together. If he can do that then, just imagine what he does when you're not around."

Silence ensues.

"Look, I don't wanna talk about him. I just wanna enjoy this dance and let you know how I feel— about you."

Kia pauses, taking in what Chance has just said but then quickly remembers their conversation being cut short outside of freshman English.

"Oh and what about that chick with the Audi? How you feel about her big booty ass?" she snipes.

"Girl, please. I just have fun with her. She means absolutely nothing to me. Besides, the only reason I even entertain any other chicks is because I can't have you. I've wanted you from day one. The day I met you. I haven't stopped wanting you."

As he holds Kia to him, Chance senses an opportunity. He stops dancing, cups her chin, and leans down to kiss her. She responds passionately, then abruptly pulls away.

"I'm sorry, Chance. I can't. I just can't. This isn't right. Deon and I are in a bad space right now, but I haven't cut that off. I don't know what's going to happen with us. I'm still trying to figure it out. But I know this just feels wrong."

Kia, confused and disappointed in herself, runs out of the party.

"Kia, please wait," Chance shouts behind her.

She does not. He quickly follows. Her concerned girlfriends are not far behind. Noticing the group exit, Chance's crew, curious, follows suit.

Kia walks purposefully across The Yard toward Deon's dormitory.

"Yo, Kia, wait up," Chance shouts again.

"Leave me alone, Chance. That was a mistake," says Kia firmly.

"Cut the bullshit, Kia. A mistake my ass. We both feel the connection. I know it's not just me. Why you fighting it? Stop fighting this. You know you want it as much as I do. Right?"

Kia slows down to a stop. She turns and faces Chance. At this point, everyone has caught up to them.

"Are you okay, sweetie?" asks Tonya. "What happened?"

"Chance kissed me on the dance floor. I didn't ask for it. But I didn't stop it right away. I feel bad about it and I'm going to tell Deon what happened. I'm not a cheater.

"I despise cheaters and I'm gonna own up to what I did," she adds with emphasis.

"Whatever happens after that happens. But I have to be honest about it and let Deon hear it from me instead of from someone else at the party."

"You gonna tell Deon what?" Big Dink asks. "Girl, are you crazy? This the same man who wanted to kill Chance just for talking to you! Imagine what his psycho ass gonna try if you tell him y'all kissed!"

"Dink is right, girl. Deon will lose his mind and there ain't no telling what he'll do," says Tonya.

"Kia, you do whatever you feel is right. Don't worry about Deon. I can handle his punk ass," offers Chance.

Kia turns and continues to walk toward Deon's dormitory. Everyone else trails behind her, primarily to intervene and protect Chance from Deon's wrath.

As they near the building, Kia spots Deon's car and thinks she observes a feminine silhouette through his tinted windows. She approaches and notices a fog growing on the glass. She realizes he is in there and is not alone. Kia yanks on the handle and the door opens. Deon's face is between a girl's legs. He looks up and is stunned. Kia instantly starts swinging at Deon.

"You bastard. I trusted you," screams Kia. She is hurt and embarrassed.

"Baby, it's not what it looks like."

Kia laughs at the absurdity.

"Oh, it's not what it looks like? Really? It looks like your fuckin' face was in this bitch's vagina. That's what it looks like."

Chance and Bird pull Kia away from the car.

"Screw you, Deon. Don't ever talk to me again in life. We are officially done! Done!"

Deon, in disbelief, sits speechless.

Kia, crying, races off, trailed by friends ready to console.

"Man, that's fucked up. She doesn't deserve that shit," Chance says to Deon.

"Man, fuck off, freshman. Mind your own fuckin' business, yo."

Chance sizes Deon up, shakes his head, and walks away.

Meanwhile, across campus in the apartment of the robust woman branded "Two Ton Tina" by Walt's friends, Walt is under the covers losing his virginity. Without clothes and body shrinking undergarments, the woman is even more obese, but the blanket covers most of her as Walt strokes. They climax in sync.

"Has anyone ever told you that you look just like Beyoncé?" Walt blissfully asks.

"No. Never," the woman answers, wondering if Walt is making fun of her.

"Well, you do." Walt pauses for a brief moment. "Oh my gosh, girl, you're the best."

Walt is greeted by silence. Expecting a response, he looks over and the woman is fast asleep and beginning to snore. He excitedly grabs his phone and sends a group text to those whom he had told tonight would be the night. The text reads, *"Yo, fellas, y'all ain't gonna believe where I am right now. I'm lying in bed with the fine ass Beyoncé-lookin' chick from the party. I just smashed the hell out of her. She's knocked out sleep. Chick has her own apartment and everything. I hit the jackpot with this one."*

Back on The Yard, Chance and his friends look at their phones as the text notifications sound in unison. As they read Walt's text, their laughter fills the nearly empty Yard, echoing up the trunk and through the leaves of the Kappa Alpha Psi tree they are standing under.

Chance texts back.

"Yo. You're the man. You just pulled one of the baddest shorties on campus. You gonna be a legend. You had a lot to drink so don't leave. Just stay over there and sleep it off. Maybe you and Beyoncé can go get some breakfast together when y'all wake up."

178

When the others read his reply another round of laughter erupts.

"Okay bet. Plus, I want to be here when we wake up so we can go for round two. Check out all these sexy ass pics I took of her."

The pictures emerge on each of their phones.

"OMG, look at Two Ton Tina," says an amused Big Dink. "She's larger than we thought."

She is sleeping, looking satisfied. Rolls of fat are seemingly everywhere. They fixate on her large breasts and buttocks, both partially covered.

Big Dink, mimicking a newscaster, announces, "It's official. This proves that, yes, a chick's ass *can* indeed be too fuckin' big."

The crew can hardly contain themselves.

"Yo," says Mad Max. "I would pay to be there when Walt wakes up sober and sees this chick don't look nothin' like Beyoncé. Walt's gonna fuckin' lose his mind."

Everyone has a witty comment. But Chance is starting to feel a little empathy for Walt—and for his bedmate.

"Yo, fellas, It's been a long night. I'm 'bout to call it. Going to my room to crash. I'll catch y'all tomorrow."

Chance daps up his friends and walks to his dormitory. Shortly after he enters his room there is a knock on the door. Tired, he grudgingly opens it. Chance is shocked to see Kia. He did not know she knew his room number.

"Kia?"

"Sorry to bother you, but I needed to see you. I hope that's okay?"

"Hell yeah it's okay, girl," he says as he puts his arm around her. "You can see me whenever you like. Are you o . . . "

Before Chance is able to finish the word "okay," Kia grabs him by the shirt and pulls his face to hers. She starts kissing him. She pushes him down on the bed and climbs on top. Chance forgets he was ever tired.

The next morning at "Two Ton Tina's" apartment, rays from the sun stream through the bedroom windows, spotlighting Walt's face. He wakes. As he sits up, yawns, and stretches, he looks over and sees long hair peeking out of the sheets. He smiles remembering he had sex with the woman of his dreams last night. A now sober Walt looks down the bed and notices that whoever is under that sheet happens to be extremely large, a lot larger than he is, and he is rather chunky.

His facial expression quickly turns from excitement to concern. Quietly and discreetly, he pulls back part of the bed sheet to see her leg. Rolls of fat plop out.

Walt jerks back and falls off of the bed. The loud thump wakes "Two Ton Tina."

"Good Morning, suga. Are you ok? Why don't you come over here and give me some more of that good lovin' from last night?"

Walt vomits right where he is. He quickly gets up and, without wasting time by getting dressed, snatches his clothes and scrambles to the door.

"Where you goin', suga?"

"I'm sorry for the misunderstanding. There's been a huge mistake. Please keep this between us. Fuck, I can't believe I did this shit. What da fuck!"

"Two Ton Tina" is puzzled.

"Did what?"

"Did you!" screams Walt without hesitation.

"What the hell you mean? You wasn't sayin' that last night when you was all up in this good pussy."

"Two Ton Tina" pulls the sheet back and reveals her entire body. Instantly, Walt vomits again and runs out of the door. He reaches the outside of the apartment building. As soon as the fresh air hits him he bends over and vomits again into a bush. He pulls out his cell phone and looks at his text thread with his friends from the night before. He rereads them and sees the pictures he sent to his crew. He puts his hands over his face in embarrassment.

"Why me, God? Why me?" he asks bewildered.

18

ISO 1000

The basketball team is hard at practice. Almost two weeks have passed since Walt lost his virginity. Big Dink still relentlessly teases him about "Two Ton Tina." This practice is the first time he has not been bombarded by jokes from Big Dink or anyone else from their crew. He is enjoying the reprieve and doesn't want practice to end. Coach Mac blows the whistle.

"Everyone, center court, take a seat on the floor. This ain't going to be quick.

"All right, fellas. The time has come. This is our last practice before our season opener on Monday. We have the talent to do some serious damage in both the MEAC and the NCAA tournament. By mixing the super talent of our freshmen with the experienced talent of our upperclassmen, we can build an awesome team here. We just need to work on the chemistry between the two groups. We need to play as one team, seamlessly.

182

"With that, I've gathered you all here because on any college campus you're going to hear things. Never forget that I have little birdies everywhere. I know everything that goes on. I don't like to get involved in people's personal lives, though. I believe in letting people do what they want as long as it doesn't start interfering with our team. I do, however, have a couple of concerns I want to address.

"We've talked about the inner team beefs and clicks, and whatnot. Initially, I asked Deon to have you guys go freshmen versus upperclassmen during open gyms. That's where the beef seemed to lie. I wanted to fuel that fire and that anger and have you guys go head-to-head. But for the past couple of weeks in practice I've been mixing you guys up so you can learn how to play as a team.

"In order for us to prevail this year, it's gonna have to be a mix of the Super Seven power with the fundamentals and experience of some of the veterans. And that can't happen if we're continuing to beef with one another and fighting over females and shit. Y'all not in high school no more.

"Chance, you're one of our star recruits. Deon, you've been the leader of this team from the moment you stepped onto this court for your first practice two years ago.

"Chance is the alpha of the freshmen. Deon, you're the alpha of the rest. If we're gonna win anything this year, we need you two to come together and lead this team to the promised land. So whatever personal shit y'all got going on, it ends right here. Right now. I don't care what beefs you have, they don't get brought onto my court—onto your teammates' court.

"This team right here is special. We have the potential to make history. Don't ever take that for granted. Don't let any outside shit interfere with that. What you do affects every one of us. Don't be selfish. Don't let your personal shit become our shit on the court."

Coach Mac turns his focus to the entire team.

"I want everyone to hear this. If they don't have their shit together, call 'em out. You have every right to expect more out of them. Y'all are a team. Each one of you has every right to expect that everyone on this team gives their all to this team. Every. Single. Time. If teammates are beefin' on the court, then they're not giving their teammates their all."

Coach Mac pauses for a moment. "We play Georgetown at the Capital One Arena on Monday. It's their home season opener, too. The place is gonna be jumpin'. If that makes you nervous, then good. It should. But I want y'all to get all those nerves out before tip-off. There's no practice tomorrow. I want

184

everyone clearing their heads and getting rest. All right, everyone bring it in. Together on three. One, two, three. Together!"

Later that evening, Chance is standing in the cafeteria line with his arm around Kia.

"You did know it was just a matter of time before I got you, right?" Chance asks playfully.

"Got me?"

"Yup, I knew from the moment I saw you that you were gonna be mine."

"Yours?" Kia asks, playing along. "So you tryin' to say I'm yours? Your what?"

"Girl, stop playin'. You know. You know you know. You my girl."

"Slow your roll there, chief. We simply hooked up during a weak emotional moment of mine. I'm just getting out of a disastrous relationship. I'm definitely not tryin' to jump right back into one. Not saying that ours would be disastrous. But you know what I mean."

Chance is taken aback. "So you sayin' you not my girl?"

"I'm saying we're kickin' it and getting to know each other for now."

"Oh, we're kickin' it," Chance repeats. "Oh okay, I see. Let me find out you tryin' to one hitta quita a brotha."

Kia laughs.

"That's definitely not the case and you know that. I'm just sayin' let's enjoy this for what it is right now and just go with the flow."

"I feel ya." Chance leans over and kisses her.

Deon and two other teammates, D.J. and Julian, are across the cafeteria. D.J. observes the kiss. He taps Deon on the shoulder and points to Chance and Kia sharing a few lingering pecks of their lips. In a huff, Deon marches over to them.

"Oh, you moved on already, Kia? As if that ain't bad enough, you messin' wit' one of my fuckin' teammates? How triflin' is that shit?"

"Boy, please. You got some nerve talkin' 'bout triflin'."

"Whateva, Kia. Do what the fuck you like. And you, Chance, didn't you hear what Coach said?"

"Yeah. I heard him loud and clear. I'm gonna keep my personal business separate and not let it interfere with my basketball or the team. You the only one makin' it an issue. Get over that shit and deal with it already."

Chance takes Kia's hand and moves forward in the food line. Deon is left standing there. He glares. "Okay. I got you, bro. Yeah, I got you for real. Just watch," he thinks to himself.

186

Howard and Georgetown fans pack the Capital One Arena for their season openers. The Georgetown cheerleaders and mascot are on the sidelines entertaining the crowd. The players are in the layup line warming up. Walt is staring off behind the Howard bench into the crowd. He looks anguished. Chance and Big Dink come up behind him and follow his gaze.

"Two Ton Tina" sits in the stands holding up a very noticeable sign that reads, "*I forgive you Walt, Love Beyoncé.*" Walt runs to the trashcan and throws up.

Big Dink pretends to console him.

"It's okay, bro, you were drunk. It's all good."

Walt looks at them unamused.

"Fuck y'all, man."

All three teammates laugh.

An animated sportscaster begins a live televised broadcast.

"There is so much buzz in the air surrounding this game, folks. Sports junkies are watching to see what the Super Seven and the rest of the Bison can do against a major program like Georgetown. This will be our first taste of what this freshman class can do at the college level. While Georgetown isn't ranked, this will still be a great test to see if Howard can hang with a big dog. Last year when they played Georgetown, they lost the game by forty-five points. This, however, is a totally different Howard team. We shall see how this one plays out. Let's now go to the public address announcer for the national anthem."

Howard players, coaches, band, and cheerleaders bend down on one knee as the national anthem is being played. At the conclusion of the anthem, the sportscaster resumes commentating.

"Looks like the Bison decided to go the Colin Kaepernick route. I'm sure that will be a topic of discussion following the game. But for now, let's go courtside for the player introductions."

Both teams' starting lineups are being introduced. Chance, Mike, Big Dink, J.J., and Deon make their entrances when called.

The jump ball is released into the air and the game begins. A perfectly executed delicate alley-oop pass from Chance to Big Dink highlights the back and forth action. The Howard fans are wild with excitement. The scoreboard at halftime reads, *"Howard 45; Georgetown 35."*

The sportscaster is impressed. During the on-air half-time recap, his remarks reflect it.

"Wow, who could have predicted this? The Howard Bison have a ten-point lead on the road against the Hoyas. Chance Knight has been on fire. He's leading both teams in scoring with twenty-five points. That's twenty-five points at the halfway mark of this game, folks, and he's a freshman.

"To say his performance has been impressive would be an understatement. I guarantee the Bison are thanking their lucky stars for his outstanding play so far because their last year's leading scorer, Deon Diggs, only has two points. He isn't having a good showing on the scoreboard. The Hoyas have found a way to shut Diggs down but have no answer for the freshman sensational phenom that is Chance Knight.

"This is shaping up to be a shocker, folks. We still have twenty minutes of basketball to play so we'll see what happens in the second half. It's unlikely he'll be able to duplicate his first half scoring performance. Since you can't expect another twenty-five points from Knight, maybe the Hoyas will be able to turn this around."

In the Howard locker room, the teammates, with one exception, are high-fiving, fist bumping, chanting, and celebrating the ten-point lead.

Yes! That's what I'm talkin' 'bout, fellas!" Chance shouts with excitement.

Deon, who is easy to read, sits sullen.

"Now that's how you play, fellas," Coach Mac says to the players. "That's the way to play together as

189

a unit. Now we need to go back out there and do the exact same thing in the second half. They're gonna come out swinging. They're gonna be all over us. They're stunned right now. Believe me their coach is rippin' them a new one as we speak.

"Expect full court presses, back court traps, and double-teams on Chance. But each time there's a trap or a double-team, what does that mean? It means someone's wide open. Keep your eyes open and find that man. The ball is dangerous in any of your hands.

"You guys are playing exceptional team ball right now. It's imperative we maintain that teamwork and unselfish play in the second half. You all are making a statement to the city right now. Let's go out there and finish this. Go add that exclamation mark!"

Their loud chants can be heard as they storm out of the locker room.

Howard inbounds the ball to start the second half. They run a play for Deon. He shoots and misses. Georgetown gets the rebound and takes it down the court. They throw an alley-oop dunk. The crowd is in a frenzy. Howard's lead is cut to eight. Deon gets the ball. Chance takes advantage of a well-executed pick. He is now wide open underneath the basket. Deon looks him off. He takes three dribbles and pulls up for a shot. Again, he misses. Georgetown gets the rebound. As all the players are running up the court, Chance looks at Deon in disbelief.

"Come on, Deon. I was wide open, man!"

"Don't even trip, we good."

Georgetown shoots a three. They drain it. The Bison lead is now cut in half.

Coach Mac calls time out and the referee blows the whistle. The Georgetown fans grow even louder as their cheerleaders perform a quick cheer. The scoreboard now reads, *"Howard 45; Georgetown 40."*

"Wow, Georgetown has come out of the locker room on fire," says the sportscaster. "Howard better settle down. Diggs has aggressively tried to get it going here in the second half, but he's just not landing his shots and it's costing his team big time. He needs to feed the hot hand of Chance Knight. The Bison have yet to score."

Back in Howard's huddle, Coach Mac is trying to remain calm.

"Now come on, fellas, do what we did in the first half that got us our lead. Let's get back to good ball movement. Deon, I'm fine with those shots *after* we've moved the ball around a bit more first. Now come on let's go."

Howard breaks the huddle. The team heads back onto the court and play resumes. Howard has possession and moves the ball. Chance now has it. He jukes his defender and drives the ball to the basket. He goes up for a powerful one-handed slam dunk. He clutches his fists, tenses his body, and yells out a fired up roar. It is an image sure to grace the cover of online articles should the Bison win. The commentators, noticing how high he appeared to jump during the execution of the dunk, use instant replay to study the different camera angles to see if his head actually got above the rim.

"Yes!" Coach Mac shouts out to the players from the sideline. "That's exactly what I'm talkin' 'bout! Great ball movement!"

"Let's go, baby!" shouts Chance.

Georgetown has the ball. They pull up for a jumper. Chance blocks the shot. Deon grabs the ball and starts a fast break. It is three-on-one. The defender follows the ball and guards Deon. Big Dink and Mad Max are now wide open for an easy layup. But Deon pulls up for the jumper, the defender in his face. He misses and Georgetown gets the rebound. They move the ball down the court and drain a three-pointer. Howard's lead is down to four. Possession is with Howard. They are demonstrating good ball movement. The ball reaches Deon. Chance makes an incredible back door cut. He heads to the basket expecting Deon to throw the alley-oop. But he does not. Deon blows him off and drives to the basket. A Georgetown defender steps in front of the drive. He quickly gets solid positioning in De-on's path. They make contact. The whistle blows. There has been a foul. A charge is called on Deon. Chance, with hands on hips, stares at Deon. He is livid.

"What da fuck you doin', yo? You gonna cost us the game."

"Man, fuck you, bitch."

Georgetown has the ball in the back court. Chance is running down the court to play defense. As he is passing the Howard bench he yells to Coach Mac.

"Coach, Deon's killing us."

"Maintain, Chance, I'll handle it."

"Come on, Deon, get your head in the game and make the open pass," Coach Mac calls out.

"My bad, Coach. I got you."

Over the next ten minutes of play there is more back and forth action until the clock on the scoreboard shows twenty seconds left in a tie game. Both teams have seventy-eight points. The shot clocks are now off.

Howard has possession. They call a thirty-sec-ond time out. Coach Mac huddles them.

"All right fellas, this is it. The game is tied and we're gonna take the last shot. Hold the ball until about ten seconds left and then run the play. We're running ISO 1000 to Chance. Chance, get open and get off a clean shot before the buzzer."

Deon rolls his eyes and sucks his teeth in displeasure.

"We've run this play a million times in practice. Y'all know it well. Now it's all about execution and attention to detail. J.J., I want you starting off with the ball up top. When the clock hits ten, you're gonna swing it to Deon. Deon, once you get the ball you'll hit Chance as he's rolling off a double screen for the game winning shot. Let's finish this shit now and shock the city."

"Let's go y'all!" screams Walt.

All the players except Deon start clapping enthusiastically as they head back out onto the court.

The sportscaster is exuberant.

"Here we go, folks. The Bison men are trying to pull off an unbelievable upset to start this season. Let's see if they can do it. Buckle your seatbelts."

The entire stadium is on their feet. The Georgetown fans are nervous, while Howard fans roar with excitement.

Big Dink inbounds the ball to J.J. He dribbles to half court. He maintains his position as he watches the clock count down to ten. He passes the ball to Deon. Deon sees Chance running, coming off a double screen. Deon inexplicably dribbles in the opposite direction. There are six seconds left on the clock. He pulls up for a jumper. The ball hits the front of the rim and bounces into the hands of Georgetown's star player.

The Georgetown player dribbles the ball down the court. Deon runs with him to try to stop him. It is one-on-one in the front court. The Georgetown player delivers a crushing crossover on Deon. Deon falls as a result. Fans on both sides ooh and aah. Undefended, the Georgetown player finger rolls the ball into the basket. The final buzzer sounds. Georgetown wins. Euphoric fans storm the court.

Howard is inside the locker room with their heads down. Coach Mac is irate. He flips over the Gatorade table. Gatorade spills everywhere and pools in an otherwise unnoticeable dip in the floor.

"Are you fuckin' kidding me, Deon? I mean seriously? You intentionally disobeyed a direct order and made a dumb ass decision that cost us the game. The level of selfishness and stupidity that was just displayed is disgusting. You're not the fuckin' coach are you? If so, then what the fuck am I doin' here? And you sure as hell ain't no leader. You don't have anyone to lead. You think this team is gonna respect someone makin' egregious decisions that cost them the win? You're officially suspended for the next game."

"But, Coach?"

"But nuffin! As a matter of fact, go wait in the hallway while I address the team. Since you want to be an individual on the court, you ain't gonna be a part of the team right now."

"But, Coach!"

"Out! Now!"

Deon snatches his towel and angrily marches out of the locker room. Coach Mac looks at his players and addresses them.

"I want to apologize to the rest of you. You guys played your asses off and did exactly what I asked of you. I noticed Deon's selfishness during the game and I made the decision to keep him in. I apologize and I put this loss on my shoulders."

The team boards the bus to return to campus. Chance does not say a word for the entire ride. They arrive back on campus and he is the first to get off. He grabs his bag from underneath the bus. Big Dink and the rest of the freshmen call after him but he ignores them and heads alone toward the dormitories. Walt grabs his bag and sprints to catch up to Chance, who is still steaming mad.

"Yo, what's up with you? You haven't said a word to anyone since the game ended."

"Bro, this is precisely the reason I wanted to go to Kentucky. I wouldn't have to deal with this type of shit."

"What kind of shit?"

"Losing to fuckin' Georgetown. If we can't beat a fuckin' unranked team then how the hell are we gonna make any noise in March Madness? Shid, that's if we can even get there."

"Man, I totally feel ya. I know you're disappointed losing our first game. Especially with all the hype surrounding us. But look at it like this, while Georgetown isn't ranked, they're still a big time historic program that blew Howard out last year. You and I both know that we had that game won. We were giving them the business until Deon went fucktard on us. He singlehandedly lost that game for us. We had it won. You played awesome and so did the team. So don't let this one early loss fuck with your mind and have you questioning your decision to come here.

"Stay positive, my brotha. We took it to Georgetown tonight. We didn't lose that game. He lost that game. Don't worry, Coach is gonna handle that. Just don't forget why you chose Howard. This is bigger than just you, Chance! Now pull your shit together and be the change that we came here to be."

Chance looks at Walt and smiles. "I hear ya, Malcolm X, I hear ya."

Walt puts his arm around Chance as they continue on toward their dormitory. Deon and some of the upperclassmen are the last players exiting the bus.

Nick, one of the upperclassmen, approaches Deon.

"Yo, Deon, man that shit wasn't cool. We been on your side this entire time. But what we saw out there today is extremely frustrating. You're the reason we lost. Your selfish actions. This would've been the biggest victory in our school's history. We could've been a part of that. We had that game won. I'm just keeping it real with you, bruh. And that last play of the game. Don't even get me started on that."

"But if my shots had fallen then it would've been all good, though, right?"

Nick scoffs.

"If my aunt had balls she would be my uncle. Bottom line is your shots weren't fallin' and Chance's were. This is your third season. You're supposed to be the team leader. You should be able to recognize who has the hot hand and feed them the ball. If your shots not fallin', pass to someone whose shots are. Damn. If the final play of the game is designed for the guy who has the hot hand, then you damn sure need to get him the ball.

"Look bro, I totally get it. We were the big men on campus, you were the star. Then these freshmen come in and it seems like everything has changed. But bottom line is we weren't winning shit. And now, when we actually can, we still ain't win shit. I know it's hard to bow down to these freshmen, especially if it takes away from your shine. I'm not saying we have to bow down completely.

"But we do, at least, need to work with them as one unit, with one common goal of winning. Imagine you and Chance as a one two punch. Man with y'all's skills working together, we could be unstoppable. I'm just sayin, bro. The writing's on the wall. Either we need to get with the program and join forces with 'em or risk being outcast, or even worse, not playing at all. We love you, bro. But we need to do what's best for the team. It's all about the team, bruh."

Deon remains silent. Nick puts his arm around him and then daps him up. Nick and the rest of the upperclassmen leave. Deon, standing alone, watches them walk away. He sits on the curb and puts his head in his hands. He feels defeated.

A few days later, after working on midterm assignments, Chance and Kia lie in bed watching Chance's small twenty-seven inch flat screen television.

"So have you and Deon had any interaction since the incident at Homecoming?"

"He tried to talk to me the other day when I was walking to class and I told him never speak to me again in life."

"Well, damn."

"One thing I don't play is cheating. I can handle many things, but cheating is not one of them." Kia cries.

"We had been together since I was a sophomore in high school," she adds. "I met him when I was visiting my cousins in Brooklyn. That's why I came to Howard, so we wouldn't have to do the long distance thing anymore. For him to cheat on me, he's such an asshole."

Chance rubs her shoulders and kisses her on her forehead.

"Coach suspended his ass for the next game."

"That's exactly what he gets. Y'all had that Georgetown game won and then he blew it. He couldn't handle you being the star and scoring all the points. He's used to being *the man*."

"Yep, I was pissed. I was so pissed that I was doubting my decision to even come here. If I can't lead a team that has so many top athletes past an unranked team, then NBA scouts might doubt me and my draft stock could slip. And as a team, if we can't win against an unranked opponent, then how the hell we gonna win against one that's ranked?"

"But y'all were winning that game and lookin' good doin' it. Y'all had it won until Deon fucked it up."

Chance laughs.

"That's exactly what Walt said. Walt's actually the one who calmed me down. He made me realize that considering Howard was blown out by George-town last year, what we did was pretty amazing. Deon needs to get over that shit. He's definitely talented and we can use his skills. But he needs to be willing to be both a role player at times and a star at other times, and know when to do which. I want us to win the whole thing. In order to do that, we need all the basketball talent we can get. I'm hoping he'll do a one-eighty and play team ball."

"If you say so."

Chance gives Kia a kiss.

"Enough about Deon's selfish ass, come here, girl." He tickles Kia and then leans in and kisses her again. They experience a climatic end to the evening.

The Howard basketball team heads onto the court for a jump ball against American University at Burr Gymnasium. A suspended Deon, wearing a dress suit, sits sullenly on the bench. The game begins and Howard executes exciting plays, including crowd pleasing dunks, blocked shots, smart passes, and consistent three-point shots. The Howard crowd can hardly believe their eyes. The cheerleaders and band rock the stands. The players on the Howard bench, with one notable exception, are standing and cheering every great play—which is almost all of them.

Howard huddles during a time-out in the second half.

"Now that's the way you play, fellas," says Coach Mac. Unselfish basketball with great ball movement. Look at the scoreboard."

The scoreboard reads, *"Howard 81; American 61"*. There are seven minutes and thirty seconds left in the game.

Coach Mac looks at the starters. "You guys have played great. I'm making substitutions now so that other players can get some time."

Walt checks into the game. As soon as Walt runs out onto the court, "Two Ton Tina," who is in the stands, holds up a sign that reads, *"I love you, Walt."* Over the remaining seven minutes, Walt shows why he is on the team. He drains shots from three-point range and drives to the basket for layups. Chance and the other starters on the bench are elated. They cannot stop yelling Walt's name. The scoreboard reads, *"Howard 98; American 75."* There are fifteen seconds left and American has the ball. The Howard crowd is chanting, "We want 100, we want 100!"

American runs a play and Walt steals the pass. The clock counts down four, three, two, one. Walt shoots a floater. It goes in at the buzzer and gives Howard 100 points. The players storm onto the court and tackle Walt. The crowd erupts! Chance is on top of him screaming.

"Hell yeah, boy. I see you. You were beastin'."

"Two Ton Tina" is jumping up and down and hollering. She is waving the "*I love you, Walt*" sign. Through the celebration, Deon, silent, sits on the bench.

Chance pushes through the players who are piled on top of him and Walt, extends a hand, and helps Walt to his feet. They both walk over to the stands where Walt's mother and Teddy are sitting. Chance extends open arms to Teddy who climbs over the railing and falls softly into his arms. He brings him onto the court. The players gather around and high-five Teddy. Teddy, now missing most of his thick, black hair as a result of chemotherapy treatments, sports a huge smile. Big Dink and Chance each holds one of Teddy's arms up in the air in a victory pose. Mrs. Williams puts her hands over her mouth and seals this moment in her heart as a forever memory.

The next day Deon, not knowing what to expect, sits in Coach Mac's office.

"Deon, I wanna talk to you about a few things. First off, I'm reinstating you effective immediately. You'll be back in uniform with us for our upcoming big game against Maryland. As you know, they're undefeated and ranked fifth. This is a chance for Howard to land on the national map in regards to respect and letting the world know we're for real. I want to make sure that you're a part of that, son.

"This is your junior year and you haven't experienced any team success. Just individual success. I know it took a while, but I finally found you the talent you—no, we—wanted to surround you with so we could win the MEAC tournament and make it to March Madness. Some of these players probably won't be around next year so we have to capitalize on their talent now."

"True, but I meant surround me with talented *role* players that could help get us there. I was still supposed to be the star."

"See, there it is. There's the problem, son," Coach Mac fires back.

"You have to get rid of that selfish *I* mentality. It's not about *you*. It's about Howard. Look at the MEAC awards you've received. You've been the man on campus for two years. You've led the team in scoring. You've done all of that. You've done everything but win.

"The talent you're surrounded with is some of the best in the nation. So who gives a fuck if you aren't the best player on the team this year? Who gives a fuck if you don't lead the team in scoring? As long as you play, contribute to the team, and we win, that's all that should matter to you. Let me ask you a question. Do you want to win the MEAC and get a championship ring?"

"Yes, sir."

"Okay. Well, do you wanna go to the NCAA tournament and have a chance at winning the national title?"

"Hell yeah, sir."

"Exactly. Well, we absolutely can win the MEAC this year. We have a realistic chance at making a run in the NCAA tournament. But only if we're able to properly gel as a team. In order for us to do that, you need to pull yourself together and become the contributor on this team that we need you to be. I have you, and all of your talent, along with what everyone calls the Super Seven. And if Walt plays like he did the other night, he might earn that title he got lumped into."

Coach Mac pauses in thought momentarily.

"But, Deon. Let me ask you another question. Are we better as a team with you guys being split and not working together, or are we better as a team using all your talents together as one unit?"

"Together as one cohesive unit, sir." Deon looks deflated. His shoulders sunken.

"Bingo."

"I'm so sorry, Coach. I've lost myself, man.

Chance took my shine and my girl. My life as I knew it is fuckin' gone right now. It's been really hard for me to cope. Bottom line is I came to Howard to play ball and to win. That's going to be my only focus moving forward. You have my word. Not being a part of that victory the other day really hurt. I just sat there and watched everything.

"To see Burr rockin' like I've never seen it rock before, and to see us blow a team out like we've never done before, it was incredible. It just made me miserable to know that I wasn't a part of that. I wasn't a part of the moment. I don't want that feeling ever again. I'm all in. I'll fit in where I fit in and I'll contribute any way I can. I'll have a positive attitude about it no matter what, Coach. Just know you won't see that selfish behavior again. I've lost my position as leader of the team. Even some of the upperclassmen don't respect me anymore. And I've lost my girl. I can't afford to lose basketball, too. Basketball is my life. It's all I have." Deon breaks down in tears.

Coach Mac is touched by Deon's remorse and anguish.

"Everything is going to be okay, son. I'm glad you opened up and I'm so glad you're finally realizing what's at stake and what needs to happen. You're capable of regaining your spot as leader of this team. You don't have to score the most points or be the best player to be the leader. All you have to do is be someone the other players look up to and respect.

"The way I see it, you can teach these freshmen a thing or two from your experience. Especially once we get to MEAC play. You know how most of our opponents play collectively as a team, and what some of the players' tendencies are. These young boys haven't studied these teams. They haven't studied these players. They only know the ones they've played against, or expected to play against, at the big schools. So, in actuality, with the right attitude and getting back in good grace with the other players, you absolutely can become the leader of this team again.

"Not to mention, you're gonna be needed big time against Maryland. These freshmen have never seen an atmosphere like they're about to see. You've seen it before. You can be a big help by preppin' them for what they're about to face."

Deon is encouraged. His face brightens. A flood of relief washes over him.

"Absolutely. Consider it done. Thanks, Coach. Thanks for this second chance and for not losing faith in me. I won't let you down."

Coach Mac and Deon both stand and shake hands. Shortly after the meeting, Deon sees Chance walking across The Yard with his arm around Kia. He approaches.

"What up, Chance? What up, Kia?" He daps up Chance and waves to Kia.

"What's good, Deon?" Chance responds.

Kia is silent.

"Just wanted to say what up. All right, I'll catch y'all later. I need to get to class."

Chance and Kia do not know what to make of the exchange.

"I thought I was gonna have to put my fists up when he was walkin' up on us. You know how he likes to swing on a brotha," Chance says jokingly.

Kia laughs.

Later on in the cafeteria, as Big Dink, Mad Max, Bird, Mike, J.J., and Walt are walking from the food line, Deon purposely makes his way to them, daps them all up with a big smile on his face, and strolls off. They are all perplexed.

During the next practice, Deon is making great passes to Chance. He floats him an alley-oop, which Chance executes effortlessly.

"Great play, bro," says Deon as he smacks Chance on the rear.

On the next play, Chance is knocked to the floor by one of the returning players. Deon is the first one over to help him up. Coach Mac, with a satisfied smile, looks over to his assistant coaches.

"We're gelling as a unit at the perfect time," he says to them.

The team is in Burr Gymnasium for the final practice before the highly anticipated matchup against the undefeated University of Maryland. Coach Mac calls them to the circle at half court.

"All right, fellas. I don't have to tell y'all how big this next game is. Winning this game will put Howard on the map and let the world know we're for real. Now let's get in here and get after it one final time. Make this practice count."

"Coach, is it all right if I say something to the team?" asks Deon with a bit of hesitation.

"Certainly, Deon. Go right ahead."

"Thanks, Coach. Fellas, I just want to start off by apologizing to everyone. I know I've been a selfish asshole."

Deon looks at his friends. He realizes that in releasing the hate, he has been liberated.

"Thanks to the upperclassmen for sticking by me initially. But even y'all came to see the light before I did. Well, I see it now and I just want all y'all to know that I'm in this to win this. The selfishness is done. I'm here to contribute in any way I can.

"Freshmen, I'm here for you if you need advice on anything. I feel that with the combination of the upperclassmen's experience and the unbelievable talent y'all have, we can do serious damage this year. We were divided in the Georgetown game and you see what that got us. I take total blame. I don't want anything like that to happen again. So, let's fully come together and be an actual cohesive unit. Oh, and one other thing, let's go kick some mutha fuckin' Terrapin ass!"

"That's what I'm talkin' 'bout, baby. Let's go!" shouts Chance.

Deon initiates an embrace with Chance. The entire team comes in behind them.

"We ready! We ready! We ready!" they all chant together as they jump up and down.

Coach Mac, elated, looks up toward the ceiling. He knows Coach Knight is looking down.

19

PARTING OF THE RED SEA

A sea of red tee shirts colors the Xfinity Center in College Park, Maryland, as the spirited Terrapin students gear up for tonight's game against Howard University. Very few fans can resist dancing to the school band's instrumental rendition of catchy songs ranging from old time classics to current Top Forty.

The lead sportscaster prepares the television audience for the impending start to the game.

"Welcome to College Park for tonight's match-up featuring the fifth ranked Maryland Terrapins facing off against the unranked Howard Bison. One of the big story lines here is Chance Knight. Remember, he was the number one recruit in the country. Maryland was one of the top three contenders when he was deciding where he wanted to play ball. The other two: Kentucky and Duke. Maryland would probably have been the favorite to win it all with Chance on their team. The students are likely to be angry he didn't choose their school. And you know how the student section can react during games. These college fans show no mercy. You can expect a lot of excitement and he can expect a lot of taunting coming from the stands."

"That's right," agrees the second sportscaster. "Chance hails from Maryland. A lot of people around here were hoping he'd choose the Terrapins. But after the tragic loss of his father during an incident with police, he chose Howard to honor his father's wish that he play for his alma mater. But don't expect the fans to show Chance any mercy. The crowd will definitely put on an exciting show. For the fans, it might almost be like they're playing against their rival. After seeing Howard's loss against an unranked Georgetown, I'm expecting an easy win for the Terrapins."

The Bison are inside the locker room counting down the minutes until they make their way onto tonight's big stage.

"Deon, I want to talk to you," says Coach Mac. The coach rests his hand on Deon's shoulder. "I just want to tell you that I'm proud of you. You've really turned your attitude around and embraced the younger players. You've been looking great in practice. The team really seems to be gelling now."

"Thanks, Coach," says Deon, grateful for the praise.

"With that being said, because this is your first game back from suspension, I'm not gonna start you. You're gonna come off the bench."

"I understand, Coach." Deon is stoic. He is trying to hide his disappointment.

"But I need you ready to go. You'll probably be subbing in fairly early on especially if we get into early trouble. These freshmen haven't seen an atmosphere like they're gonna see tonight. But you have. They haven't faced off against a powerhouse like this either. But you have. I'm gonna need you to use your experience to lead and calm them down when necessary. So, you ready?"

"Yes, sir!"

The Howard Bison stand in the Xfinity Center hallway gearing up to run out onto the floor for pregame warm up.

"This is it, fellas," Chance says with excitement in his voice. "This is what it's all about. We have an opportunity of a lifetime right here. We're about to face the fifth ranked team in all the land. Imagine the reaction when we knock them off."

"Let's go, baby!" exclaims Walt.

"All right, fellas, let's go shake up DI basketball."

Chance leads them out onto the court. They are met with deafening boos. Maryland's team runs out onto the court and the crowd erupts! A Maryland player bumps into Chance as they pass.

"You made the wrong choice, chump. Get ready to face payback," he warns.

Chance looks at him and continues to warm up. Deon witnesses the exchange and is surprised that Chance does not quip back.

"Don't let them get in your head. That's their goal. Play your game. Give it to him on the court. Don't get caught up in any other nonsense that they'll try to distract you with."

"Thanks, man. Not to worry. Let's go, baby!"

Chance and Deon bump chests.

The national anthem begins and the Howard players, coaches, cheerleaders, and band take a knee. Some of the fans are enraged. As the anthem ends, a spattering of boos are heard.

"Have some respect for your country and military!" yells a middle-aged spectator.

Surrounding fans applaud.

Chance, Big Dink, J.J., Mike Jones, and Bird walk out onto the court to meet the Maryland starters for the jump ball. Maryland earns the opening tip. They quickly move the ball toward the basket. The point guard throws a spectacular alley-oop to their small forward. The small forward dunks it right over Chance's head. The crowd goes berserk.

The small forward is the same player who taunted Chance during warmups. He does not stop.

"Welcome to the next level, freshman. I knew you weren't ready for this. This ain't mutha fuckin' high school, my nigga."

Chance remains collected and doesn't engage him.

Howard inbounds the ball. J.J. takes it down court. He passes to Chance who is fresh off of a pick. The small forward picks him up and is now defending him and relentlessly goading him.

"What you got, freshman? What you got?"

Chance attempts a crossover move. The defender steals it. He dribbles down court. He gets to the basket and slams down a monstrous dunk. The crowd is on their feet. Howard now has the ball. They initiate an inbound pass. It is stolen by a defender who kicks it out to one of their shooters. The shooter drains a three-pointer. In under a few minutes, the score is seven to zero.

"Time out!" yells Coach Mac.

The nearest referee blows his whistle and grants Howard a full time out. The starters take a seat on the bench and look at their coach who looks back at them and smiles.

"Welcome to top notch Division I basketball, fellas. You guys are fine. Just relax. We just need to calm down, breathe, and play our game. This is a top notch team. This ain't gonna be easy. But we're more than capable of beating them if we play our game. Now go out there and show them what we're made of."

Howard goes back out and the crowd watches an expected lopsided performance. Howard is making unforced errors. For several minutes Coach Mac allows his team to try to find themselves. He realizes it is not happening and is now visibly frustrated. He calls another time out.

"Well, folks, Howard has called their second time out," says the lead sportscaster. "Their coach needs to find a way to fire up the Bison. They're on the verge of getting blown out of this arena. Let's recap. The score is Terrapins twenty-five and Bison twelve. There are ten minutes and twenty-two seconds left in the half. Howard needs to turn things around before halftime if they want to have any chance of pulling off the upset. If not, they might as well not even come back out on the court."

The second sportscaster chimes in. "Exactly. Right now it looks as if the so-called Super Seven and the rest of their team are intimidated and unsure of themselves among the raucous in the sea of red. They're being out-played and outworked in every single aspect of the game."

"And they're clearly getting out fanned."

Both sportscasters laugh.

Coach Mac looks around and signals Deon.

"Deon, let's go. You're in. Take a seat, Bird."

Deon and the other four players walk onto the court. Deon motions them to gather around him.

"Look, fellas, this is where the game is gonna change. Together we can beat these mutha fuckas. Now let's go play team ball and get back in this game. We gotta do it now. Now!"

Over the next few minutes Howard goes on a major run. On offense they move the ball beautifully and execute plays perfectly with picks opening up players for swished jump shots, dunks, and consistency from three-point range. On defense they virtually shut the Terrapins down with blocked shots, several steals, and a drawn charge. Deon is the change factor.

The spectators are stunned. The sea of red that always appears to be in motion has stilled as the fans remain quiet in their seats.

Maryland calls a time out. Howard players spring up from their bench and run onto the court to chest bump and high-five Deon and the others.

"Wow!" says the lead sportscaster. His excitement is evident. "Now that is impressive. Junior Deon Diggs came in and sparked the visiting Bison. The combination of Deon and Chance has just been too much for the Terrapins to handle. There's one minute and twenty-two seconds to go in the half and the Maryland lead has been cut to one. This is unbelievable! Last year Maryland beat Howard by fifty-two points. Howard obviously didn't have the Super Seven, but this showing tonight is just incredible. Even with some of the best ranked freshmen in the nation, this just isn't fathomable against a team like Maryland. This game is shaping up to be a thriller."

"That's right," the second sportscaster says in agreement. "Nobody would have predicted this. I have never seen the stands in the Xfinity Center so somber. But the question remains; is this a fleeting moment closing out the first half, or can the Bison actually keep this up in the second?"

Coach Mac talks to the team in the huddle, his voice a pitch higher than usual.

"You see that? You guys belong here. You're on their level. This is the moment you guys need to realize who you are. This is the moment you gotta say hello to the mutha fuckin' world. Now go get the lead! And keep it! Do it now!"

218

"Let's go," exclaims Deon as he leads the pumped up players onto the court.

Howard showcases breathtaking skills and closes out the half in the lead. This time it is the Maryland coach who flips over the Gatorade table in the locker room.

When play resumes in the second half, competitive action between the two teams incites the crowd. J.J. has the ball and sets Chance up for an alley-oop. He dunks the ball over the trash talking defending small forward. As Chance runs by him, he smacks the guy on his rear end and smirks. On the next Howard possession, J.J. feeds the ball to Mike inside the paint using a no look pass. Mike, invoking his super human power, slams the ball through the hoop on top of two defenders. The dunk beckons involuntary oohs and aahs from both teams and their fans. The teams counter dunk after dunk, three-pointer after three-pointer. Maryland fans are witnessing a battle they were not expecting. The Howard fans are uncontrollable.

The sportscasters are no less intrigued than the fans and recognize that this may be a turning point for HBCUs and Division I college sports.

"Well, folks," says the lead sportscaster. "It has all come down to this. The Terrapins are in an unexpected fight for their lives against the Bison, the unranked Bison. Howard is down by one point with fifteen seconds left. Fasten your seatbelts, folks. Here we go."

The Howard team is huddling during their most important time out of the game.

"All right, fellas. We are exactly where we want to be. This is the situation we all dream about. This is the situation that we've all simulated on the playground, where you hit the game winning shot. We've all simulated the countdown game winning buzzer beater. Four, three, two, one! It's good! The crowd goes wild!

"Y'all know I ain't lyin'." Coach Mac laughs. "All right, let's get serious. Listen up. We're going to run the exact same play we planned at the end of the Georgetown game, ISO 1000 to Chance. J.J., you're gonna get the ball and hold it till about eleven seconds. Then you're gonna pass to Deon. Deon's gonna look for Chance who'll be comin' off a double screen with about six seconds left. Deon, you pass to Chance. Chance, you take the shot. It's the game winning shot so make sure you drain it."

Everyone in the huddle shoots Deon an inquiring look. Deon laughs and shakes his head.

"Don't worry y'all. I got ya. I'm not gonna fuck us up again. The ball's going to Chance no matter what. I don't care if that mutha fucka got four defenders on him."

Everyone laughs.

"All right, together on three. One, two, three. Together!"

Not one seat is occupied in the entire stadium; everyone is on their feet and making noise. "Defense! Defense! Defense," chants the Maryland crowd.

Big Dink inbounds the ball to J.J. He holds the ball for a few seconds and then passes it to Deon. The game clock is down to eleven seconds. Deon looks at Chance and then drives to his right. He crosses over, gets set, and pulls up for a shot. It is a pump fake. He passes it to Chance who is coming off of the double screen. Chance is wide open. He catches the ball and goes up to shoot with four seconds left. The ball leaves his hands, three, two, one, swish! The ball goes through the net just as the buzzer sounds. Howard wins the game ninety-two to ninety-one.

The Howard players rush the court and tackle Chance. They are in a frenzy; crazy with excitement. The Maryland players are in disbelief. Most of the fans' faces match their red tee shirts as the shock settles in. Their chins are dropped, eyebrows raised, and facial expressions puzzled as they triple-take the final score and search one another's faces trying to make sense of what just happened.

"Howard wins! Howard wins!" the sportscasters scream into their microphones.

"The Howard Bison, who lost this game last year by fifty-two points, have just knocked off the undefeated and fifth-ranked Maryland Terrapins in an absolute thriller," exclaims the lead sportscaster.

"I guess they answered the question. They kept their play up in the second half to finish with a remarkable win. Chance Knight, who hit the game winning shot at the buzzer, led the Bison with twenty-two points and eight rebounds. A few other major contributors were Jason Jacks, Deon Diggs, and, of course, Mike Jones. Jason finished with sixteen points and an impressive thirteen assists. Talk about a point guard with the ability to see the court and find the open shot."

"That's right," says the second sportscaster. "But Diggs had the most important assist of the game—the pass to Knight to win it. He finished the game with fifteen points and six rebounds."

"Yes, that young man played his heart out tonight. And Mike finished with seventeen points, five blocked shots, and eleven rebounds. He was all over the boards tonight."

"No surprise there. He's expected to be one of the best power forwards in college basketball."

"What we saw tonight from these young men makes it clear that this is college sports history in the making."

A petite television reporter approaches Chance and Deon who are still on the court.

"What do you guys have to say after your miraculous win?" she asks as she extends her arm to push the microphone under Chance's face.

Chance smiles.

"This is just the beginning, baby. Y'all haven't seen anything yet. Howard Bison. Get used to hearing that name. H-UUUUU! You Know!"

"What about you, Deon?" The reporter repositions the microphone.

"I just want to say that it was a great team win! I was here last year when we got blown out. This payback victory feels terrific."

"How did you guys pull off such a huge upset?"

Chance and Deon look at each other. "Teamwork!" they exclaim simultaneously.

Deon leaves the court. Chance sticks around for another interview.

Back in the locker room, with music blasting, the Howard players, coaches, and team managers are celebrating like they never have before. They dance, jump, high-five, fist bump, dap each other up, and re-count all of the winning plays. Walt leads a chant. "We Ready! We Ready!"

Coach Mac, looking solemn, walks in the room, stops, and stares at everyone. As word spreads that he seems upset, the music is turned off and the players quiet. After a few seconds of awkward silence, Coach Mac grins.

"Got ya."

He runs to the middle where everyone is celebrating and joins in, jumping up and down. The partying continues as well as the chant. "We ready! We ready! We ready!"

"All right, fellas, listen up," Coach Mac says as he claps his hands to command attention. "Great win. You guys played incredible team ball and if we continue to play like that then we can beat anyone. When you get back to your rooms tonight, I want each of you to watch *Sports Highlight Center*."

"Yup, we probably gonna be the lead story," says Big Dink.

"I just want y'all to see the impact that you can have this year. We're talkin' national impact. Not just local."

At 10:59 p.m., Chance, Walt, Big Dink, and Mad Max wish that Chance's flat screen were bigger as they eagerly await the start of the sports show. A minute later the show begins.

"Welcome to *Sports Highlight Center*, everyone. As usual, tonight I'll start off with the coolest thing I saw today. You guys know I'm a Maryland University alumnus so I wasn't happy about this. But considering the magnitude of this upset and the awesome backstories, I had to make it the coolest thing I saw today.

"First, let me give some background. In case you've been living under a rock, the Howard University men's basketball team landed the top recruiting class in the nation. This is unheard of for an historically black college or university. Typically, that honor goes to the likes of a Kentucky, Duke, UNC, you get my drift. Chance Knight, who is a kid from Prince George's County in Maryland, was the nation's number one ranked high school player. He had narrowed his selections to Kentucky, Maryland, and Duke. Eventually, he privately verbally committed to Kentucky.

"Then, tragically his father, Craig Knight, who was also his AAU coach, was killed during a police traffic stop involving some of the players he coached. Chance's dad always wanted Chance to attend Howard University, his alma mater. He was also a former basketball player there. In light of Chance's dad's death, Chance elected to honor his wishes."

Walt looks over at Chance who is perfectly still as the anchor continues.

"His father always felt that top level African American athletes should go to HBCUs as opposed to the big power schools. His vision was that their presence would lead to a transfer of power with respect to revenue and all that comes with it. He wanted a seismic change in Division I college sports."

Chance is fixated on every word uttered. The anchor pauses as if in reflection, and then continues.

"Well, maybe he was right. I don't know. It's still too early to tell. But all I can say is it has already made an impact for Howard. Other top recruits who played on his AAU team decided to join forces and go with him to Howard. That's how much Craig Knight was loved and respected by those kids. Two other top recruits, his cousin Mike Jones and friend Jason Jacks, who played on a rival AAU team from the West Coast, were inspired by Craig's dream and decided to join Chance and be a part of the movement. Some of you may remember when the Fab Five went to Michigan. Well this is essentially the same thing, but instead it's seven players, the Super Seven, and they chose Howard. Well tonight, folks, Chance's dad looks like a genius. The Howard Bison knocked off the fifth-ranked Maryland Terrapins on the road in a hostile environment."

He pauses again before resuming.

"Unfortunately, this brilliant win by the Howard Bison did not come without controversy. During tonight's national anthem, the Bison players and coaches all took a knee in support of Colin Kaepernick. Even the Howard band and cheerleaders. As you all know, the anthem has been a huge topic of discussion in the NFL. It has drawn attention from everyone, including the president who likes to tweet about it from time to time. I wonder if the president will tweet about the Bison men kneeling tonight and call them *sons of bitches*. We shall see.

"I want to play a very interesting clip of Chance Knight being asked by our correspondent, Sherri Greene, about the anthem protest after the game."

The video features an attractive, thirty-something-year-old reporter interviewing Chance.

"Chance, congrats on this victory. This was a spectacular performance by an amazing group of young men. How does it feel?"

"It feels great, ma'am. We worked very hard for this and it feels so good to win a game that puts Howard basketball on the map."

"Yes, absolutely. You guys are going to make all types of headlines after this huge win." The reporter then pivots to what she really wants to ask. "But one of those headlines won't be basketball related.

Your team knelt for the anthem. You want to speak on that at all?"

Chance does not flinch.

"Most folks already know the story of Kaep and why he kneeled. Kaep is out of an NFL job now because of the stance he took. The reason he's out of a job is because the people in power, who are the decision makers, don't look like him and don't support the cause.

"So after my pops became one of those unarmed black men that fell victim to the police, I decided to attend his alma mater to honor him. The reason I'm able to take a knee without consequence is because at Howard my coach is black and believes in the same cause. Our school president is black and believes in the same cause. The MEAC commissioner is black and believes in the same cause. So this is something I want all five- and four-star black athletes to see. Shoot, all black athletes for that matter.

"If I'd chosen Duke or Kentucky and started kneeling for the anthem, it would probably end up being a Kaep situation, which is extremely sad. But at an HBCU, I don't have that problem. I'm able to peacefully protest and not be villainized or blackballed because of it."

Chance turns to the camera.

"I want to make something very clear. We in no way are disrespecting the military by kneeling during the anthem. I'm a big supporter of the military and so was my father. My uncles were in the military. I have the utmost respect for our men and women in uniform and am forever grateful for them.

"Our president is the one who changed the narrative. He falsely accused Kaep and anyone who kneels as disrespecting our military and country. That couldn't be further from the truth. I know one thing, if we win at Howard just like we did tonight against the best in the country, then maybe more top black athletes will follow.

"I just want minority athletes to see the power in numbers and realize the power we have to make change. Just imagine if all the other black NFL players took the same stance as Kaep and stood by him in unity. The NFL would then have to blackball seventy percent of their league. That would destroy their product and the league's bottom line."

The reporter was not expecting that response.

"Chance, not only are you one of the best basketball talents in the country, but you clearly are one of the most conscientious. Congrats again and I wish you all the best."

"Thank you."

The video ends.

"Man, this kid is really impressive y'all. But I guess it's not too surprising. The kid did graduate high school with a 4.0 GPA and a high SAT score. Just saying.

"Now as painful as it is for me, let's go straight to the final play of tonight's game. Maryland is up by one with fifteen seconds to play and then this happens." The video ends with Chance's game winning shot and the ensuing pandemonium.

Walt turns to Chance and pats him on the back. They hear cheers from nearby dormitory rooms.

"Okay, I have to wrap up this segment and move on. I'll leave you with this, I can't predict the future, but I think Chance's father was on to something here. Look at what Howard just did with these top recruits. Last year Howard lost to Maryland by fifty-two points. So if recruits of this caliber start going to HBCUs in significant numbers, then what you saw tonight potentially will be much more common.

"If that trend were to continue, you could start seeing television network money flowing to these schools, a revitalization of the HBCUs as we know them. Kudos to the Super Seven, potential trailblazers. But even if this works, they won't reap the benefits. Change takes time and this is a huge risk. The fact that these kids took a stand and sacrificed all that the big schools offer is very impressive.

"Their passion and character are undeniable. More impressive than their win tonight. I tip my hat to them. They should be very proud. This is why the Howard Bison win over my Maryland Terrapins was the coolest thing I saw tonight."

20
THE REAL HU

The Howard Bison have been on a miraculous run following the Maryland Terrapins upset. They have won five consecutive games, stopped only in their last game by the number two ranked Michigan State Spartans. Today the Bison are mentally preparing to face a familiar opponent, their long-standing nemesis—the Hampton University Pirates. The Howard versus Hampton game has historically been the most heated rivalry in the MEAC until recent years when the Pirates exited the conference to join the Big South. The switch does not detract from the fact that, *to them*, there can only be one *real* HU. They are playing for that title. This game is personal for both the teams and their fans.

The local demand for this game is like none other and the media attention reflects it. Today's headline from the sports section in The *Washington City Paper* reads, "Former MEAC Rival Powers to Face-Off.

Who's the Real HU?" *The Washington Times* reads, "Battle of the HUs, Game Sold Out!"

Judgement night has arrived. The game is being played at Washington, DC's newly built Entertainment and Sports Arena, which stretches over 118,000 square feet and seats 4,200. The Bison are huddled inside the locker room and their attention is focused on Coach Mac.

"All right, fellas. Y'all freshmen haven't played against this opponent. But let me tell you, this isn't an ordinary game. The rest of you know what I'm talking about, especially you, Deon. I don't have to tell you guys that no matter what the teams' records are, in a rivalry game, anything can happen. We are coming off of a hard fought loss on the road. You know I'm proud of how you played, but I know you want a gimme to get that winning feeling back. I can assure you this game isn't it.

"Tonight's game is a different animal. You're gonna have to be ready for war. Think Redskins versus Cowboys. Ohio State versus Michigan. New York Yankees versus Boston Red Sox. That's Howard versus Hampton. You newbies are a part of a rivalry like nothing you've experienced before.

"It still pains me that Hampton's no longer part of the MEAC. Their president believes the Big South

Conference will enhance their profile and visibility. They're hoping that will enhance their revenue.

"This is a direct result of the continuing financial decline of many HBCUs. You have one of the HBCU powers leaving to go join a non-HBCU conference in search of more revenue.

"This is precisely why the decision you youngins made, and you Deon, to attend Howard is so vitally important. By you guys winning and bringing national attention to HBCUs, we can potentially accomplish what Hampton is seeking without leaving the MEAC—a black conference, which is exactly where we belong. And where *they* belong. We're gonna show them, and everyone, that if our top black athletes attend HBCUs, then the financial benefits will follow. Each and every last one of you are trailblazers. And that takes true guts! And I'm not just talking about the Super Seven and Deon. Everyone is a contributor and everyone has sacrificed.

"Now let's go out here and show this city who the *real* HU is. Everyone bring it in. Real HU on three. One, two, three. Real HU!"

The Bison and Pirates run out onto the court. As expected, the entire arena is in a frenzy. The atmosphere for this game is indeed living up to the hype.

Every seat is filled and every single person in them is rowdy. Although the game is in the District of Columbia, the fan support is not lopsided. Hampton representation is in full force.

Chance and the other starting Bison walk onto the court for the jump ball. The Pirates' starters follow. The jump ball goes up and the game begins. Howard earns the first possession. Big Dink has the ball just above the top of the key. He takes two strong dribbles and, while making contact with a defender set in his position, pulls up for a jumper just outside of the charge zone. He makes the shot as the referee blows his whistle. The crowd is so loud the whistle goes unnoticed and the Bison run down the court to position themselves for defense only to realize a foul has been called on Big Dink.

The Hampton Pirates take advantage and go on a quick seven point run. Coach Mac has not broken a sweat. He does not call a time out until five minutes left in the half.

"Fellas, what did I tell you before this game? Outside of March Madness there is no game like playing a game against your rival. I told you it was going to be war and war is what you're in, and you're losing. I'm not worried though. I knew you would be caught off guard by this experience, but I know you get it now. So go back out there and close out this half right. You're only down by five. I

235

expect you to be winning after the next five minutes. Now go out there and play some ball. Have fun with it."

The Howard Bison do just that. Going into the second half they are up by four points. J.J. shows off his "playground" basketball handling skills, causing Hampton defenders to fall to the ground, sprain ankles, and "break their necks" trying to figure out where the ball has gone. Mike shows off his inside and outside game, dunking over any player in his path and draining three pointers while double-teamed. His defense matches, blocking shots anywhere in his radius of play. And Chance shows off his dominant yet playful side, playing every offensive position with ease and with a lot of extra flare. He finishes with thirty-seven points, J.J. finishes with sixteen assists, and Mike finishes with twenty points and five blocked shots.

After the game the Howard Bison dance at center court chanting, "Real HU! Real HU! Real HU!" Surrounding them are bouncing cheerleaders, excited band members, and screaming fans who have stormed onto the court to join in.

The dejected Hampton players, heads low, walk back to the locker room. On this particular night there is no question as to who is the *real* HU. The Howard Bison made sure of that. The end of game scoreboard reflects, *"Howard 100; Hampton 67."*

21

THIS HERE'S MISSISSIPPI

The Bison are inside the Mississippi State visitor's locker room. Coach Mac huddles everyone together.

"All right, fellas. We're eight and two through our first ten games. We've only lost to Georgetown and Michigan State. The Georgetown loss was inexcusable, but you should still feel good about Michigan State. It was a road game, they're undefeated, and they're ranked number two.

"You all played great ball. Today is our last game before winter break. If we can go out here and knock them off, then we'll have beaten another ranked team.

"So far this is the best record Howard has ever had at this point in any season. I'm so proud of you fellas. Now let's go out there and kick some ass. Let's go!"

Howard stands at the front of the tunnel waiting to run out onto the court for warmups. A Mississippi State fan looks down at them from the stands and yells.

"Why don't you unpatriotic niggers go back to Africa? If you're not going to respect the flag, then get the fuck outta our country. This here's Mississippi. We honor the flag down here. Don't even think about kneeling in here or there'll be consequences."

Coach Mac's head snaps up.

"Hey. Who the hell do you think you're talkin' to? You have no right to threaten these young men. They'll continue to do what they believe in. We won't tolerate disrespect from a redneck bigot like you."

"Fuck you, boy. This the South right here, boy. Y'all in the wrong place tonight."

The arena police notice the unruly fan and quickly come over to escort him out of the building. As he is being escorted away he continues to yell profanities and spits in the direction of the Bison.

"Let's stay focused on the task at hand, gentlemen. Use this incident as fuel. Take the anger you feel right now out against our opponents. Let's play angry tonight and kick some ass. Let's go," Coach Mac says in an effort to rally his players, although he is himself rattled.

The Howard team runs out onto the floor for warmups. After warmups, everyone takes their place for the national anthem. Once again, Howard players, cheerleaders, managers, trainers, and coaches all take a knee. They are instantly met by boos from the crowd before the anthem even starts. As the anthem is ending, an unopened plastic water bottle flies out of the stands and hits Walt in the back of his neck. Security runs in the direction of where the bottle was thrown from the crowd. A few of the Mississippi State fans point out the guy who threw the bottle. He is escorted out.

The team trainer examines Walt's head and neck and determines he only appears to have a bruise. He gives Coach Mac a nod.

"Everyone bring it in," instructs Coach Mac. "All right, fellas. No distractions from outside nonsense. Don't pay attention to these racist ass fans. Focus on what we came here to do. We came here to get a big victory over a really good top twenty team. Let's put a hurtin' on 'em from the jump."

Following the game, as the Howard University team bus pulls slowly out of the stadium parking lot, eggs splatter the windows. A small group of enraged egg-throwing fans yell obscenities. Their faces are ugly with hate. Most of the Howard players have never experienced such a blatant display of loathing. They simply stare at the strangers who despise them. Coach Mac looks around at his players, wondering if they are afraid as the bus beeps its way through the angry crowd. He knows he is. He looks down at the floor and shakes his head. The bus finally pulls away from the campus and onto the main road.

Coach Mac feels compelled to address his players and stands up at the front of the bus.

"I want to commend you guys for the way you handled everything tonight. You weren't only goin' up against the seventeenth-ranked team in the land, you were also goin' up against an ignorant crowd in a hostile environment. Despite all that, you kept your composure, stayed together as a unit, and went out there and kicked ass. A win by fifteen points is convincing. Very convincing.

"It just saddens me that in 2018, we as a people, still have to endure such racist shit. You, too, Bird. I know for a lot of you this was your first time experiencing racial hostility on this level. You've never been to the deep South. That type of stuff is, unfortunately, common in certain areas out here," he says in a slightly lowered voice. "Hell, it wasn't too long ago when some Ole Miss frat boys were hanging a noose around the neck of James Merideth's statue on their campus. He was the first black student there and had to be protected by Federal troops. In the end, it took over 31,000 Federal Marshals and National Guardsmen to secure his place.

"Forget all that, though," he says as his voice is getting louder. "We accomplished what we came here to do. We're nine and two heading into winter break. I couldn't be any prouder of you fellas. I want y'all to enjoy your short break and then we'll get right back into it. MEAC play begins as soon as we return from the holidays. You guys have already proven to everyone that you can go toe-to-toe with the best teams in the country.

"With that type of recognition comes expectations. And one of those expectations now is that we should run through the MEAC unfazed. And that's not gonna be an easy task because we're now the hunted. Teams are going to come for us night after night. We gotta stay ready."

22 REACQUAINTED

Chance is enjoying his mother's buttermilk pancakes, scrambled cheese eggs, and uncured hickory smoked bacon. His mother and sister, thrilled to have him home for part of winter break, watch in amazement at how much food he consumes over breakfast. They tease him mercilessly until their jokes are interrupted by a ringing cell phone. Chance reaches into his pocket and pulls out his phone. His face lights up when he sees the name. Chance does not usually answer the phone at the table while eating with his family, but for this call he makes an exception.

"Hey, you."

Kia imagines his smile.

"Hi, Chance. I need to see you. I'm missing you already. Let's hang out today."

"All right, bet. Come scoop me in about an hour or so."

Exactly an hour later, a small car pulls up and parks in the driveway. Kia springs out and rings the doorbell. Chance opens the door and greets Kia in the foyer with an embrace and restrained kiss.

"Mom, this is Kia. Kia, this is my mother and my little sister, Amaia."

"Hello, Kia," says Mrs. Knight. "It's a pleasure to meet you. May I offer you anything?"

"No thank you, Mrs. Knight. It's a pleasure to meet the both of you." Kia is nervous, wanting to make a good impression.

Mrs. Knight smiles warmly.

"Well come on in and make yourself at home, sweetie."

"Thank you, ma'am."

As they make their way to the living room, Kia notices family pictures displayed on the wall.

"Oh my gosh! Is that you when you were in elementary school?

"Yep."

"Aww, you were so cute!"

"Thank you. This my pops right here." Chance still chokes up somewhat when referring to his father.

"You have such a beautiful family, babe." Kia means it.

Over the next hour or so Kia converses with Mrs. Knight and Amaia. They share lighthearted moments, punctuated by a few polite but personal questions from Mrs. Knight. Kia shares that she is an only child. Her father graduated from Georgetown University Medical School. Her mother graduated from Howard University's College of Nursing. Mrs. Knight is impressed. After further inquiry, she realizes she graduated the year before Kia's mother entered Howard. Amaia is more interested in Kia's defensive specialist position on her volleyball team.

"Babe, we're running late," says Chance. "We gotta go."

"Mrs. Knight, thank you so much for opening up your home. I had such a good time meeting you and Amaia and hearing so many of your family stories."

"It was our pleasure, Kia. You two have fun at the movies."

"Thanks, Mom. Love y'all." Chance kisses his family goodbye.

Having lost track of time, and having stayed a little too long at Chance's house, Kia skillfully winds her Mini Cooper in and out of traffic in order to catch a comedy at the Magic Johnson Theater in Largo, Maryland.

Inside the theater, Chance and Kia wait in the concessions line.

"Have you had their popcorn before?" Chance asks.

"Nope. Never been here before. But I'm not really big on popcorn."

"What? Girl, you crazy! This is the best popcorn you'll ever have in your life. Just wait until I'm done buttering and salting it up. You'll want to come get this popcorn every day."

"Boy, please." Kia rolls her eyes. "It can't be all that. But it better be good since your hyping it up."

A few hours later they pull up to Chance's house.

"I still can't believe how good that popcorn was."

"I told you. And I see how much you liked it. I go to the restroom and the bag is practically gone."

"Can you blame me?" Kia laughs.

"Come inside with me so we can have a little fun. My mom and sister are out Christmas shopping and won't be back for a couple of more hours."

"Boy, are you crazy? I'm not about to have sex in your momma's house."

"Girl, I've had sex plenty of . . ." He quickly catches himself.

"You've had plenty of *what*, where?" Kia looks at him with an attitude.

Chance laughs and covers his face.

"Look. My momma ain't comin' home no time soon. Now I want some of that ass, so come on."

"But I'm scared."

"Woman, come on."

"Okay, fine. But if your momma comes home while we're doin' it, I will literally kill you."

"Oh trust me, she won't."

A little later Chance and Kia, both content, lie in bed.

"How much time do we have before your mom and sis get home?"

Chance looks at the plain round wall clock that has hung in his room since he was nine.

"They won't be home for another hour or so."

"Okay, cool, we have some time then. So you know how I told you my family and I always go to New York for the holidays to celebrate with our family up there?

"Well, we're leaving on Friday and won't be back until right before school starts back up. I'm going to miss you so much. I've never felt like this before where I kinda don't want to go."

"I feel ya." Chance is disappointed. "I'm gonna miss you, too. I'm really enjoying the time we've been spending together."

"I know, me too."

"I want you to go enjoy the holidays with your family. Just don't hook up with Deon."

Kia hits him with the pillow.

"I'll see you when you get back," says Chance. "But I want to see you again before you leave, if that works for you."

"Well I'm going to have to get back to you on that. I need to check my schedule. I'll try to see if I can fit you in anywhere before we leave."

"Oh, for real. That's how you gonna play me?"

Chance leans in to kiss Kia and their temperatures rise.

"Oh we going for round two, huh?" Kia coyly asks.

"Hell yeah."

They start back at it again.

While Chance and Kia are making love, Kia hears a noise that startles her. It sounds like a car pulling into the driveway. She stops her rhythm with Chance and pops up. Her face looks stricken.

"What is that?"

Chance sits up. In total panic, he jumps up and runs quickly to the window to peek out.

"Oh shit! It's them!"

"I'm going to fuckin' kill you!"

"You won't have to because my mother's gonna kill both of us!"

"Shit!"

Both Kia and Chance are frantic as they scurry to put on their clothes.

The front door opens as Mrs. Knight and Amaia walk in. Mrs. Knight, who noticed Kia's car, immediately makes a sniffing gesture as if she smells something out of the ordinary.

"Baby, go in the kitchen and make yourself a sandwich. I'll be right back."

Amaia dutifully heads for the kitchen. She watches her mother walk purposefully up the steps and disappear. She is intrigued by the look her mom has—as if she is about to kill someone. Mrs. Knight reaches the top of the stairs and notices that Chance's bedroom door is open. She approaches the door at a quickening pace. She peers into the room. The bed is perfectly made. Chance is fully dressed. He is sitting at his computer desk pecking on the keyboard. Kia, also fully dressed, is sitting primly on the corner of the bed looking at a Knight family photo album.

"Oh, hi, Mom, how did everything go?" Chance smiles at his mother.

"Hi, Mrs. Knight." Kia smiles, big dimples showing in her flawless heart-shaped face.

Mrs. Knight stands suspicious. She takes a couple of sniffs while looking Chance and Kia up and down—eyeing them.

"Hi y'all," Mrs. Knight says coolly. The hint of distrust in her voice and on her face is not lost on her son. She turns and leaves the room.

Chance and Kia look at each other and each releases a big exhale.

Chance is in his room ironing his clothes in preparation for a New Year's Eve house party being thrown by one of his high school friends. The evening news is broadcasting on the television. Chance looks up when the reporter announces breaking news and begins his report.

"The police officer involved in the shooting death of the young black male in Seat Pleasant, Maryland, has been cleared on all charges. That's all the information we have right now, but we will update you as soon as we get more details."

Chance stares blankly at the television for a moment. He stiffens. The verdict is no surprise to him, yet he still feels a sting of disbelief. He puts on his clothes and walks into the living room. His mother is reclined in his father's chair watching the same evening news. Chance walks over to her and gives her a kiss goodbye. Just as he gets to the door, he turns back.

"Mom, what's the latest with what's going to happen to the cop that killed pops? I mean, has the trial date been set yet?"

"The trial's scheduled for March. I just found out Christmas Eve. I didn't want to bring it up until after the holidays. You've been smiling so much lately and I didn't want to take that from you. I haven't seen you smile this much since, well, you know, before. The prosecutor will meet with you and Dink again to prep you for your testimony."

Chance says nothing. His body feels weighted by the thought of reliving that night. But he also feels a measure of relief that judgment day has been set. He remains faithful to the notion that, unlike the countless cases that have come before, the outcome of his father's case will be a just one. He kisses his mother once more and walks out of the house.

Chance, Big Dink, and Walt emerge from Big Dink's SUV and walk into the party.

"Man, this shit is lit," declares Big Dink. "There's ass everywhere."

"Yup, sure is," Walt agrees quickly. "Speaking of ass, guess who's up in here?"

"Who?" asks Chance.

"Sexy ass Tasha."

Chance's heart stops.

"Oh, shit. I didn't even think about her being here."

"You better stay away or Kia will fuck you up, son," warns Big Dink.

"Kia and I are kickin' it hard, but we not official. So technically I'm still single, bro."

"So right now while Kia is in New York, is she technically single? Can she fuck a dude tonight if she wants?"

"Oh shit. Good point man. Hell naw." Chance chuckles. "I'm 'bout to call her ass right now."

He pulls out his phone and starts to dial Kia's number when Big Dink abruptly snatches the phone.

"Man, put that shit away. We're here to have fun and bring in the new year, right? Ain't gonna be none of that phone bonin' and kissy face talk goin' on tonight."

"Yeah, you right, man."

Tasha spots the three young men and walks straight over—pulled to Chance like a magnet.

"What up, fellas?"

Chance and Big Dink look at each other and share a silent *"oh shit"* moment while Walt shyly smiles back at Tasha.

Not long after, Chance is outside of the party in Big Dink's SUV. He sits in the passenger seat with the seat reclined as far as it will go. His eyes are closed. Tasha's head emerges from his lap.

"No, don't stop, please don't stop," whispers Chance. He takes his hand and guides Tasha's head back down.

Later on that night, Chance, Walt, and Big Dink are inside the SUV on their way home. "Man, there better not be any pussy juice on my seats, bro."

Chance laughs.

"Naw, you good, bro. But check this out. Why Tasha say she's transferring to Howard."

"Oh, word," Walt says with a huge smile.

"Get da fuck outta here?" asks Big Dink.

"No bull. She's gonna be at Howard with us as soon as we come back from winter break."

"Yoooo. You gonna have ass on call anytime you want it."

"Man, I ain't gonna be messin' with her once the new semester starts. I'm finally where I wanna be with Kia. I'm not trying to mess that up. I think Kia and I could be something special."

"Well since you done wit' sexy ass Tasha, you don't mind if I get at her, right?"

"That's all you, bruh. Have at it."

Big Dink looks back at Walt in disgust. "Walt, you do know she just had this man's dick in her mouth, don't you?"

Walt grimaces.

"I'm just sayin', yo. But do you, Walt. Do you. Chance, you know you shouldn't have hooked up with her tonight. What you should've done is tell her ass about Kia. You don't want no confusion next semester."

"Duh. Of course I would've done that if I knew ahead of time that she was coming to Howard. But as far as I'm concerned, I was just gettin' me some head and would simply keep it movin'."

"Damn, yo. This 'bout to get real interesting. Just make sure your chick drama doesn't spill over to our team like the you, Deon, and Kia drama did."

"Naw, that ain't happenin'. I can assure you of that. Deon let that shit happen. Not me."

Kia pulls into Chance's driveway. He comes out, climbs into her car, and eagerly embraces her.

"Damn, I missed you, boy. Two weeks is a long time to go without seeing you."

"I missed you, too, boo. How was the trip?"

"It was really good. Relaxing. I got plenty of quality family time and lots of rest. How was your time off?"

"Honestly, it was difficult being the first holiday season without pops. Knowing that the end of the year marked my last year with him. So from that perspective, it was tough. We started practice back

253

up pretty early because we got our first MEAC game on Monday. I'm pumped about that. And I'm also pumped you back. I missed you. I need you."

"What you need, boy?" Kia asks flirtatiously.

Chance evokes his Rico Suave voice. "You." He leans in and kisses her passionately. Kia pulls back a little too soon for Chance's liking.

"I need you too, but it's gonna have to wait till after lunch 'cause I'm starving. Let's go. And besides, you were probably getting your dick sucked by some hoe while I was gone anyway."

Chance's face tightens, but he laughs it off.

"Girl, you a trip."

"Yeah, whatever. I'm watchin' you, boy."

"And I'm watchin' yo ass, too."

They both laugh.

"I got you something."

"Got me something for what?" asks a surprised Chance.

"Umm, Christmas maybe."

"But, babe, you said we're just kicking it. Getting to know each other. I wasn't expecting to do a gift exchange or anything."

"Relax, chief." Kia smiles. "I wanted to get you something so I got you something. You weren't expected to get me anything." She hands Chance a wrapped present.

"Thank you, baby girl. Damn, now I feel so bad I didn't get you anything."

"Boy, just open the damn gift already."

Chance opens the gift and pulls out a watch.

"Yoooooo. This shit is fire. I'll definitely be rockin' this, all the time." He reaches over and gives Kia a kiss. "Thank you so much."

"You're more than welcome, sir. Now let's go get some grub before I starve to death."

"Wait a second. What the heck is this in my pocket that keeps bothering me?"

Kia looks down at Chance's pocket. Chance reaches in and pulls out a small black bag and hands it to Kia. She is surprised and delighted.

"I have no idea what that is. Open it."

Kia unties the bag and pulls out a silver necklace with a slightly bigger than average silver heart-shaped charm. The charm is engraved, *"For my Mo Co Girl from your PG Guy."* She laughs out loud. A nanosecond later she is in tears.

"Why you cryin'?" Chance is confused, afraid he did something wrong. Afraid the gift was too much—he overstepped.

"'Cause this is so sweet and well thought out."

Relieved, Chance wipes away her tears as Kia stares into his eyes. Kia and Chance repeat that passionate kiss but for much longer.

23

THE HUNTED

Howard is wrapping up their last practice in advance of their highly anticipated MEAC season opener against the Morgan State Bears.

"All right, fellas. I'm not going to give you another long speech. This will be short and direct."

The players applaud in jest.

"HA. HA. HA. Very funny, fellas. Winter break is about over. Classes start on Monday. So with all the students back on campus, Burr is gonna be rockin'. You freshmen haven't seen Burr rock how it's 'bout to rock now that we're in MEAC play.

"Y'all put Howard on the map this year with your wins over nationally ranked teams. Even the close loss to Michigan State showcased how dangerous this team is. But as I already told you, with that type of recognition comes expectations. And, again, one of those expectations is pretty much a perfect winning record in the MEAC.

"That means come Monday night we not goin' into the game *hoping* for a win. We're goin' in expecting it. The fans are expecting it. The media is expecting it. And let me be clear, I'm expecting we win big. I mean blowout style. The mentality I want y'all havin' during every MEAC game is blow them the fuck out!"

Coach Mac's words resonate with the players and incite fire inside of them. Their chants could not be louder nor their claps harder or faster. They are believers. They feel they are on the periphery of something exceptional. Coach Mac takes in all of the excitement for a brief moment before he continues. He is confident the new recruits know what is at stake, but he needs everyone to own it.

"Settle down, fellas, settle down. There's one last thing." He pauses and surveys his players. "I was notified today that we made it onto the board. We're now ranked number twenty-five in the country." Coach Mac maintains his cool. "It will be announced in the new rankings coming out on Monday."

Shocked, the players look at each other as if searching for confirmation they heard what they thought they heard. It sinks in and they go berserk. They run around, hug one another, and jump in jubilation. The atmosphere is euphoric. Coach Mac looks over at Chance and they exchange a knowing smile. They walk toward each other and share a triumphant embrace.

It is game night in Burr Gymnasium. The game is sold out and the stadium has standing room only. The Howard basketball team congregates in the tunnel at the bottom of the stairs that leads out onto the court. Morgan State, chanting loudly in a deep tone and clapping in unison, jog by the Bison as they make their way up the steps and onto the court for warmups. As they pass, they glare and grimace at the Bison, looking them directly in their eyes and then up and down. Their intent to intimidate is evident. So is their focus and confidence. It is written all over their cool demeanors.

"I hope y'all saw that look in their eyes; they fuckin' came to play," says Coach Mac, verbalizing what the players are thinking. "I hope y'all realize that you're now the hunted. There's never been a MEAC team—in history—to be ranked in the top twenty-five of the national rankings until now. The target is on your back. The same way y'all are pumped up and hyped to knock off ranked teams, that's the feelin' MEAC teams will have playin' you. So you gotta be ready to absorb every team's best shot.

"Morgan State is an experienced team. They have four seniors and one junior in their starting lineup. They've been playing together as a unit for the past few years. That means we gotta be ready. Let's focus and remember to move the ball and play together. Don't get sloppy because this is the MEAC. Don't sleep on the talent in this league. All right, fellas! It's time! The MEAC starts now! Let's go!"

The Howard Bison sprint up the steps and race onto the floor. They are greeted with cheers and stomps by the fans, both so loud that it almost feels like an earthquake. Band members are jamming on their instruments and cheerleaders are cheering, doing backflips along the sideline, executing lifts, and stepping in sync with one another. The combination has riled the crowd into a frenzy.

"Two Ton Tina" is in the front row of the stands across from the Bison bench. She is holding up a sign that reads, *"Hi, Walt. It's me. Your boo thang."* Walt has never returned her calls, but she refuses to believe he regrets their passionate encounter.

The teams go through their usual layup line routines. The buzzer goes off, signaling the end of the warmup period. The public address announcer booms through the speaker system.

"Ladies and Gentlemen, please remove your hats for the singing of our national anthem. Tonight's singer will be Howard University's own, Walt Williams."

"That's my baby! Go head, boo. Sing that thang," screams "Two Ton Tina," forever hopeful.

Walt accepts the microphone and takes a knee at center court. Every player and coach from Howard and Morgan State also take a knee. Walt, from a kneeling position, reaches deep into his diaphragm and belts out a moving rendition of The Star Spangled Banner. The crowd roars its approval.

"Two Ton Tina" proudly holds her sign up again and waves it from side-to-side.

"That's my boo! That's my boo!" she declares.

Walt walks back over to his teammates and is greeted with fist bumps and pats on the back.

"Man, you ripped it, bro," says Chance.

Walt grins. He knows somewhere in the stands his mother is enjoying a rare happy moment. Another Howard male student leads the fans in singing the Negro national anthem, "Lift Every Voice." He does not disappoint either and also receives a rousing applause.

At the completion of the last anthem, the game starters walk to center court for the jump ball. The Morgan State players' eyes project a practiced intensity. The Bears grab the jump ball. They make two passes and throw an alley-oop for the first two points of the game. The Bison get possession and turn the ball over. The Bears dribble the ball down the court and quickly earn three points to take a five to zero lead. Mike in-bounds the ball to J.J. J.J. passes to Chance who passes to Deon. Deon releases a jumper. He misses. The Bears rebound, move the ball down the court, and make a couple of passes. The third pass affords them an easy layup. The Bison now have possession. J.J. brings the ball down. He passes to Deon who passes to Chance. He also misses. The Bears grab the rebound. The shooting guard, on a fast break, abruptly stops at the top of the perimeter. He pulls up for a shot and drains the wide open three-pointer. The lead is now ten to zero.

"Time out, Ref," Coach Mac yells from the sideline. He is livid.

The referee blows his whistle and charges the Bison with a thirty second time-out.

"This is exactly what we just talked about pre-game! We literally just had this fuckin' discussion! I said they had fire in their eyes. That they're a solid, experienced team that's gonna come out looking to destroy you! That's exactly what they're doing right now! You're the fuckin' twenty-fifth ranked team! In the country! If you want to stay ranked, then your asses better go back out there and start playing like it! But you have to go do it now!" He pauses. "Now!"

Coach Mac lit the fuse. From that point on How-ard dominates the game through crowd erupting dunks and alley-oops, as well as textbook steals and blocked shots. Midway through the second half, Chance has the ball on a fast break. He leaps into the air, maneuvers the basketball between his legs and ferociously slams it through the basketball hoop. The crowd is on their feet. The Bison lead the Bears by twenty points going into the fourth quarter. Coach Mac takes the starters out of the game for a well-earned rest. Because of their absence on the court, Morgan State is able to cut the lead in half making the final score a bit more respectable for them. The scoreboard reads, *"Howard 92, Morgan 82"*.

24 MINUTE MAN

Walt sits at his desk in class. Tasha sashays into the room and to Walt's delight, settles in the chair next to him.

"What up, boy?"

"What up, gorgeous? I mean, Tasha."

"You so silly. Nice win last night. Y'all put a whoopin' on Morgan State. And you sounded pretty good, too." Tasha winks.

"Thanks, Tasha." Walt cannot believe that Tasha Sellers reserved a wink just for him. "Where's my man at?"

"Your man? Who's your man?" He knows trouble is coming.

"My boy toy, Chance. Where's his sexy ass at? I heard he registered for this class."

Walt looks out of the window and sees that Chance and Kia have crossed The Yard and are about to enter the building.

"Oh, Chance's gonna be here in just a sec. He's gonna be so excited—and surprised—you're in this class," says a mischievous Walt.

"Yep, I can't wait to see his face."

"Yup. Me neither." Walt suppresses a chuckle.

Shortly after, Chance walks in with Kia by his side. To Tasha's chagrin, it is obvious that they both appear very comfortable and familiar with each other.

"Yo, who da fuck is that bitch?" Tasha asks Walt in a whisper.

"That's Chance's friend Kia."

Tasha glares at them. Chance feels eyes on him, turns in her direction, and acknowledges her with a nod.

After class, Chance, Walt, and Kia linger on The Yard and discuss their assignment. Tasha comes up from behind and pinches Chance's rear.

"What's up, Big Daddy?"

Kia's eyebrows rise.

"Oh, what up, Tash? Tasha, this is Kia. Kia, this is Tasha."

"Hey, girl," says Tasha.

"Hello," returns Kia.

"Chance and I go way back. We went to high school together."

"Oh, nice."

"Yeah, we just had a little reunion on New Year's Eve," Tasha eagerly offers with a smirk on her face. She knows what she says next will rub Kia the wrong way and that is exactly what she wants.

"Me, Chance, Walt, and some of our other friends from high school had a freakin' blast. We were all, like, seriously fucked up. You remember how much fun we had, right, Chance?"

Kia turns cold. Walt notices Kia's expression and quickly changes the course of the conversation.

"Come on, Tasha. Let me show you around campus."

"Okay, bet. Nice seeing you, Big Daddy."

Kia winces.

"Nice meeting you, sweetie," Tasha says dismissively to Kia.

Kia wants to respond, *"Bitch, get the fuck out of here."* Her upbringing restrains her.

"Nice meeting you too, *sweetie*," she says mockingly." She had to at least give a hint of displeasure meeting Tasha.

Tasha gives Chance a look that suggests she wants to do something indecent to him and then confidently sashays away with Walt. Kia's heart feels a pang. She turns to Chance, hoping he will make that pang disappear.

"Would you like to explain who the hell that is and what the hell's going on?"

Chance stands there lost for words, but his pained face says a lot.

Up ahead, Tasha and Walt continue walking together across The Yard. Tasha stops and touches Walt's arm. She looks up at him.

"I know Chance and I weren't *together* in high school, but we did hook up quite a few times and the shit was always amazing. And then we kinda hooked up at the party on New Year's Eve. I just want that to continue and see where it leads. The only reason I transferred to Howard is because I wanna be around him more. But he seems more interested in that Kia bitch. So what the fuck's going on, Walt?"

"Look, Tash. I'm just gonna be straight up with you. We all think you're freakin' sexy. Sexy as hell. Especially me," Walt smiles bashfully.

"But I gotta be honest. For Chance, it's strictly physical between y'all. Whereas with Kia, he's really into her." Walt gets even more direct. "Look, bottom line is Chance and Kia are tight now. I don't think they're official, but they might as well be. So you need to get Chance out of your mind." Testing the water, he playfully but pointedly adds, "And focus on me and you."

Tasha, undeterred and unamused, looks at the husky, borderline chubby Walt with a salty expression before responding.

"Boy, bye. You a trip you know."

On the other side of The Yard, Kia is waiting for her response from Chance. Chance finds his words.

"Tasha went to high school with us and she's always liked me. Yes, we have a history together. Nothing serious, though."

"Well, what about this party she was talking about? She sure made it sound like y'all had a *fun* time."

"Babe, we all had a good time. Everyone just caught up with one another and had fun. That's it. Now get her out of your head and realize that you're who I want. I've been after you from the first day I saw you, in case you forgot. Now come here."

Chance leans in and kisses Kia on the lips and then puts his arm around her as they walk away. Kia smiles slightly, but the pang has not quite receded.

Later that weekend, Chance, Kia, Walt, Big Dink, Mad Max, Bird, J.J., Mike, and a few young ladies are in the corner at a party having an exceptionally good time joking and laughing.

"I'm 'bout to run to the ladies room real quick, babe," Kia says softly.

"Okay, I'm 'bout to go get me a bottled water. You want somethin'?"

"Grab me one, too, please."

Kia walks toward the restroom and Chance walks to where the bottled water is being chilled. He bends down and reaches into the large ice-filled bucket and pulls out two bottles. As he comes back up and starts to turn around, Tasha, appearing from nowhere, blocks his path.

"What up, Chance?" coos an always seductive Tasha.

"Oh, what up, Tash?"

Tasha stands on her tippy-toes and pulls on Chance, guiding his ear toward her mouth.

"I'm gonna need you to come dance with me, sexy," she whispers.

"Naw, I can't do that right now."

Tasha puts her hand on Chance's chest and slowly moves it downward towards his waistline.

"But I need you right now, Big Daddy."

"Look, Tash, it's not a good time right now," he says as he removes Tasha's hand from his body.

Tasha frowns and her forehead furrows. "Why? Is it 'cause of that bitch, Kia?"

"Tasha, look. I gotta go. And don't call her that."

Kia looks ahead as she emerges from the restroom. Chance and Tasha are in her line of sight. She stands immobile and watches. Chance attempts to walk around Tasha, but she grabs his arm, throws her arms around him, and tries to pull him in for a kiss. Chance pulls back firmly.

"Look, Tasha. I told you I'm good. Now chill, all right?"

"Oh, now you actin' brand new? You too good for me all of a sudden?"

Kia has seen enough. She nearly flies to where they are standing and finds herself in Tasha's face.

"Look, chick. You heard what he said. So why don't you just fall your thirsty thot ass back, hoe." Kia is surprised by what just came out of her mouth.

Tasha pushes Kia to the floor and jumps on her. They are wrestling and pulling each other's hair. Movement stops in the room as all eyes turn to the two girls fighting. Walt grabs Tasha and pulls her off while Chance grabs Kia.

"Yo, Tasha, chill the fuck out, yo," orders Chance. He places his arm around Kia and they move quickly toward the exit.

"Fuck you, Chance! That's fucked up! You weren't actin' like this when I was suckin' your dick at the New Year's Eve party, now were you?" screams Tasha. She is enraged.

The room is now eerily silent under the veil of music blasting throughout the house. Those close enough to hear the details of the exchange, find Tasha's loud announcement to the room shocking. Kia comes to a halt and pushes away from Chance.

"Is that shit true? Was that bitch givin' you head at the party?"

Chance looks at Kia and then looks over at Tasha. Tasha is smug.

"Man, hell naw that ain't true. She's obviously mad right now and would say anything." Chance looks straight into Kia's eyes. "She's lying because she wants to take me from you. Can't you see that? It's that simple. Pay her crazy ass no mind. Now let's get out of here."

Chance takes Kia's hand and they exit the building. An angry and embarrassed Tasha walks over to a bucket of ice and beer, grabs a Corona, and starts guzzling it down.

"Yo, you okay?" Walt asks Tasha, concerned.

Tasha looks at Walt and chugs the rest of the Corona. She tosses the bottle in the trash and then grabs him. They start kissing on her lead. Tasha ends the kiss and Walt stays in position—eyes closed, glasses crooked, and lips pursed. Tasha grabs Walt by the hand and pulls him with her toward the exit.

"I see you, Big Walt," Big Dink yells out.

"You da man, Walt," shouts Mad Max.

Later that night, Tasha is on top of Walt in his bed.

"Oh, thank you, God," Walt mutters under his breath. "Thank you so very much."

Tasha slides her tongue into Walt's mouth as she reaches under the covers and guides him inside of her.

"Boy, I'm 'bout to ride the shit out you."

She starts to show Walt what real experience is.

"Oh shit, girl," cries out Walt a minute later before letting out a long moan, "Ohhhhhhhhhhh, shiiiiid-ddddddd."

He exhales.

Tasha stops abruptly and looks down at him. She doesn't hide her disappointment. "Nigga, I know you didn't cum already?"

"I'm so sorry," he says apologetically. "It's totally your fault, tho."

"How da fuck is it my fault?"

"'Cause you got dat bomb, girl."

Walt and Tasha laugh. Tasha climbs off of Walt and lies beside him.

"You gotta make that shit up to me."

"Whatever you want, girl, you got it."

"All right, bet. Imma let you know. Don't be fakin' either. Especially if you ever want some more of this."

"Girl, hell yeah. I got you."

"Ten mutha fuckin' seconds, though, yo. Really?" Tasha says teasingly.

She throws the pillow over Walt's face.

The next morning Walt's alarm clock rings at six thirty. Exhausted, he reaches over and turns it off. He looks over and sees Tasha. The memory of last night puts a wide grin on his face, even though he wishes he had performed better. He gets up to dress. Tasha awakes and rolls over.

"Where you going?"

"I got practice, sexy. But you can stay in bed if you like."

"Thanks but I gotta get outta here."

"Okay, bet. When can we hook up so I can bring you that thunder again?"

Tasha realizes that she never noticed Walt is so funny.

"Boy, please. I'll find you when and if I'm interested in some more ten second lovin'."

Walt laughs.

Tasha throws on her clothes and gives Walt a kiss on his cheek.

"Holla at you later, boy. Don't forget you gotta buy me something to make up for last night."

"Buy?" asks Walt, taken aback. The hesitation is fleeting. "You know I got you, girl."

Tasha smiles and leaves. Just as Tasha closes the door behind her, Chance walks down the hallway headed for his room to change for practice. He stops in his tracks. Tasha brushes by him smiling. She turns back and looks at Chance who is now turned around staring at her in disbelief.

"Tell your roommate thanks for an amazing time. He really knows how to handle his business." She smiles and walks away.

Chance walks into the room and sees Walt standing there with an oversized grin.

Chance, Kia, Walt, Mad Max, Big Dink, and Bird ride the metro and engage in lighthearted banter making fun of one another in every way they can think of, from clothes to their intelligence to people they've dated or bedded.

Walt gets serious. "I know I've said this before, but, man, I just wanna thank y'all for coming to see Teddy with me."

"You know I'm always gonna be there for y'all," says Chance.

"Hell yeah, man. You know we always got you," adds Big Dink.

"I'm excited to meet him. I feel like I know him already," chimes in Kia.

Walt smiles. "Thank you, Kia."

Chance notices Walt's eyes—lids abruptly lowering and then opening wide until they lower one final time and remain closed.

"Yo, Walt, are you literally falling asleep as we're having a conversation?"

Walt's eyes fling open. "Yeah, bro, I'm so tired, man," he says—barely discernible through his yawn. "I hardly got any sleep last night and then having to wake up early for practice didn't help. I need to be in bed right now, y'all. Wake me when we get there."

"My man, Walt, was putting in that work last night," says Mad Max with a congratulatory tone.

"Yes, sir," says Big Dink. "The brotha finally took Tasha down! His fantasy finally came true."

Kia's eyebrows rise.

"The same Tasha from last night?" Kia asks Chance in a whisper.

"Yep. She let Walt smash after the party," he whispers back.

"Wow. She sure is a thot."

Chance and Kia share a private chuckle.

The metro car comes to a stop at the next station. The doors open and a homeless woman gets on. She catches Kia's attention. She thinks the woman appears to be in her late fifties. Then again, she looks and smells as if she has lived a hard-partying life, so she could actually be in her forties. Maybe even thirties. She smells of cheap wine, a strong cigarette habit, and a need for a long-overdue shower. She is donned in a long early nineties style plaid dress coat. The opening of the coat reveals a dingy tee-shirt and worn out sweat pants. Surprisingly, she has on clean, somewhat stylish Nike sneakers. They look a bit big for her scrawny, short frame—suggesting she recently received a shoe donation.

"Y'all have any spare change to help a sista out?" begs the homeless woman as she approaches the Howard students.

Big Dink looks over at Walt. Walt is sitting in the seat knocked out snoring with his mouth wide open. A mischievous smile appears on Big Dink's face.

"I'll give you a few dollars if you do somethin' for me."

"Well, wait now, I ain't no prostitute or nuffin'. What type of shit you got on your mind?"

Everyone laughs.

"Naw, nuffin like that, lady. I just want you to go sit in that empty seat right there next to that sleepin' brotha."

"Yo, Big Dink, what you doin', man?" asks Chance. "I can't take the smell any longer."

"Yo, chill, cuz. It's only for a sec. Trust me."

The homeless lady nods and then sits next to Walt.

"All right now," says Big Dink as his excitement rises. "Okay, lay your head on his shoulder and just smile for the camera."

Big Dink pulls out his cell phone and snaps. He reviews the picture and laughs.

"Yo, I'm postin' all types of memes for this shit," he says.

Mad Max and Bird laugh along with Big Dink.

"Y'all a trip. Oh my gosh. Come on y'all, cut it out," says Kia.

"Yo, y'all buggin'," says Chance.

Big Dink is by no means finished.

"All right, that was perfect. Now I want you to kiss him on his cheek as I take another picture."

The homeless lady kisses Walt on the cheek and then quickly becomes more animated. She seems to be enjoying the attention from the students. She takes initiative and starts licking and gently sucking Walt's right ear. Walt smiles with his eyes still closed and starts mumbling in his sleep, "Yes, Tasha. Yes, baby girl, just like that."

His friends, including Chance and Kia who had been less enthusiastic about the prank, are now hysterical with laughter. The homeless lady aims for a kiss on the lips. Just before it lands, Walt opens his eyes and, startled out of his sleep, instinctively pushes her away. He jumps up and starts screaming.

"What the fuck, yo!"

Even a few observant passengers chuckle.

"Well hello, suga'."

"Get the hell away from me!" yells Walt as he looks at the lady, not quite sure what is happening.

She stiffens, rises, and opens her hand to Big Dink. He pulls out a five-dollar bill and gives it to her, careful not to make skin-to-skin contact.

"Five dollars? That's it? I put on a twenty-dollar performance, nigga," she says as she snatches the money.

"Well, thank you, sweetie. I guess it was nice doing business with ya," she says after quickly changing her attitude.

She continues down the aisle begging for money.

Walt looks at Big Dink after the exchange.

"Mutha fucka!"

The group tries to surpress their laughter as Walt vigorously wipes his face while asking passengers for hand sanitizer or wet wipes.

25
KING

Over the next few weeks Howard University dominates their MEAC opponents. A headline from the sports section in The *Washington City Paper* reads, "Undefeated MEAC Powers to Face-Off." The first line of the article reads, "The undefeated number twenty three ranked Howard Bison will face the undefeated defending Mid-Eastern Athletic Conference champions, the North Carolina Central Eagles."

The Bison are preparing for the big MEAC game. They huddle at half court as their Saturday morning practice comes to a close.

"All right, fellas. That was a great practice. You guys are playing exceptionally well. Up until this point we've been winning MEAC games with ease.

"Monday night's road game at North Carolina Central University has the potential to be very different. Most of the MEAC teams have been afraid of you. Central, like us, is undefeated in the MEAC. And they're the two time defending conference champs with five returning starters—all seniors. They've got a highly decorated and respected head coach who clearly knows how to get the best out of his players. They're not gonna back down. They see y'all as a threat. A threat to their crown. They're gonna come at you hard right from the jump. Get it in your head now that Monday night's gonna be an epic conference battle. It's gonna have the intensity and feel of a March Madness game. Anything can happen—ranked or not ranked—doesn't matter.

"I want you to take it easy for the rest of today and tomorrow. No distractions. Fresh legs for Monday. All right now. Together on three. One, two, three. Together!"

The highly anticipated game night finally arrives. The Howard players sit on the locker room benches waiting to walk out for warmups. The distance to the gym does not diminish the sound of the cheering Central students.

Coach Mac, dressed in his finest game day suit, takes center stage in front of his players.

"I've already given y'all the pep talk. Now it's time to go out there and do what we do. As you can hear from all the way down here, the atmosphere is crazy up there. Central's gonna be the fiercest conference competition you're gonna face. You know what you gotta do. So go do it!"

The Howard basketball team walks down the dimly lit hallway. The Eagles team lines each side of the corridor. They are clapping in unison and chanting, "back to back." In order to reach the court, the Howard players have to walk through the Eagles' team chant. As they make their way through, players on both teams use eye contact as their weapon of intimidation. One of the coldest stares is owned by Central's William Parker and he reserves it for Chance. William is better known as Billy. Billy is six feet, eight inches tall and is last year's MEAC Player of the Year. He averages twenty-seven points and twelve rebounds per game. He is as impressive as they come in the MEAC.

"So this is the nation's number one recruit, huh?" Billy asks sarcastically as Chance walks by. "Well, this ain't high school, bitch. The MEAC's ours. Always has been. Always will be. Get ready, young blood, 'cause you 'bout to feel the pain, nigga."

"Whateva, bruh," Chance says as he stares down Billy.

Billy steps to Chance's face and the Bison assistant coaches jump in and break it up before it starts. The Howard Bison players run onto the court and are greeted by blaring boos. The NCCU Eagles emerge and the crowd's cheering can be heard from outside of the arena. Billy passes by Chance and bumps his shoulder.

"All right, fellas, I told you this place was gonna be nuts," Coach Mac says in the team huddle right before the start of the game. "The crowd's hype and Central's angry, and motivated. Pay attention to where Billy is at all times. He's a threat in and out of the paint. Let's get out there and give these mutha fuckas their first conference loss. In order for us to be the champs, we gotta beat the champs. Right here, right now, is where we stake our claim. We let everyone else in the MEAC know who's king. King on three. One, two, three. King!"

Chance and the other starting Bison walk onto the court for the jump ball. Kia is in the crowd with her friends as are Tasha and her friends.

"Let's go, Chance! Do work, boy!" Kia yells out.

Tasha hopes no one notices that she steals a glance at Kia. She is becoming an expert at masking her jealousy.

The game begins as the jump ball goes up. The action up and down the basketball court excites the crowd. The scoreboard reads, *"North Carolina Central 32; Howard 25,"* and shows six minutes left in the half.

Coach Mac calls a full time out and the Bison huddle. He is enraged and has a lot to say before the sixty seconds are up.

"Are you guys fuckin' serious? You're nationally ranked and you're fuckin' losing to North Carolina Central? To North Carolina Central? Yes, they're really good, but they ain't ranked. Not even close. The number twenty-three ranked team shouldn't be losing this game. Kentucky beat Central earlier this year by forty-five fuckin' points. The way we're performing now, what the hell do you think they'd do to us? If you guys wanna be considered the best, and ranked among the best, then you better start playin' like it. Just getting to this point isn't enough to be satisfied. Just being ranked in the top twenty-five is not enough to settle and think we've made it. You gotta bust your ass every single game and prove to the world that Howard is the real deal. Y'all betta' get your shit together now, or risk losing it all! Now go show these mutha fuckas who the real MEAC champion is!"

"Let's go, baby!" Chance yells out.

Howard begins showing the Eagles why they are ranked. Billy and Chance go back and forth, exchanging insults at every opportunity. Chance schools Billy and Billy takes it out on his teammates. Central's frustration shows. In the last play of the game, Chance steals the ball from Billy and takes it down the court where he meets a lone defender. Chance fakes left and then beautifully executes a spin move to the right, takes off into the air, and throws down an instant replay worthy two-handed savage dunk. The final score is Howard—ninety-four, North Carolina Central—seventy-five. The Eagles crowd is quiet over the loss but they recognize that what they have just witnessed is a part of something bigger—something extraordinary.

26

SPORTS TALK

Over the next few weeks Howard ignites quite a buzz on *Sports Talk Radio*.

"Welcome to the *Sports Talk Radio Show* and thanks for tuning in. I'm Marlo A. Jackson. Today I'm going to start by getting something off my chest. I'm not sure how many of y'all have been paying attention to what's going on in college basketball right now. There's something happening that's very special and the start of something that could change collegiate sports as we know it. As you all know, I attended an HBCU. I also played basketball there—Winston Salem State University. HBCUs are near and dear to my heart. So what's currently going on at Howard University is of great interest to me.

"Remember the Fab Five at Michigan, to include Chris Webber, Jalen Rose, and Juwan Howard? They were a group of top-level college recruits who decided to play for the same school. That was one of the first times top recruits joined forces and attended the same university. They made headlines and ended up going to the national championship two years in a row before some of them left to go pro. They were arguably the top recruiting class of all time. Imagine if the Fab Five had chosen an HBCU instead of a big power school like Michigan?

"Let's just look at last season as an example. Duke had the number one recruiting class. They landed four top ten five-star recruits: R.J. Barrett, number one rated player in the nation; Zion Williamson rated number two; Cam Reddish, number three; and Tre Jones, rated number ten. Now just envision these super athletes playing for an HBCU. Talk about shaking up the world of college basketball instantly!

"Well, that's exactly what happened at Howard University. I know not everyone follows HBCU college basketball so a lot of people may not know that Howard signed the nation's number one high school player, Chance Knight, along with a group of other nationally ranked players. If they continue to play the way they are, they could potentially be better than the Fab Five and that Duke squad.

"I know that's a bold statement. But hear me out. They have Chance Knight, who's pretty unanimously considered to be the best player out of high school since LeBron James. Combine his talent with other top recruits and . . . *whew*! Not to mention, they've been dominating their conference and have even knocked off top schools. They beat Maryland when they were ranked number five and fell just short of beating number two ranked Michigan State. They've beaten enough schools to make history and be ranked within the top twenty-five. That might not sound like a lot if you're not familiar with HBCUs. But for them to be able to accomplish what they've been accomplishing and not be doing it with a big name school is unprecedented.

"Most HBCUs don't have a lot of money, especially these days. They don't have the money big schools have for the fancy facilities such as state-of-the-art weight rooms, practice facilities, and arenas. They don't have nationally televised games, national prestige, the list goes on. They also don't have the history of sending many top basketball players to the pros. So for them to land the talent they did, and for them to be doing what they're doing. I mean, wow. Again it's unprecedented. If you're wondering how some of the best freshmen in the country came to choose an HBCU over the best college basketball programs in the world, well then let me tell you.

"Chance Knight had all but signed with Kentucky when tragedy struck. He witnessed his father, Craig Knight, die at the hands of police. Chance's father attended and played ball at Howard. He always wanted his son to follow in his footsteps. So Chance, after his father's death, decided to honor him by attending Howard. His AAU teammates, and even a couple of top recruit opponents—one being his cousin—decided to follow him to Howard. They decided to be change agents.

"One of their acts as change agents was to bring kneeling for the national anthem front and center in college basketball. Howard began kneeling and some of the other MEAC teams quickly followed to show their support for Colin Kaepernick. They're standing up against injustices such as the police killings of unarmed black men like Chance's father.

"Normally, the fact that kneeling is going on in the MEAC probably would have stayed under the radar. But with all the hoopla surrounding Howard's recruiting class, and especially after knocking off top ranked teams during televised games, their kneeling has picked up attention. They're proud of what they're doing.

"After seeing what Howard's doing right now, it has me, and everyone else, asking the unthinkable, the unimaginable. What if top black athletes see this and realize they don't necessarily have to go to traditional power schools to win and be seen by the pros? What if the top black athletes start taking a stand and start attending HBCUs? Do you realize the impact this could have on college sports?

"First the winning will come. Then the exposure. The national attention. Then the money and the TV deals. Then new facilities and arenas. The possibilities are endless. Folks, this is serious. Howard should be on your radar. Pay attention to this as it unfolds. If Howard continues this miraculous run, then they're sure to make some noise during March Madness. You can't count them out. Oh boy! Watch out! That's all I'm gonna say.

"Wow! This is clearly a hot topic because my phone lines are lighting up. And this isn't even the call-in portion of the show. I'll tell you what, since the phone lines are blowing up, let's go ahead and take some calls on this now. Let's see what the callers have to say. Hello caller, state your name and where you're from."

"Hello. My name is Chuck calling from South Carolina."

"Hi, Chuck. What's your comment?"

"Man, I think this is a joke. I love basketball, okay? If it ain't broke, then why try to fix it? College basketball is just fine the way it is *now*. The best talent goes to the best schools with the best facilities.

"No one is pointing a gun to these kids' heads and telling them where to go. They're the ones choosing big schools. If blacks start playing for black schools, then it would ruin college basketball. And I damn sure wouldn't watch it anymore. But I ain't worried because it will never happen.

"This school you're talking about today—— what's its name? Howard? I've never heard of it. They have no chance come NCAA tournament time. Yeah, they might be doing well now, but they don't stand a chance against the likes of Kentucky or Duke. So let's get off all this crap and just appreciate things the way they are and always have been. That's it. I'm done. Thanks."

"Okay, thanks for your call, Chuck. Well, that's certainly one opinion. Let's go to the next caller. Caller, state your name, where you're from, and your comment."

"Hello?"

"Yes, you're on the air."

"Oh, hi. My name is Harry from Ohio. My comment is, this is not the way it's always been. There was a time when blacks couldn't even play for the big schools or get the exposure that lands them in the NBA. They should be grateful that they're allowed to do that now and get the best education while they're at it. Why turn back the clock? I don't mean any disrespect, but, what they need to do, as Laura Ingraham told LeBron, is just shut up and dribble. Just shut the hell up is what I say."

"Thank you, Harry. Everyone is entitled to their opinion on this show. Let's move on to the next caller. Caller, you're on the air. Name and where you're from."

"Hey, Marlo. I'm Cliff from Pennsylvania. I'm just going to be honest. We're all grown ups here. It's the kneeling that pisses me off. This so-called unjust treatment. Let's just face the facts. If black people would just stop committing crimes and doing drugs, then police wouldn't fear them. And if the blacks didn't resist arrest, there wouldn't be any issues. Period."

"I've said all opinions are welcome, but let's keep it real. Most black people don't commit crimes, but they are *all* treated as if they do. If institutional racism has systemically *and* generationally deprived black people of opportunity, from the *cradle*, then you have crime. Black people are more fearful of the police than the police are of them. But sometimes they are just tired of being harassed and disrespected—and something clicks—and they resist. They don't deserve to be killed because of it. I've been stopped many times for driving while black, and it's hard to contain my anger, I'm just saying. Let's take the next caller, please."

"Marlo, hi, yes, this is Jabari from Florida. I went to Florida A&M, which is an HBCU, and my roommate and I used to always say how awesome it would be if our top black athletes chose HBCUs. I think this Howard story is great and I really hope this becomes the norm. It always pisses me off when I see big power schools obliterating HBCUs in the beginning of the season. They refer to HBCU games on their schedule as the cupcakes. It's easy for them to destroy us and to ridicule us when they're using our very own athletes against us. That's why it's so good to hear this story. It's the perfect example of what happens when the tables are turned. Thanks for taking my call."

"Amen, my brotha. Thank you. Okay, let's go to the next caller."

"Yeah, my name is Maleek and I attended Maryland University. While this might be a fun story for this one year, I just don't think it's sustainable over time. I think the power schools will stay on top. Thanks for taking my call."

"Thank you, Maleek. I have to disagree with you there. If this Howard Super Seven succeeds, then I think it's very realistic that we'll see a trend of this moving forward. Because of its social injustice awareness aspect, I can see this becoming a movement. Next caller, you're on the air. Go."

"Hello, I'm a white guy born and raised in Wisconsin so I'm not familiar with HBCUs. But I think the fact that Chance Knight made this move to honor his father is truly special. I can relate. I also lost my father when I was in high school. He always wanted me to join the military because he was in the military and instilled in me that there is no higher honor than that of serving your country and protecting the freedom of those who occupy it. So when my father passed away at a rather young age, I made the decision to enlist. It's a decision that I'm proud of to this very day. I think this is a wonderful story about Howard. Thanks for taking my call, Mr. Jackson."

"Wow, now that *is* special. Thank you for your story and thank you for your service to this country. Let me ask you a question. How do you feel about Howard kneeling during the anthem? As a veteran, does that action make you feel disrespected?"

"I don't feel personally affected. They're not kneeling in protest of me or my service to the country. I don't believe it has anything to do with that. I would never personally kneel for it or advocate kneeling. But I don't feel disrespected. That's what I was fighting for—freedom. And that includes the freedom to protest. In their own way, they are fighting peacefully for this country—for what it can and should be—and for those who occupy it. But that's just me."

"Thank you, friend. I appreciate your openness and ability to see the larger picture. Okay, folks. I have time for one more call before we need to take a commercial break. Caller, you're on the line. Go ahead."

"Yeah, I'm a retired Division I men's basketball coach. I'm from Boston and I'm not liking what I'm hearing. The idea of all the African American top athletes flocking to HBCUs and no longer playing for the big schools is frightening. That could change the current landscape of college basketball. The NCAA will never allow this to happen. Big time Division I coaches will scramble and think of something to counter this. I don't know what that something is, but you better believe they will come together and figure out how to stop this. Thank you."

"Man, we're going to have to dedicate an entire show to this topic. My phone lines are on fire! Let's take a quick commercial break and then we'll be right back with *Sports Talk Radio*."

Walt turns down the volume and, turning over on his bed, reaches for the phone to make a call. Chance answers and Walt tells him what he just heard. Walt then makes another call. Tasha answers.

"What up, sexy lady?"

"Just chillin'. What's good?"

"You tell me. I'm tryin' to see ya today. Can we make that happen?"

"Look. If you take me to Georgetown and buy me some stuff, then you can definitely see me."

"For sure. I'll get Big Dink's SUV and come scoop you in 'bout an hour."

"Bet."

Several hours later, Walt and Tasha, each holding shopping bags, walk into Tasha's dormitory room.

"Thanks, Walt. Now that's how you take care of a woman. The sneakers you got me are awesome and this necklace is the shit."

"Girl, I aim to please."

"Well since you're in a pleasing type of mood, why don't you come over here and please me some more?"

Tasha walks over to the bed as a smile overtakes Walt's face. He walks toward her and starts taking off his clothes.

"Wait. Get down on your knees," Tasha pulls down her pants. She takes off her panties and spreads her legs. "Come and get something to eat, boy."

Walt gets down on his knees, puts his face in between her legs, and starts going to work.

"Oh, hell yeah, boy. That shit feel good," says Tasha while firmly holding Walt's head down as he is servicing her.

As Walt's head is down, Tasha scrolls through her phone and finds a picture of Chance.

"Oh, hell yeah, boy. You 'bout to make me cum," she says while looking at the picture.

The next morning, Walt enters the cafeteria grinning. He looks over and sees Chance, Kia, Mad Max, Big Dink, and Bird at the table eating. Walt hurriedly grabs food and then heads over to the table to join them.

"What up good peoples?" Walt asks.

"Hey, Walt," responds Kia.

"Why the hell you so chipper and what's up with that goofy big ass smile on your face?" Chance asks.

"Don't bring me down, my brotha. I'm just out here livin' my best life. That's all."

Walt and Chance share a laugh.

"But I do have some good news," says Walt.

"Spit it out, bro," says Big Dink.

"Tasha and I are now officially together."

"Oh wow, congratulations, Walt. That's great," says Kia.

Kia finds a small sense of relief. She ponders the possibility that maybe Tasha isn't secretly scheming to get Chance.

Walt's teammates look at one another and laugh.

"What the fuck are y'all laughing at?" Walt asks.

"Man, you know damn well you can't turn no hoe into a housewife," says Big Dink.

The guys laugh again.

"Don't talk about my girl like that. Ya hear me? She ain't even like that no more. I really like this girl. Why can't y'all just be happy for me?" Walt storms out, breakfast uneaten.

Kia is not amused. "Come on you guys. Really? How old are y'all?" Kia gets up and runs after Walt. She catches up to him outside.

"Walt, don't mind those guys. They're assholes and they're probably jealous because they don't have a girlfriend."

"True, but aren't you and Chance girlfriend and boyfriend now, though?"

Kia considers Walt's question a while. As she is about to respond, Walt spots Tasha off in the distance.

"Excuse me, Kia, and thanks for being nice. I definitely feel better now thanks to you. But I gotta run." Walt sprints over to Tasha.

Chance leaves the cafeteria and catches up to Kia.

"Is Walt okay?" Chance asks.

"Yeah, he's good now."

"Oh, okay, cool. Thanks for talkin' to him."

"No prob. But can I ask you a question?"

"Girl, you don't even have to ask. Of course we can go back to the room right now so I can give you some."

Kia does not laugh. She looks at Chance with annoyance. He realizes his mistake.

"Or not. Okay, this must be a serious question. What's up?"

"What are we? Are we boyfriend and girlfriend? Are we friends with benefits? What are we?"

"What do you want us to be? Last time I asked about us you basically said we're just kickin' it."

Kia looks at Chance and marvels again how handsome he is, with eyelashes so long that she wonders how he can see past them. She knows his heart is kind, even if he tries to be hard so much of the time. And with the grade point average he effortlessly maintains, he could be anything even without basketball.

"I'm ready to be your girlfriend. I've been ready."

"Wait one sec," says Chance as he holds up his index finger.

"Ummm, okay."

Chance runs back into the cafeteria while Kia waits alone outside. He asks for a piece of paper and pen from the first person he sees with a book bag. He then scribbles a few words. He folds the paper and runs back outside to Kia. He takes her by the hand and walks her across The Yard while saying nothing.

After a few seconds of silence, Kia, slightly apprehensive, looks at him.

"Ummm, are you gonna ever answer my question?"

"What question?" Chance plays dumb.

"I'm serious, Chance," says Kia as she punches him in his right arm.

"Ow, that's my shooting arm, girrrl. You could be costing Howard wins if you hurt this arm."

Kia, again, is not amused. Chance reaches into his pocket.

"Oh, wait. What's this?" He pulls out a folded piece of paper and gives it to her.

She looks at him curiously and notices the note has a lever that reads, *"Pull me."* Kia smiles and pulls it. The paper unfolds and reveals hastily written handwriting that reads, *"Kia, will you be my girl? If Yes, check this box. If No, check this box. If Maybe, check this box."*

Kia cannot contain her smile and feels as if she is floating. Chance hands her a pen. Kia snatches the pen and pretends she has to think about it. She is *really* thinking that she should pinch herself to make sure this is really happening. Finally, she checks the "Yes" box. Chance and Kia attract attention from passersby as they share a long, sensual kiss in the middle of The Yard.

"Now make sure you go tell all dem other chicks and groupies that yo ass is officially taken."

"You the only girl I want and you the only girl I need. Now give me dem juicy lips again."

27

WASTED

The Howard Bison wrap up another MEAC victory and, although Teddy is always on his mind, Walt is feeling good. Tasha waits for him outside of the locker room. When he spots her, he feels even better.

"That was a great game, babe. Y'all kicked Delaware State's ass and you represented when you got in there."

"Thanks, babe," says Walt, thinking how lucky he is to have her.

"Let's take the short cut through the alley."

Walt stops midstride.

"Naw, babe, it's too dangerous. I already told you I got jumped and robbed around here before. I'm definitely not tryin' to put your fine ass at risk."

"I feel ya. But the game just let out so people are all over campus. No one's gonna try nuthin' with all these people nearby."

Walt considers what Tasha just said.

"Okay, fine. You're probably right."

Walt and Tasha, recapping Walt's plays in the game, walk down the poorly lit alley. They are unaware that they are walking toward an armed man hidden by an alley pocket veiled in complete darkness. As Tasha and Walt approach, the armed man pulls out a single action revolver, slowly raises the gun and aims at Walt. With his thumb, he pulls back on the hammer until he hears, "Click, Click" signaling that his gun is now fully cocked. His finger on the trigger is just starting to squeeze when it stops and the gun is lowered. A campus police car pulls up next to Walt and Tasha. The driver's side window rolls down.

"Great win tonight, Walt."

"Thank you, sir."

"Let me give y'all a ride home. We get a lot of robberies and assaults reported in this alley. Delinquent locals seem to pick it as their on campus hunting ground. I guess because they can quickly escape off campus in those two different directions," he says as he points out two exits that provide ready access to dark streets neighboring the campus. "We patrol this alley a lot now. When I spotted you two, I headed straight over. You're a very tall, big guy, Walt, but no match for a gang or a gun."

"Wow, thank you, Officer. All right, come on, Tash."

Tasha eagerly follows.

The person holding the gun stays hidden as Walt and Tasha climb into the back of the vehicle. As the campus policeman whisks Walt and Tasha away, the armed man steps out of the shadows and reveals himself. Red stands with Tarik and Tyrone.

"Fuck," says Red.

"Fuck, man," says Tarik. "It's all good. We'll get that mutha fucka eventually. We know their home game schedule and we know their practice schedule. His time will come."

The team loads their travel bags on the bus headed to the airport for a trip to Tallahassee to play Florida A&M.

"Have a safe trip, Chance," says Kia. "Good luck and hurry up and get back home to me." She gives him a kiss and then he returns a lingering hug.

As Walt is stepping onto the bus, he stops and turns his head to glance at Tasha.

"Bye, babe," says Tasha. "I'm gonna head to the airport shortly. See you in Florida."

"Okay, babe, safe travels. See you there." Walt blows Tasha a kiss and then gets on the bus. Tasha makes eye contact with Kia, gives her a forced smile, and heads off. Kia, having overheard Tasha talking to Walt, is not thrilled Tasha is going on the trip.

The team arrives in Florida. Their plane taxies on the runway until reaching the gate. The players and coaches retrieve their carry-ons from the overhead compartments and exit the plane. They are greeted by a sign that reads, "Welcome to Tallahassee." On the way to the hotel they take in the numerous tall cabbage palm trees weighted down by the heavy rain. After a fifteen-minute ride in two rental vans, they are appreciative that the bright warm sun has parted the dark grey clouds as they enter the hotel.

Chance and Walt settle into their shared room.

"All right, my brotha, I'm headed to Tasha's room. I'll probably be there most of the time but will make sure to be in here when the coaches do room checks for evening curfew."

"All right, bro. Do ya thing. Be safe."

"Always, bro."

They dap each other up and Walt leaves.

Chance is looking forward to having the room to himself to catch up on schoolwork. Before he has a chance to get to a book, his cell phone rings. He sees Kia's picture on the screen and answers.

"Hi, beautiful."

Simply hearing his voice warms her. "Hey, babe. Just checking to make sure y'all got there safely."

"Yup, got here safe and all checked into the hotel. What you up to?"

"Just sittin' here missin' you. Who you roomed with?"

"My main man, Walt."

Kia can't suppress a nagging feeling. "Speaking of Walt, Tasha's down there with y'all?"

"Yeah. She flew out here. She's staying in our hotel. Walt just left a few minutes ago to kick it with her. He said he'll be in her room most of the time. That girl has him whipped!"

"Well, I'm not crazy about that girl being there and I damn sure ain't crazy about her staying in the same hotel as you."

"Babe, you ain't got a damn thing to worry 'bout. For one, I don't want nuthin' to do with that girl, and two, do you think for one second that Walt is gonna let that girl outta his sight during this entire trip?"

"Good point."

"Shit. I couldn't even get to that girl if I wanted to. Walt got her on 24/7 watch."

Feeling more relieved, Kia laughs. "You ain't lyin'."

"Look, girl. Bottom line is you're my girlfriend and you're the only girl I want. You're the only girl I need. From the first day I laid eyes on you, I knew you were gonna be mine. After all my chasing and fighting for you, do you think I'd do anything to jeopardize what I've worked so hard to get? Girl, please. I ain't crazy."

"Well, that better be the case. Just know that I've got no problem whatsoever jumpin' on a plane to come down there to whup your ass and Tasha's ass."

"Oh trust me, I know. Believe me I know."

They both laugh.

The next day, following the Florida A&M game, the Bison are in the locker room. Coach Mac is on a high.

"Great game, fellas. You came ready to play and you didn't play down to your opponent. This thirty-point victory for a conference game is the type of result I like to see. I'm very proud of this performance.

"Now, I'm hearing all the whispers about there being a party tonight. And I know Florida A&M versus Howard after-parties are a big thing down here so I'll allow you guys to go. But a few of our coaches will be there along with a local cop we know. That way you guys can have fun, but there'll be eyes on you in case any shit pops off."

The team claps and whistles at Coach Mac's approval.

"Thanks, Coach," says Chance.

"No prob. Y'all just be responsible, have fun, and be safe. Please remember you're representing Howard University at all times. All right, now everyone bring it in."

Later that night, the team joins a full crowd of partygoers. As Mad Max, Big Dink, Bird, Mike, J.J., and Chance make their way through the crowd, girls stare, smile, and wink. The more aggressive young women slap and pinch their rear ends as they walk by. The players' eyes light up as they take in the Florida A&M coeds.

"Man, Florida A&M got mad shawties, yo," says Big Dink.

"Hell yeah," says Mike.

"And it seems as if they love them some vanilla," says Bird as his eyes scan the faces and bodies of the ladies looking his way.

His friends laugh.

"Chance, you was smart as hell to leave your girl at home," says Mad Max. "Unlike Walt's dumb ass. Look at him over there all bunned up with Tasha."

The players observe Walt protectively holding Tasha's hand and keeping her close as they maneuver through the crowded room.

"Man, I'm chillin'. I'm behaving myself tonight, fellas. I got my baby waiting for me when I get back to DC and I ain't gettin' into no shit out here. Kia's made me a changed man."

Right then, a pretty brown-skinned coed grabs Chance's hand and pulls him toward the dance floor. Chance can't help but notice her exterior assets, particularly her posterior asset.

"Yup, that's what we thought," says Mad Max.

Big Dink, J.J., Mike, and Bird chuckle. Walt and Tasha, each with a clear cup filled with a red drink in their hands, come up to where the young men are standing.

"Yo, one of the A&M players told me that the red punch over there is spiked," says Walt. "That's what we drinkin' and it's so good! Just wanted to let y'all know."

"Oh, hell yeah. Good lookin' out," says Big Dink.

"Where's Chance?" asks Walt.

"On the dance floor getting grinded on by that baddie right there," says J.J. while pointing his finger in the direction of the attractive girl dancing with Chance.

Tasha sips her drink as she stares wistfully at Chance.

By the end of the night, Mike and J.J. have left the party with two young ladies. Walt is inebriated and Big Dink has to hold him up and guide him out of the party. Mad Max is helping a drunken Chance. A wasted

Tasha is getting a piggyback ride from Bird. They all reach the hotel and make their way to Chance's room. Big Dink throws Walt down on his bed. He's knocked out and already snoring as Big Dink takes off his boots.

"Man, Walt is done," says Big Dink. "How many glasses of punch did this dude have? I mean damn."

Mad Max helps Chance to his bed and takes off his sneakers.

"Thank you, my brotha," says Chance in a slur of words.

"Sounds like you had too many punches, too," says Big Dink. "But at least you're still awake and functioning—well somewhat functioning—unlike Walt over here who's completely out."

At the same time Big Dink and Mad Max are taking off Walt and Chance's shoes, Tasha jumps down off Bird's back, loses her balance, and falls to the floor. She attempts to get up but stumbles a bit again.

The guys are amused.

"Damn, all y'all mutha fuckas is fucked up," says Big Dink.

"I ain't fucked up. I'm just a little tipsy," says Tasha.

"If you say so, shawty. You need us to take you to your room?"

"Naw, I gotta stay here and take care of my man."

"It's all good, Tash. I got him," says Chance.

"I was talkin' 'bout takin' care of you. You know I gotta take care of my man."

"Well on that note, that's our cue," says Big Dink. "Come on y'all, let's go out front and see if those A&M chicks are here yet."

Big Dink, Mad Max, and Bird leave the room. Tasha staggers over to Chance's bed and gets on top of him. She starts kissing him.

"Wait, Tasha, no. We can't. We're both drunk and Walt is right there."

"Boy, stop trippin'. Walt's passed out and ain't waking up for nuffin. Now just lay there and let me take care of you."

Chance tries to get up, but Tasha aggressively pushes him back down. She pulls up his shirt and starts licking his chest. She gradually goes farther down toward his belly button.

"Aw fuck, girl."

"Yeah that's right, boy. You know you want it."

"This ain't right, girl. We can't."

Tasha's head goes further down and starts to bob up and down.

"Ohhhh Fuckkkkkkk," says Chance.

Tasha takes off her clothes, pulls Chance's pants off, gets on top of him, places his penis inside of her, and starts riding him.

"We can't be doing this."

"Boy, shut the hell up and come on."

"Damn that shit feel good. Fuck!"

Tasha, as she is riding Chance, bends down and whispers in his ear.

"This all yours, Chance. You hear me. All. Yours."

Walt lays in the next bed still fast asleep as Tasha and Chance go at it.

The morning sunlight shines through the hotel window and onto Walt's face. He squints his eyes, and then stretches and yawns simultaneously. He rolls over, sees Tasha next to him, and smiles. He leans over and lightly kisses her full lips. She opens her eyes, smiles, and then cuddles up against him. He rubs her arm and pulls her even closer to him, savoring the moment. Chance's snores provide the only background noise.

28

TWO TON TINA

A few weeks have passed since Howard played Florida A&M and they have continued to dominate the MEAC and garner media attention. The MAGA hat guy, Charlie, is enjoying his evening playing pool and drinking beer with his friends at their local Alexandria, Virginia, dive bar. The six o'clock news broadcast is visible on a big screen television affixed to the wall parallel to the pool table. The volume is muted to not disturb customer conversation. A picture of the Howard University Super Seven displays in the top right corner of the screen adjacent to the newscaster. Just as Charlie leans down toward the pool table, cue stick in hand, and is setting up to take his next strike, he glances up and notices Walt's face. Stunned, he drops the cue stick.

"Billy, pause that TV for a sec," says Charlie.

Billy obliges.

"Mother fucker."

"What?"

"That's that fucking nigger who took my hat on the metro."

"Are you sure that's him?"

"You damn right I am. I never forget a face. He was staring right at me holding my hat after the doors closed. Unpause and rewind it."

Billy obliges again.

"Can you really be sure?"

"Shut up for a second and let me hear the TV. Turn it up."

A perky, ginger-haired television reporter begins her report standing outside of Burr Gymnasium.

"Tonight we're putting the *Local Spotlight* on the Howard University men's basketball program and their Super Seven. These guys have become a hurricane in the DMV and are starting to make waves throughout the rest of the country. Tonight they play their final MEAC—that's the Mid-Eastern Athletic Conference—season game at home against the North Carolina Central University Eagles. NCCU has only lost one MEAC game and that was to the Howard Bison. If the Bison win tonight, then they will finish their overall season with a record of twenty-four and two, and they will finish undefeated in their conference. This is their best record in school history. It would also be their first time winning the MEAC regular season title in over seventeen years. The Howard University Bison are ranked fifteenth in the nation. This is the highest ranking for Howard or any HBCU—short for Historically Black Colleges and Universities—ever!

"As a matter of fact, it's the first time that an HBCU has ever been ranked in the top twenty-five. And it's largely because of the Super Seven, a group predominately comprised of national all-stars, including the number one ranked recruit coming out of high school—Chance Knight. He is often compared to a LeBron James and is easily that caliber of an athlete. This has been a magical and historic year for Howard basketball. Over to you, Jim."

"Thank you, Andrea."

Jim Makowski, the news anchor, a bit more mundane than the reporter, repeats what every other television and radio personality who highlights the Bison team reports.

"But this season has not come without some controversy for the team. They have also made headlines for kneeling during the national anthem. And let's not forget, as we reported last spring when it happened, Craig Knight, the father of Chance Knight, was tragically killed by police. Howard University is where Craig Knight went to school and it's where he always wanted Chance to attend. Chance, and a small group of other high school national all-stars, the Super Seven as Andrea reported, decided to play for Howard in honor of Chance's father. I should point out that Bobby Banks, who is not African American, proudly wears the Bison jersey.

"Not only is the Howard basketball program having an historic season, but they might also be having an historic and cascading impact on collegiate basketball. It has been reported that a number of high school five-star athletes are strongly considering attending HBCUs next year. The current number one ranked high school basketball senior has said his top three schools are Kentucky, Florida State, and Florida A&M. This was unimaginable a year ago. Good luck tonight, fellas. The game tips off at seven o'clock tonight at Howard's Burr Gymnasium. What a great *Local Spotlight* story. Go Bison!"

Billy mutes the television.

"Those mother fucking niggers snatched my MAGA hat off and took it, and now they disrespect our country's flag. Hell no. Fuck that."

"Chill the fuck out, Charlie. They're fucking kids. Your ass is forty somethin' years old. Let that shit go, brother. Some fuckin' niggers snatched off your stupid ass MAGA hat and are protesting the flag. So what? Brother, let that shit go."

313

"Let it go? The day it happened, wasn't it you telling me what they did was disrespectful and if I found him you would help me take care of him?"

"Charlie, I was just talking. We were all just talking. Nobody was actually serious. Except for you, apparently."

Charlie goes silent. Minutes pass. He has not said a word, but his silence is unnerving. Billy tries to break the ice.

"Come on dude, it's your shot. Any day now."

Charlie, still silent, turns and looks directly at Billy. He takes the cue stick and breaks it over his knee. He throws the broken stick on the table and it scrambles the balls. Grabbing his nearly full glass of beer, he walks toward the exit.

"That fucker is crazy. His ass clearly isn't taking his meds," Billy says to the others.

Charlie pushes open the exit door hard, causing it to bang the wall on his way out and slam shut. The bartender yells after him that he cannot leave with the beer, but it is too late.

The crowd begins to funnel into Burr Gymnasium at six o'clock. By six thirty the gym is filled to capacity and latecomers are being turned away. A young off-duty policeman from the Midwest, hired for tonight to serve as security, monitors the crowd along with his partner, an African American born and reared in the District of Columbia.

"I can't believe this atmosphere," says the Midwestener while running his hand over his short blond crew cut. "It's out of this world. I've never heard a band like this, or seen cheerleaders move like that. I wanna get down like everybody else here."

His partner laughs.

"Welcome to Howard University."

ESPN2 cameramen are getting into position for a live broadcast. Cameramen from multiple local news channels are also jockeying for space. A section of the bleachers is reserved and roped off for NBA scouts.

The NCCU Eagles run out onto the floor to the anticipated chorus of boos. When the Bison emerge wearing black tee-shirts that read, *"HBUCs Matter,"* there is no containing the crowd. The cheers last for what seems like an eternity to the Bison. They cannot get enough of it and play to the crowd during warmups.

"Ladies and Gentlemen, please rise and remove your caps as we honor our country with the singing of our national anthem," says the public announcer.

Walt walks out to center court, takes the microphone, and gets down on one knee. All players, coaches, trainers, managers, cheerleaders, and band members follow his lead and kneel. For the first time, the entire student body takes a knee. Walt's tenor rendition of the anthem is reminiscent of Marvin Gaye's. He reaches the climactic part of the song and as he hits the last note, ESPN2 shows a wide-angle view of Burr Gymnasium. Even the cameraman is captivated by the display in the gymnasium. Walt receives a standing ovation.

Tasha is mesmerized by Walt as he walks off. She is on her feet clapping proudly and loudly. Walt looks up at Tasha and blows her a kiss. She catches the kiss and Walt returns the smile. "Two Ton Tina," still pining for Walt, notices the exchange as she has over the last few weeks. Reality bites her. Walt is not playing hard to get. He is just not in to her. The strength of her emotions pushes her out of her seat and out of the gymnasium. She rips up her sign and places it in the trashcan outside before weeping back to her car. Meanwhile, Tasha sits in her seat and tears start flowing as she puts her face down in her hands remembering how she cheated on Walt with Chance, his best friend. She feels something she has never felt before—guilt.

A young coed from the Howard University Choir follows Walt's performance and sings The National Negro Anthem with an operatic flair. The fans respond again with a standing ovation and appreciate that even before the main event, they have witnessed a spectacular show.

The starters walk out to center court and assume their positions. The jump ball goes up and the game begins.

Later on that night, Coach Mac is sitting in his office by himself smoking a cigar and sipping his second glass of Cîroc on the rocks. He looks at old photos of himself and Coach Knight that he had pulled out of an album and has not yet put back. He fingers various pictures from their college heyday and remembers clowning on The Yard, pledging Omega Psi Phi, and sitting in the freshman dormitory lounge with a group of friends. He both smiles and releases built up tears. He looks up toward the ceiling.

"You would be so proud of Chance. Damn, I wish you were here to see what your son is doing, and the change he's leading. He's making your dream come true. He's making *our* dream come true. It's a beautiful sight to see, my brotha. So many firsts inspired by him."

He wipes his tears as he glances over at the clock and sees that it is already eleven o'clock. He hurriedly grabs the remote control and changes the channel just in time to hear the sportscaster begin the program.

"Thank you all for tuning in to *Sports Highlight Center*. Y'all know I like to start off the night with the coolest thing I saw today. This is the second time in the past two months that Howard basketball has made this segment. The number fifteen ranked Howard Bison beat the North Carolina Central Eagles by a convincing twenty-three points tonight to win the regular season MEAC championship for the first time in over seventeen years. Chance Knight scored a career high forty-eight points to go along with fifteen rebounds. Yes, you heard that right. I said he scored forty-eight points to go along with fifteen rebounds. I predict this kid is going to be the number one pick in this year's NBA draft. Mark my words. He is flat out incredible. Superhuman.

"But the coolest thing I saw tonight was this picture of the entire gymnasium taking a knee during the national anthem. I mean look at this shot. To be clear, I'm not condoning taking a knee during the anthem. I believe in standing for our flag, but at the same time, I believe that everyone has a right to express their opinion and make their own decisions. That's what freedom means. That's what the flag means. No matter how you feel about what they're doing, there's no denying the power of this picture."

Coach Mac turns off the television with the remote control, takes a puff of his cigar, and blows smoke into the air. He smiles. He looks toward the ceiling once more, nods a couple of times, and thinks, "Perfect ending to a perfect day. Thank you, Jesus."

29
GOD'S HANDS

The Howard Bison are finishing their first practice since closing out the MEAC season undefeated. Coach Mac blows his whistle.

"All right, fellas. Let's bring it in. Great practice today. There's no letting up now. The MEAC tournament is one week away. We accomplished our first goal, which was to knock off some nationally ranked teams to let the world know that we're a force to be reckoned with. That's done. We just accomplished our second goal of winning the MEAC regular season. Check and Check.

"We still have three goals left. The next goal within reach is to win the MEAC tournament. I don't have to tell y'all that it's extremely difficult to beat a team three times in one season. But that's what we're gonna have to do in order to win. Winning the MEAC puts us in the NCAA tournament, which sets us up for a chance at the fourth goal—winning the national championship."

Coach Mac hears a few whispers of doubt but lets it slide for now.

"When I came up with these goals, I assumed that we had to accomplish the first four in order for the fifth to be achieved—HBCUs as a reality for top black athletes. While that's still likely the case, I'm proud to announce that I'm already seeing signs of goal five starting to happen. Because of your success, I already have a commitment from a five-star recruit from Cali for next year. He was gonna sign with UCLA, but when he saw us on *Sports Highlight Center* and learned about the movement, *he* reached out to *me*. He's the number three ranked center in the country."

Coach Mac savors the whistles and cheers from the team.

"I hope you told that mutha fucka that he'll be my back up," says Big Dink. "Because I don't care who he is and what he's ranked, he ain't takin' my mutha fuckin' startin' spot next year."

Everyone laughs.

"I also had two four-star recruits reach out to me about coming here. I had to tell them I have to wait and see how many scholarships will be available. Just contemplate that for a moment. I had to tell *four-star* recruits that they may not be able to come here, to Howard University. But I told them if we're full, then they should consider reaching out to other MEAC schools. I know any of them would love to have 'em. So you see, fellas. You guys are doing something extremely meaningful here. Something powerful. Something that could go down in history books. You, as African American athletes. And you, too, Bird."

Bird gets jabbed with elbows by a few players sitting next to him.

"Coach Knight would be so proud of y'all. Y'all are trailblazers. Now let's go out and finish this thing. No letdowns. No leftovers. No getting over confident. Let's take it one game at a time. All right, bring it in. Finish it on three. One, two, three. Finish it!"

Chance walks by himself on The Yard lost in his thoughts about the next game and his next exam. His phone rings. He loves hearing the voice on the other end.

"Hey, babe. Just calling to see if you're down for a quickie and then we can grab some lunch before my next class."

"Am I down? Girl, you silly. I know Walt said he and Tasha were 'bout to go shopping. So they should be 'bout to leave if they haven't already. Meet me at my room. I'm headed there now."

"Okay, cool. See ya soon."

As Walt and Tasha are walking out of Walt's bedroom, Chance walks into the dormitory room.

"Oh, what's up y'all?"

"What up, my brotha?"

"Hey, Chance," says Tasha, more quietly than usual.

"Y'all headed out?"

"Yeah, I'm 'bout to take Miss Thang here shopping for some new shades."

"Oh, okay. Bet. Well, y'all have fun."

Holding hands, Walt and Tasha head down the hallway.

"Oh, shit. I left my phone in the room, babe," says Tasha.

"All right. Let's go back and get it."

"I'll go get it. You go ahead outside and grab me some cocoa bread and a lemonade from the corner truck, please. I'll meet you out there in a sec."

"Yeah, some cocoa bread does sound good right about now. Okay. Bet."

Walt walks down the dormitory steps leading to the sidewalk as Kia is walking up them.

"What up, girl?"

"What's up, Walt? Where's your girlfriend? Chance said y'all goin' shopping."

"Yup. She had to run back to the room real quick to get her phone."

"Oh, okay. Well, I'm gonna go on up."

"Okay. Take care."

"Thanks. You, too, Walt." As she enters the building, Kia thinks how truly fond she is of Walt.

There is a knock on Chance's door. Expecting Kia, he opens it without asking who is there. He is surprised to see Tasha.

"Chance, we need to talk for a sec."

"Where's Walt?"

"He's waiting for me at the corner truck getting us some cocoa bread."

"Well this is gonna have to wait 'cause Kia's 'bout to be here."

Kia, anticipating her afternoon rendezvous in bed with Chance, quickens her pace down the hallway.

"Sorry, but this can't wait. It'll only take a sec."

"Ugh. What is it, Tash?"

"I'm pregnant, Chance."

"You're what?"

Kia reaches the door of Chance's room and notices that the door is partially open. Just as she goes to push it open the rest of the way, she hears Tasha's voice and stops.

"I said I'm pregnant, Chance. Pregnant!"

"Well, congratulations. I'm happy for you and Walt. Now you gotta get outta here. Kia's gonna be here any second."

"You're not understanding me. I'm pregnant and I fuckin' don't know if the baby is yours or Walt's."

"Uh. I can answer that for you. It's definitely Walt's. How could it be mine? You only gave me head in Florida."

Kia is outside of the door hearing every syllable. She is holding her hands over her mouth and can't believe what she is hearing. Tears start to trickle down her face.

"Nigga, I knew you was tipsy, but I ain't know you was that fucked up to not remember all of it. Yeah, I was givin' you head at first, but then I got on top of you and rode you until you nutted all up inside me."

The door opens and a devastated Kia, with tears cascading down her face, stands there. She is momentarily speechless and can hardly breathe in the room that is now closing in and suffocating her. She looks at Tasha and then looks at Chance.

"How could you?" she asks. "How could you do this to me? It's over. We're over!" She runs out.

"Thanks a fucking lot, Tash. Fuck!" He looks at Tasha as if he could kill her. Right then. Right there. And then races after Kia. "Kia, wait!"

Tasha falls on Walt's bed and cries into the pillow.

Meanwhile, Walt is walking back toward the dormitory with the cocoa bread and lemonade in his hands. Kia storms past Walt.

"Yo, Kia, what's the matter? You okay?"

Kia stops and turns around, still crying.

"No! I am not okay! Your stupid slut, dick catching girlfriend, Tasha, fucked Chance! And she's pregnant! So, no! I'm not fucking okay!" She rushes off, even more upset knowing that she has devastated Walt.

Walt loosens his grip on the food and drinks and they fall to the ground. He puts both hands on top of his head slowly walking in circles as if he is lost and cannot find his way. He can't believe what is happening. Walt spots Chance running in his direction as he chases after Kia. Just as Chance is running by, Walt snaps out of his daze, tackles Chance and starts pounding on him.

"How could you fuckin' do this to me?" yells Walt.

Kia races pass Deon and Nick.

"Kia!" shouts Deon. "Are you okay?"

Kia stops and turns around. "Fuck you. Fuck all you cheatin,' lyin' ass basketball players. Y'all are *all* jerks!" She turns back around and continues to storm off.

Deon wonders what Chance did, or rather who he did. Then he hears a commotion and turns to see Walt pounding Chance, who is not fighting back.

Deon and Nick run over to Chance and pull Walt off of him. Tasha, who has managed to pull herself together and has now made her way outside to talk to Walt, rushes over to where they are and tries to calm Walt down.

"Baby, stop it! You've gotta let me explain."

Deon has his answer.

"Explain what? Explain how you fucked my best friend? How you fucked my roommate who's like a brother to me?"

Walt turns his attention back to Chance.

"How could you do this to me, bro?" We're like blood. How could you do that knowing what I'm dealing with, like Teddy being sick? You know how much Tasha means to me, and always has. I finally had something special with her that made me happy and helped me cope with everything else. And you knew this. For *you,* of all people, to take that shit away from me is what hurts so bad." Walt falls to his knees and breaks down.

Chance puts his hand on Walt's shoulder.

"Walt, listen to me."

Walt shakes him off.

"Stay the fuck away from me, Chance!"

Walt gets up and walks briskly away. Tasha chases after him. A few minutes later, her short quick strides finally catch up to his, which have been long and steady.

"I need you to listen to me, baby. I've got bad news and good news, but I can assure you that you're gonna love the good news. You just gotta hear me out."

"You know what, Tasha. Just go ahead. Have at it. I'm so drained right now. Just go ahead and say what you've gotta say. I don't even have the energy to walk anymore."

"So the bad news is when you, Chance, and I all got drunk at the Florida A&M party, Chance and I ended up screwing around while you were passed out. We were both drunk as hell and it meant absolutely nothing to either of us. I barely even remember the shit."

Tasha pauses for a very brief moment.

"The other bad news is I was using you in the beginning just to make Chance jealous. And I was using you to buy me things."

"Well damn, Tash. What the fuck is the goddamn good news?"

"The good news is that during our time together, I actually fell in love with you. I mean, I'm totally truly in love with you right now. That's why it's killin' me that this one drunken mistake is causin' all this pain. I would never intentionally hurt you. I'm so proud to be your girl. I just want us to be together and get past this."

"Really? You fell in love with me? You honestly love me?"

"Yes, baby, yes." She moves closer to Walt and kisses him gently.

"Wait, I haven't even finished the good news. So guess what?"

"What?"

"I'm pregnant! And I am 95 percent positive it's yours."

Walt looks at Tasha with a blank expression.

"Well, aren't you gonna say something?"

"I'm gonna be a daddy, y'all!" Walt gets down on his knees and starts kissing Tasha's belly.

"There's no doubt in my mind that this baby's mine. We're gonna be parents, Tash."

"I know, Walt. You're gonna be a great father."

Walt hugs Tasha's belly. Tasha bends down, hugs Walt, and falls apart.

"So you forgive me and will still be with me, baby?"

"I forgive you, girl. I ain't going nowhere."

Walt and Tasha stand and share a passionate kiss that produces more electricity between them than they have ever experienced with anyone else before, or even with each other.

Chance, who followed behind Walt and Tasha while keeping his distance, now walks over to them. He gets close to Walt and looks him directly in his eyes.

"Look, bro. I feel terrible about what happened. Tasha and I were super drunk. I don't even remember most of that night. I would never intentionally do anything to hurt you and you know that. We're practically family. Shit. Fuck that. We *are* family."

"I forgive you, bro. It's gonna take me some time to fully forgive you. But for now I kinda forgive you. And both of you mutha fuckas better hope this is my baby. 'Cause if it isn't then I'm done with both of you. We need to do whateva' we need to do ASAP to confirm this baby mine. Somebody call Maury. I want that fool to look at Chance and say, 'You are *not* the father.' And then my ass is gonna jump up an' down like a crazy person celebrating and dancin' 'cause that means I *am* the father."

Chance and Tasha laugh.

"There's no doubt in my mind that you're my baby's father, Walt. And you'll see."

"Yeah, man. As much as y'all be fuckin', that baby definitely yours, bro."

Walt smiles and then drops down to his knees and starts kissing Tasha's belly again.

"Daddy's right here. I'm right here."

Tasha looks at Chance as though uncertain and scared, Chance returns the gaze, puts his hands in the prayer position, and walks away.

Chance walks the three blocks to the corner and turns. Looking off into the distance, he immediately finds the needle in the haystack. He sees Kia sitting on a bench crying. He makes his way over to her.

Tasha and Walt, after sharing a few lingering embraces and affirmations of love, hold hands and head toward Tasha's dormitory.

"Man, my feet are killin' me," says Tasha.

"That's that pregnant life starting to kick in."

"Boy, I ain't even showing yet."

"Oh yeah, true."

They laugh and Walt squeezes her hand.

"Since your feet hurt, let's take a short cut through the alley real quick."

Tasha hesitates.

"Don't you remember what the campus police said the last time? About people getting attacked and robbed in there?"

"Yeah, but it's the middle of the day. It's not nighttime like the last time."

"True. My feet *are* killing me. Okay. Let's do it."

"Bet."

Walt and Tasha walk into the alley. Someone holding a gun stares at them from a hidden corner.

"I'm so happy with you, baby," says Tasha. "We're about to be parents. This is so exciting!"

"Babe, I'm not going to lie. It still hurts. But I can't help how much I love you. I know this is my baby. There's no doubt."

"Me, too. I know it's yours."

"With all that's going on with my brother, Teddy, and his cancer, I really needed this good news. I think this child is a blessing from God. I really needed this right now, Tash. Thank you for this blessing."

"No. Thank *you*, Walt. I'm the one who should be thankin' you for forgivin' me. You've always treated me special. Like a lady. Not many guys have in the past. Falling in love with you has completely changed me. I'm ashamed of how I was."

Without warning, three locals emerge from nowhere. Two of them grab Tasha and pull her to the side as the other one aims a gun at Walt. Tasha starts screaming. Walt recognizes them. His stomach drops. His heart pumps vigorously; he can feel it.

"Tasha!" yells Walt.

"Don't move, mutha fucka," says Red while keeping the gun firmly pointed at him.

Chance is standing next to Kia as she sits on the bench.

"Look. I know you're pissed. But I can assure you that the baby isn't mine."

"If this baby isn't yours, do you think for one minute that makes everything okay?"

"Not at all. Kia, I'm crazy about you. I made a drunken mistake. A terrible mistake. I was so drunk I hardly even remember it. I know being drunk isn't a good excuse. But I swear to you that something like this will never happen again. I would never let it. I swear that on my father's grave, yo."

Chance reaches out and grabs Kia's hand. She allows him to hold it. She looks at him and a single tear escapes her eye, tracing her cheek downward until absorbed by her skin, leaving behind just a faint wet trail. She stands up quietly and heads toward her dormitory. Chance follows.

Back in the alley, Tarik and Tyrone pull Tasha into a more secluded area behind a large garbage dumpster. They throw her to the ground.

"Come over here and watch what's about to happen to your precious little girlfriend," Red says, gun still pointed at Walt.

"Mutha fuckas, I will kill you!"

"Nigga, you ain't gonna do shit but shut the fuck up and watch as we take turns on your bitch."

"No! I'm pregnant! Please don't hurt my baby!"

Tarik holds her down. As Tyrone starts to pull her pants down three gunshots ring out. Pop! Pop! Pop!

Chance and Kia hear three close by gunshots and instantly hit the ground. Kia screams. Chance instinctively wraps his arms around her, shielding her as she fearfully latches on.

"Are you okay, babe?"

Kia nods.

"Oh no! Walt!" exclaims Chance. He immediately fears for his friend. The shots were coming from the direction Walt could have been walking, and there was no love lost between those local boys and Walt.

In the alley, Tasha lies on the ground emitting wails she never knew were in her. Blood splatter paints her face and clothes. She looks down and sees blood all over her stomach.

"My baby! No!"

The three locals lie still with gunshot wounds to their heads. A man with a hooded sweatshirt is holding a gun standing over their bodies.

Walt runs over to Tasha and assesses her.

"It's not your blood, babe! It's not your blood! You and the baby are fine!"

Tasha, hysterical, grips onto Walt as he protectively hugs and squeezes her.

Walt stands up and looks over at the man with the gun.

"Thank you! Thank you! You saved our lives! My girl and I, we just can't thank you enough."

The man pulls the hood of his sweatshirt down and reveals his face. He's wearing a new MAGA hat that was concealed under his hood. Walt squints and looks at the guy closely. He vaguely recognizes him but cannot recall from where. Then it clicks. He knows who he is. And he knows that look in his eyes. He recognizes the evil.

"Oh, no! Tasha, run!"

Back around the corner, Chance and Kia desperately race to find Walt. They hear another gun shot. Pop! They once again hit the ground. Kia is increasingly frightened, as are the other nearby students.

"What the hell's happening?" asks Kia.

"Come on, babe."

They get back up and break into a full sprint.

"Hold up, Chance, I'm outta breath."

They stop. They both bend over and put their hands on their knees as they try to catch their breaths for a few seconds. Kia looks up and sees the alley directly in her line of sight.

"Chance, look! Is that Tasha?"

Chance squints and peers down the alley where he sees Tasha bending over what looks to him like a body. He takes off again and races toward her. Kia tries to keep up. He reaches Tasha and finds Walt lying unconscious and bleeding. Chance is terrified.

"Walt! Walt! Walt!" screams Chance as he bends down and cradles him. "Get up, Walt! Get up! Somebody help!"

Tasha, shaking, is in shock.

"What happened, Tasha?" yells Chance.

Tasha, still shaking, stands mute.

Kia finally reaches them.

"Oh, God! Walt!" she cries.

"Kia, call 911 right now!" Chance orders.

Kia pulls out her cell phone to dial 911 as Walt lies still, bleeding profusely from his head. Chance continues to cradle Walt in his arms, holding his head up, and trying desperately to stop the blood flow by exerting pressure.

"Don't you leave me, Walt. Don't you fuckin' leave me. You hear me? Stay with me, Walt. Teddy needs his big brother. And I need my brother. Oh, God!"

Tears are pouring from Chance's eyes, as he once again screams repeatedly for help. Walt's full body weight rests in Chance's arms. He feels and looks lifeless.

At Children's National Hospital, Mrs. Williams is sitting with Teddy watching cartoons. A call comes in on her phone. A few seconds later, she is gripped by terror.

"Dear God, no!" Mrs. Williams shrieks.

The phone falls from her hands, hits the floor, and shatters.

Walt fights for his life at Howard University Hospital. The waiting room is standing room only as Walt's family and friends continue to pack in. The Bison basketball team stands silently alongside the coaching staff. Walt's mother sits surrounded by her sisters and brothers, nieces and nephews. The tall slender surgeon enters the waiting area looking for Mrs. Williams. She jumps up and moves toward him.

"Tell me something, Doctor," she says.

"Walt is out of surgery and in recovery. While he remains in critical condition, he's very fortunate that the bullet missed his brain completely, which means no brain damage. The problem is the bullet wound was still significant and he lost a tremendous amount of blood, which can lead to other complications. We did manage to eventually stop the bleeding and replenish some of the blood through transfusions. He'll remain in ICU. We're monitoring him closely to determine if he'll need more surgeries. The next twenty-four hours are critical and will be very revealing. If you believe in God, please ask everyone to keep Walt in prayer. Walt's in His hands for the next twenty-four hours."

Mrs. Williams melts onto the floor. Chance drops down to pick her up and attempts to console her. She looks up at the doctor.

"When can I see him?" she asks.

"You can see him now but only you. He's still unconscious, but you can be in there with him."

Mrs. Williams turns to everyone in the waiting room.

"Please pray for my baby! Please! Pray for my baby. I thank you all for being here."

Mrs. Williams follows the surgeon into the recovery room. Kia and Chance remain in the waiting room stroking each other's backs for comfort. Coach Mac walks by and places his hand on Chance's shoulder for a moment without saying anything, and then heads to the chapel.

Chance is easily awakened from a restless sleep when his cell phone rings. He does not recognize the number. Usually he would not answer for an unknown caller, but today something compels him. Two days have passed since Walt was shot so he is anxious when he recognizes Mrs. Williams' voice on the other end of the call.

"Good morning, Chance."

"Good morning, ma'am. I didn't recognize the number. I'm glad I answered. Are you calling from the hospital?"

"I am. I just wanted to let you know one of the detectives called me early this morning. They found the man who shot Walt and the three boys. They caught the monster who shot my baby."

"Oh, wow! That's great news!"

"Yes, praise Jesus! Believe it or not, his friend turned him in. Apparently he's always had anger problems and mental issues. He talked *crazy* from time to time, but his friends never thought he would actually do any of the insane stuff he threatened to do.

"Howard recently installed a security camera in that alley to deter robberies, thankfully. The camera showed footage of a guy in a MAGA hat holding a gun running away from the direction of the shootings. Police released the footage to the local news stations and it aired on the eleven o'clock news last night.

"One of the guy's friends saw it and, just that quickly, called the police. He gave them his name and address. He said he was afraid for his own life and afraid that his friend would hurt himself or more people."

"Did they get the actual shooting on tape?"

"No. The shooting was in a blind spot. But they got enough on camera to know it was him."

"I'm just so relieved that mad man is off the streets now. Now maybe we can get some justice for Walt."

"You and me both. Whether he's crazy or not, I hope he rots in hell for what he did to my son. Now both of my boys are battling for their lives. You know, the detective told me they're investigating this as a hate crime. It's unbelievable. You have to be very careful, Chance. A lot of people think the outbreak of this kind of violence is directly related to the president's hateful rhetoric. It hurts to think that my son is lying in a hospital bed fighting for his life because of the president's words and actions, or lack thereof. It's like he's a virus that's spreading quickly."

"I will. I promise. How's Walt today? Is he awake?"

"Last night, he was fully conscious."

"Thank God!"

"You were the second person he asked for."

"Who was the first?" Chance already knows the answer.

"Do you really have to ask?"

"Tasha."

"That's right."

Mrs. Williams and Chance share a chuckle, grateful for a moment of levity.

"Tasha was released from the hospital yesterday," says Mrs. Williams. "She was really shaken up. They treated her for shock and provided her a list of counselors. Walt's doctors, with my permission, allowed her to sneak in here for a few minutes to see him. I gave them their privacy. Walt was relieved she was okay and very happy to see her. I'm glad he got that time with her. Now he seems a little more at ease and focused on his recovery."

"Oh, that's great. I'm glad he's alert and concentrating on getting better."

"Well, he was also hoping to see *you* today, but in the middle of the night, he started complaining about headaches and irritating pain around the area on his head where he was shot."

Mrs. Williams pauses, thinking to herself that saying the words "he was shot" when referring to her son is surreal.

"Early this morning, the pain worsened. The doctors determined he has an infection. So he won't be able to have visitors for at least three to four more days. He's very disappointed, of course. But the doctors are doing all they can. He's heavily sedated now and being given antibiotics through an IV."

Chance's heart sinks.

"He mentioned that the MEAC tournament is in three days. He was hoping to tell you this himself, but obviously now he can't. He wants you to promise him that you guys are going to make it to the NCAA tournament."

"Please tell Walt not to worry. I'll take care of it for him. Please make sure to tell him to hurry up and get well so that he can come watch us play in it."

"Absolutely, Chance. We love you. Good luck in the tournament, sweetie."

"Thank you, Mrs. Williams. I love y'all, too. Please keep me posted and please call me as soon as he can have visitors. Is your family with Teddy?"

"My sister, Robyn. We go back and forth. Teddy is being released today. Thanks for asking. Take care."

"You too, Mrs. Williams."

Chance ends the phone call and lies back down. He glances over to his desk and finds what he is looking for. A framed picture of himself with Walt in the weight room. They had posed for the camera, his arm around Walt. He thinks about Teddy now having to worry about his big brother. That can't be good.

31

WHO'S YOUR DADDY?

Although the last few days have been excruciatingly tough on the entire Howard University basketball team and coaching staff, preparation for the MEAC tournament has continued. Chance, returning from early morning practice, needs to talk to Kia. He picks up his cell phone and punches in the numbers.

"Hello?" Kia manages to say, barely awake.

"Hey, babe. I know it's early. I'm sorry."

"It's okay. I have a class in a bit so I need to get up. Everything okay?"

"I don't know. I feel like I'm struggling. I just don't want anything to happen to Walt. I just feel like everything is my fault."

"Babe, that's nonsense. How could anything be your fault?"

"You don't understand. When my pops died, the only reason we were there is because I was hungry and wanted pizza. If we'd gone anywhere else or if I had suggested it earlier, he'd still be here. And Walt, the only reason he's at Howard is because of me. If I'd never come here, he wouldn't have come here, and this never would have happened." Chance breaks down.

"Babe, listen to me. None of this is your fault. None of it! I'm coming over. I'll skip class."

"No, don't do that. I just need a minute to myself. Go to class. I'll meet you for lunch after."

"I love you, Chance."

Kia has never said that to him before, nor has he to her. It just slipped out, but she means it. The phone goes quiet and the beat of Kia's heart has paused as she waits out the silence.

"I love you, too. You have no idea how much. I don't know how I would get through this without you."

Kia's heart resumes beating. She knows she loves this man and he loves her. She will do anything to help relieve his pain.

Over lunch in the cafeteria, Kia tries to raise Chance's spirits.

"So are you excited that the MEAC tournament is starting tomorrow?" she asks.

"It's bitter sweet. I'm excited, but I'm still trippin' that Walt won't be there with us."

"Yeah, I feel ya. You just gotta make sure you go and win this tournament so that you can bring the championship trophy with you to the hospital for him to see."

"You know, that's a great idea. I'm definitely gonna do that. Big Dink, Bird, Mad Max, Mike, J.J., and I will take it to him."

Tasha walks into the cafeteria and scans the tables for Chance and Kia. She knows they typically are at lunch around this time. She spots them, but is tentative on approach.

"Hi, guys. Is it okay if I say something to the both of you?" she asks.

Kia raises her eyebrows.

"Can you believe the audacity of this chick?" Kia asks Chance while staring at Tasha.

"Look, Tasha. My girl's finally forgiven me. I messed up badly because I was drunk. I'm never making a mistake like that again. No one will ever come between Kia and me again. She's my girl, I love her, and that's that."

"Well, that's just it. I can see that. You guys are clearly meant for each other. Kia, Chance, I can't apologize enough for the mistake I caused. Kia, I just want you to know that I was the aggressor. I was the one who initiated everything and forced my way on Chance. I was extremely drunk and it wasn't a good look. I just wanted to look both of you in your eyes and give you a sincere apology from the bottom of my heart. I don't expect you to forget, but I still hope that one day you two will find it in your hearts to forgive me."

Tasha's eyes well up with tears.

"I was initially jealous of y'all's relationship because I had no idea that Chance was seeing anyone. But I can assure you that I no longer have any desire to come between you guys. I admitted to Walt that I was using him initially," Tasha says as she lowers her head.

"But during this entire process I ended up falling in love with him. He's such a sincere and genuinely caring guy. No one has ever loved me like he does. I'll never forgive myself for hurting him like this. Especially with his fuckin' best friend who's like his brother. I feel so terrible about myself, about everything I've done. I'm so sorry."

She raises her eyes to look at them.

"But, I do have some good news to share that will interest you both," says Tasha. "While I was in the hospital, I told the doctor about my situation. Considering Walt was also there and having all types of bloodwork done, I asked if they could do a blood test to see if Walt's the father. Once they were able to discreetly get

Walt's consent without his mom knowing, they ran the test. Walt *is* the father!"

Chance breathes a big sigh of relief. Kia smiles, elated, and hugs him.

"Well thank you, Tasha. I'm very happy for you and Walt and wish y'all the best," says Chance.

"Thank you. I'll leave y'all be, but wanted to make sure I apologized to both of you face-to-face and passed along the baby news. Y'all take care and good luck tomorrow, Chance."

Tasha walks off and is out of ear shot.

"All right, boy. You're in the clear now that I know the baby's not yours. I'll forgive, but I won't forget. I can't help but have some bitterness, but as much as I can, I'm willing to move on."

"Thank you, babe," Chance says softly as he hugs her. "I screwed up terribly and it will never happen again. Thank you so much for sticking by my side through all this shit. You won't be sorry. I'll never forget this."

"So when you find out I messed around on you, just remember this exact moment."

"Shhhiiiiittt. Woman, don't play with me. You ain't tryin' ta die."

Kia laughs.

"Oh so it's a double standard, huh?"

"Girl, stop playin' with me and come here."

The next few days prove eventful. Walt sits up alertly in his hospital room as he laughs with Teddy. Their mother sits off to the side counting her blessings that both boys are alive and moving along the path to becoming well.

32

TWO AND A HALF MINUTES

The Scope Arena in Norfolk, Virginia, is host to the MEAC tournament and holds its own when compared to other impressive venues that have hosted the Bison. Its massive concrete dome supported by twenty-four artfully crafted and strategically placed flying buttresses is particularly distinctive—the combination of the two elements make for an architecturally stunning arena. Howard, as expected by most sports fans, easily wins their first tournament game against South Carolina State with a final score of ninety-two to fifty. They follow with another easy win against Norfolk State, boasting a final score of eighty-seven to fifty-six.

Having not worked up much of a sweat, they advance to the championship game to take on North Carolina Central University. The game is broadcasting over Walt's tiny hospital television mounted on the facing wall. Tasha, on top of the covers, is next to Walt in bed. Teddy is snuggled on his mother's lap as she sits upright in a new looking mint green recliner. Walt is very quiet watching Howard warming up. After the singing of the national and black anthems, the starters move to center court for the opening tipoff. The jump ball goes up as the MEAC championship begins.

The next afternoon, Walt is sitting up in bed with his mother by his side.

"How ya feelin', honey?"

"I feel good. I'm actually feelin' much better physically and ready to get outta here and back to a normal life."

"The doc said you should be able to leave any day now."

"I just wanna get outta here and go see my teammates. It killed me to see them celebrating after winning the tournament last night and not be able to experience it, too. Obviously, I'm thrilled that Chance delivered on his promise. Ya know, to get us to the NCAA tournament. But I just wanna feel a part of the celebration with my team. I wanna at least be with them for March Madness. It sucks that the doc said I can't play."

Although she has a totally different perspective, grateful her son is still breathing, his mother empathizes with him.

"I totally understand, honey."

A text message chimes on Mrs. Williams' phone. About ten seconds later, they hear a knock on the door.

"Who's that?" Walt asks his mom.

"Why don't we find out." She raises her voice, "Come on in, y'all."

Walt is puzzled. "Y'all?"

The door slowly opens and Chance, holding the championship trophy, walks in followed by the rest of his teammates and coaching staff.

Walt looks at his mom in surprise. His teammates take turns greeting him—some with a hug and some with a fist bump. Walt's mother is grateful that the hospital room is practically a suite, but knows it is still a tight squeeze for so many tall and physically imposing young men.

"Y'all did it, man. Y'all really did it," says Walt as he shares an emotional embrace with Chance.

"We did it for you, bro. For you and my pops."

Chance hands the trophy to Walt, who cradles and kisses it. Everyone is clapping and cheering. Coach Mac tells them to quiet down, reminding them they are in a hospital. Walt's mother is overcome with appreciation.

"All right, fellas, let me get a picture of everyone together," says Mrs. Williams.

They gather around Walt who is in the middle holding the trophy. Walt's mom holds up her cell phone, puts it in camera mode, and turns on the flash feature.

"All right, everyone, smile on three. One, two, three."

Over the next few days, headline after headline, not all good, feature Howard's basketball team.

> "Howard Bison Defeat Defending MEAC Champs NCCU, Advance to Big Dance"
> "Howard Bison Reach March Madness, First Time in 17 Years"
> "Son Fulfills Slain Father's Wish"
> "Howard University Could Make Noise in the NCAA Tournament"
> "Anthem Protest Could be Issue with Networks"
> "Howard Basketball Player Shot in Alleged Hate Crime Recovering"
> "Four- and Five-Star Athletes Commit to HBCUs Next Year"
> "Howard to Learn NCAA First Round Opponent, March Madness Selection Show"

The team and coaching staff are settled into the dining area of Walt's hospital to watch the *March Madness Selection Show* with him on a much larger flat screen television than the one in his room. Howard cheerleaders also trickle in for an impromptu March Madness selection party. Hospital staff on break gather their food trays to move closer in to hear the announcement.

"All right, fellas, this is it. We're about to find out who we're facing first."

These days Coach Mac seems to wear a perpetual grin on his face, and this moment is no exception. He turns up the television volume.

"Next up in the South bracket playing in Lexington, Kentucky, will be the number three seed West Virginia Mountaineers facing off against the number fourteen seed Howard Bison," announces the show's commentator.

The excitement in the cafeteria erupts.

"That's what I'm talkin' 'bout, baby!" Walt screams. "We're going to Lexington. Bye bye hospital. Kentucky, here I come! I know I can't play but it's gonna feel so good to just be with y'all at the game."

"That's right, baby. God is good. We're going to have our guy Walt back with us," says Chance.

"Yup. I'm gonna be there every step of the way. I had to miss the conference tournament, but I ain't missin' March Madness for nuffin. This is a dream come true, y'all."

"Walt's back in the house, y'all. We ready! We ready! We ready!" Big Dink says in his rich, deep voice.

The Howard students and staff start jumping and chanting, "We ready! We ready!" Even Walt is on his feet jumping with them. The cheerleaders use the aisles to squeeze in a few moves, to the delight of the hospital staff. Walt savors this moment as one that will forever bond the team. He pauses for a second and senses that something is not right. The room starts spinning and he feels disoriented and scared. Coach Mac notices Walt struggling to balance himself.

"Walt, are you okay?"

Walt does not respond. His mom is panicked and alarmed.

"Baby, what's wrong?" she asks.

Walt's eyes roll into the back of his head and he collapses. He shakes uncontrollably. The hospital staff who, until this moment had been celebrating with them, rush to Walt and spring into action. One of the younger nurses pages Walt's doctor. Another nurse clears Walt's path of all obstacles. A third one turns Walt on his side so he will not choke if he vomits. The fourth rushes to get a pillow and props it under his head. Walt's mom is now frantic. Coach Mac tries to console her. She hears a hospital staff member say "seizure."

Walt's doctor rushes into the cafeteria.

"Everyone back, please," the doctor sternly says to Walt's family and friends.

"What's happening? Walt! What's happening to my baby?"

Teddy stares, scared and confused.

Walt continues to convulse. Chance drops to his knees and begins to pray. The doctors and nurses wait out the seizure. Two and a half minutes later, it is over.

33

SEE YOU IN KENTUCKY

"I'm home, y'all," Chance announces.

"Chance!" says Amaia as she runs and leaps into his arms.

"What up, Sis? So good to see you. How's everything?"

"Everything's good, Bro. I'm so sorry 'bout Walt. Sorry I couldn't be at the March Madness party. How is he?"

"Y'all, come into the kitchen. Lunch is almost ready," their mom calls out to them.

"Come on." He motions Amaia. "I'll tell you and Mom together."

Chance slowly inhales the aromas floating out of his mother's kitchen.

"Man, this is what I'm talkin' 'bout. It smells good up in here. Ain't nuffin like some home cookin'."

Chance's mom hugs him tightly.

"Y'all get ready to sit on down to eat," she says. "So what's the latest on Walt, sweetie?"

A dejected Chance slumps in his chair as if the weight of the world is on him.

"Mom, it's awful. You know he had a seizure yesterday and then slipped into a coma. Mrs. Williams said the doctors been runnin' all types of tests to determine the cause. It could be something from the gunshot wound itself, the surgery, or the infection he developed. They don't have any answers yet, but they said they hope to know something definitively over the next few days." Chance looks up at his mother and sighs heavily.

"He obviously won't be going with us to March Madness. I'm devastated for him. He was so excited. We've dreamed about playing together in this tournament since we were kids. He dealt with the fact that he wasn't gonna play, but it never occurred to any of us that he wouldn't get to be there. Even though Walt's more of a role player, he's a major contributor to our team spirit, personality, and swag. His absence might actually hurt us on the court."

Chance sighs again and begins to eat his food. Once done, he rinses off his plate, places it in the sink, and sits back down at the table.

"We fly out to Kentucky tomorrow. Ya'll coming the next day, right?" he asks.

"Yes, we'll be there, baby. Your father would have been so proud. What you and your teammates are doing is extraordinary. Just getting to this point is a huge accomplishment. But if you guys keep winning and go further in this tournament, then there's no telling what will follow."

"Thanks, Mom. Speaking of Pops. When he was trying to keep me from choosing Kentucky, he said they were the last team to recruit black players. That didn't really mean anything to me then. But now I can't help but think of the irony. Our first round games are gonna be played at Rupp Arena, named after the Kentucky coach who made it his mission to keep us out. Best believe our team is extra motivated to go in there and kick some ass!"

"Language, Son."

"My bad."

"Yes, baby. You know your grandfather was from Kentucky. And you know how passionate he was about college basketball. My whole life I heard about 'Adolph Rupp.' I can hear it in my head. Every college basketball season, 'Rupp was the last coach to integrate. I'm so glad that the '66 Texas Western team beat them in the national championship.' That's the exact statement he said every year. Boy, your grandfather would be so proud of you."

"I've never heard that story. Why did you never tell me?"

"I knew how much you wanted to go to Kentucky. As a mother, my only priority is to make sure you're happy and can succeed in life. Your father and I discussed it. I just wanted you to go where you wanted to go. Knowing how close you were to your grandfather, I didn't want to put his feelings on you. Your father respected that. As I respected him at least wanting you to know Kentucky was the last to integrate."

"So what was it about that Texas Western school? They had black players?"

"They were the first white college to start five black players in the championship game. They're now called UTEP, University of Texas at El Paso."

"Wow. So we're gonna be playing for Walt and Pops, and *I'm* also gonna be playing for Pop Pop. Texas Western might have been the first historically white school to have five black starters and beat Kentucky in an NCAA tournament, but we 'bout to be the first HBCU to beat they asses!"

"Again, language, Son!"

"My bad, Mom. My bad."

"Your father *and* grandfather would be so proud. Now, how's Teddy doing?"

"Oh, yes, thank you. Sorry, but with all this Walt being in a coma stuff I totally forgot to mention that Teddy's cancer is in remission!"

"Thank you, Jesus! Oh that's music to my ears."

"I know, right. Walt's mom was gonna tell him after the March Madness selection when they were by themselves. Obviously that didn't happen. When we were in the waiting room she told me. She can't wait to tell Walt once he wakes up. If anything can make Walt feel better and get him back healthy again, it will be hearing that."

Mrs. Knight sits across from her son, studies his face, and worries. His father died, and now possibly his best friend. As exciting as basketball is, there is no substitute for either.

34

"I WEAR #7"

The excitement at March Madness transcends the atmosphere of every game that had come before. The camaraderie and competitiveness in the crowd melds every race, gender, class, and religion. They are all "in it to win it," but also feel kinship in the journey taken to reach this point.

The Howard cheerleaders and band stir fans, young and old, to dance in place wherever they are, whether on their way to concessions or in their seats.

The sportscaster begins his telecast.

"Welcome, everyone, to today's first round matchup between the number fourteen seed Howard Bison and the number three seed West Virginia Mountaineers.

"Typically, the number fourteen seed versus the number three seed matchup is expected to be one-sided. But not this year, folks. Howard University has the number one ranked recruiting class in the nation, a first for an HBCU. Not surprisingly, they went undefeated in their MEAC conference. The team representing the MEAC normally would be a sixteen seed in the NCAA tournament. But as I already stated, this isn't a typical year. There are, however, some people who feel Howard's been disrespected by landing such a low seed. Not Howard though. Their team, thrilled to be a part of March Madness for the first time in over seventeen years, didn't argue that seeding one bit.

"I have to mention the growing controversy over the anthem. This is the first time we're seeing major headlines about kneeling outside of the NFL. Now that we're in March Madness, it will stand out even more if Howard continues to protest on such a big stage like this, with the nation watching. They've already faced adversity playing opponents at away games. Some of the backlash and responses have the feel of the 1968 Olympics when Tommie Smith and John Carlos each raised a black-gloved fist when the anthem was played. It has to be rough on these kids but, whether you agree with it or not, it's impressive that they continue to do it and stand up for what they believe in at such a young age.

"And here they come out for warmups. Well, folks, it looks like the Bison are definitely here to make a statement. Let's get a close-up of their shirts. They're wearing all black tee shirts that read, *"HBCUs Matter"* on the front, and the back appears to read, *"Walt/Strong."* For those of you who don't know, their teammate, Walt Williams, was shot in the head by a Caucasian man wearing a Make America Great Again hat in a targeted attack that can only be classified as a hate crime. I think it's safe to assume *"Walt/Strong"* is in honor of him and in support of his difficult recovery. I mean it's one thing to disagree with someone's message, but to try to kill somebody over it, my God. Our thoughts and prayers go out to Walt and his family."

"Let's now get ready for the singing of our national anthem," says the public announcer.

"It's interesting," says the sportscaster. "Although the Bison are becoming known for kneeling during the anthem, Walt Williams often sang it before their games. I attended one of them and I must say, even down on one knee where I imagine it's hard to engage the whole diaphragm, he sang it beautifully. Let's pray he can do so again soon. If the front of the team's tee-shirts is an indication of what's to come, I think we can expect that they *will* be taking a knee momentarily."

A young girl in her very early teens walks to the center of the court to sing the anthem. Predictably, the Howard basketball team, coaches, band, cheerleaders, and some students take a knee. The crowd, referees, and West Virginia team stand with hands on hearts or behind their backs. The jumbotron captures the Bison kneeling. At the end of the anthem, the polite applause for the singer is followed by boos, loud and long, directed at Howard University.

The game begins with captivating basketball action up and down the court. Chance struggles a bit, but Deon, Mike, and J.J. pick up the slack and keep Howard in the game. There is a time out. Coach Mac uses this opportunity to keep his players focused.

"All right, fellas. You guys are hanging in there. Chance, man, your head hasn't been in the game not one second of the sixteen minutes you've been on the court. I know you got Walt and the trial on your mind, but you gotta focus. I need you to focus! You hear me? We worked all season for this. This is one and done for you. If you lose now, your season's over. There's no coming back. You've gotta get it together and you gotta get it together now. Now! There are four minutes to go in the half and we're down five. Now come on, fellas! Let's go play like we know we can."

Chance continues to struggle and just can't seem to pull himself out of his slump, but his teammates are playing exceptional basketball. With fifty-five seconds left in the game, the scoreboard illuminates, *"Howard 87; West Virginia 86."* West Virginia gets the ball and the player who Chance is guarding takes him off the dribble and throws down a fierce one-handed slam dunk. The crowd erupts and Howard calls a timeout. The scoreboard now reads, *"Howard 87; West Virginia 88"* with 28 seconds left to play. Coach Mac's face glistens with sweat.

"We've been in this scenario at the end of a game before, fellas," he says. "We're fine. Chance, I know you're in a funk right now, but we're going to you for the win. So for this one moment, I need you to focus and free your mind from all the worry you got going on. All right, y'all, the play is Bison Blue for Chance. Chance, I got faith in you. Knock this shot down and let's move on to the next round."

"This is your team now," says Deon while slapping Chance on his rear end. "Lead us to the promised land, baby. You got this."

As the Bison are walking back onto the court, Coach Mac stops Chance and places his arm around his shoulders.

"I know how worried you are about Walt right now and understandably so," he whispers. "Remember how he told you to promise to get us to March Madness?"

"Yes, sir." Chance's eyes are moist.

"Walt is still in a coma. If we lose tonight he won't have the chance to see us play a March Madness game. So snap the fuck outta this funk and go win us this damn game!"

Coach Mac thinks he sees the fire return to Chance's eyes. He prays he is right. The inbound pass comes in to Chance and he dribbles the ball for a while before passing it to Deon. They run the play and the clock reads ten, nine, eight, and seven. The ball finds its way back to Chance. The clock ticks five, four, three and Chance drives right. He has a defender in his face. He steps back and releases the ball for a jump shot. The ball flies toward the basket. All eyes in the stadium follow its path in the air. Time seems to be moving in slow motion. Then they hear a sound as the ball enters the net. Swish. Pandemonium breaks out. The players run onto the court and jump onto Chance, inadvertently tackling him. The Mountaineers are in disbelief. The final score reads, *"Howard 89; West Virginia 88."* Chance smiles, thinking this one is for Walt.

After the game, Chance, Deon, and Coach Mac sit at a table to field questions from the press. They each have a table microphone in front of them. Coach Mac calls on a reporter in the first row.

"First, congratulations on an historic win for Howard University. Coach, how does it feel to have Howard's first ever NCAA tournament win?"

"It feels amazing. But we had particular goals and expectations this year. So while it feels great, and we appreciate the magnitude of the win, it's simply a first round win for us. At the risk of sounding cocky or over confident, we expected to win this game. This is no disrespect to West Virginia because everyone knows how great they are. But we have a special group of players here. We have NBA talent on this team. There's no reason we can't compete with the top schools in the nation. I don't want to start preaching or anything."

"Here we go," Chance says, rolling his eyes and throwing up his hands.

The room laughs.

"Don't worry, I'm just going to make one quick point. Howard University and many other HBCUs are losing money as we speak. The sports facilities at most HBCUs are not great. But this year Howard accomplished the impossible. We managed to get the top recruiting class in the nation. Look what has happened since. We won the MEAC. We made it to the NCAA tournament. We just won our first round game against a number three seed. We've received national media coverage and attention. We knocked off the then number five ranked Maryland on their home court. I've already had five- and four-star recruits reach out to me about coming here next year. Let that sink in for a moment.

Some of the most sought after, highly recruited, high school players in the nation are reaching out to *me*, the coach of an HBCU, to tell *me* that *they* want to play for Howard. Top recruits are starting to include HBCUs on their list of top contenders of where they want to play.

"This is the result of just one single season," Coach Mac says holding up his pointer finger for emphasis. "Imagine the ripple effects if this trend continues. HBCUs will benefit exponentially in exposure and revenue. Do you know what that means? Top facilities, top faculty, top research, and scholarships for kids who can't go to college any other way. We've had networks scrambling to add us to the national TV schedule this year. The NBA scouts have come to quite a few of our games. I want high school talent to realize the power and control that they hold as top-level athletes. I want them to realize that they have the power to stand up and create change. I want them to realize that it's okay to go against tradition. It's okay to create your own path, especially if it's for the greater good. The power is within *us*. This was the vision of Chance's father, God rest his soul.

"Okay. Okay. I've gone on enough about this for now. Today's about the players and today's victory. But since, as an HBCU coach, I don't usually have a national stage and platform, this was an opportunity I had to capitalize on. Thank you."

A few of the African American reporters in the room stand up and applaud. Chance leans forward into his microphone.

"Great point, Coach, and I would like to add something. We often choose schools that don't represent us. But as you can see we have other options. But a perfect example is who we play next. The defending national champs. As you all know, UVA is where the white nationalists held that hateful rally in 2017, only about two and a half years ago. So I ask myself, as an African American, why would I want to attend a school that would allow that type of rally to take place on their campus?" Staring at the reporters, he pauses as he takes a moment to choose his next words.

"And not just that. Police are killing unarmed black men. My *own* father became one of the victims. I wear number seven on my jersey in solidarity with Colin Kaepernick. Kaep led his team to play in a Super Bowl and now that he's decided to take a stand against all this hate toward black people and police killings of black people, he's being punished; black-balled by the entire league. And in a country that's supposed to, and should, represent freedom and equality for all. This is a shame. A flat out travesty! A black man standing up for the rights and lives of other black people is considered wrong?

"You *know* why that is. You *know* the reason he's blackballed. The people making the decisions to hire him don't look like him. Not one of the NFL owners looks like him or can relate to what he's fighting for. The Commissioner of the League doesn't look like him. There are no black people in any power to do anything about that. That's part of the reason why I decided to attend an HBCU. I knew I wouldn't have to worry about repercussions for kneeling. For taking a stand. The MEAC's president and people in power all look like me. They can relate to me. They understand the struggle. That's why I want all top black high school athletes to hear this press conference and understand what I'm saying. Believe me, I know firsthand how scary it is to do something different. But understand, we have the power to create change. We need to realize that. And not just in sports. In business. In life.

"So back to my point, why would I, as a young black athlete, go to UVA knowing it allowed what was essentially a hate rally to be held on its campus? Do you realize that these top black athletes playing for Virginia and Florida, which also sanctioned a hate rally on its campus, are generating tremendous revenue for these schools?

"Virginia just won the national title last year for crying out loud. One of their key starters was an African American freshman four-star recruit. He was the number four NBA draft pick. He could have gone to an HBCU but didn't. He chose Virginia. I'll be dammed if I'm gonna use my talent to generate money for a university that allows hate to be preached on its campus grounds. Hell no! Oh, and I forgot about Mississippi. Ole Miss allowed confederate celebration rallies on its campus. Why are you, as a black athlete, contributing to generating money and athletic success and prestige for universities that allow these rallies to take place?"

A smattering of applause interrupts Chance but encourages him to continue.

"As far as I'm concerned, every black athlete at Florida, Virginia, and Old Miss should've protested immediately. They should've taken a stand right away, without hesitation. And transferring should be something they consider. I know we've gotten way off topic but these issues need to be addressed. Like what Coach was saying, this is a national platform. What better place to discuss them than right here, right now? I can guarantee you there are thousands of high school black athletes watching this press conference. I would call that mission accomplished."

More black reporters in the room stand up and applaud. After digesting all that was said by Coach Mac and Chance, a local reporter poses a question.

"I can imagine that some big universities might take offense to the implication that they're making money on the backs of black athletes, but may not value the lives of black people in general, or respect their black athletes enough to disallow demonstrations of freedom of speech on their campus. One can argue that they honor the laws of the land and that doesn't mean that they endorse the beliefs of demonstrators, but rather they believe in the meaning behind the national anthem and First Amendment. What would you say to those universities?"

Chance does not get a full word out before Deon interrupts to answer the question.

"We appreciate the question. Look, this isn't really about those schools. They're not the focus. Black lives are the focus. Whether it's trying to stay alive when getting pulled over by the cops, or trying to make sure we have the opportunity to go to college and get a great education with state-of-the-art educational tools, it's about bettering ourselves. We're not saying black athletes can't go there. We're not implying big schools hate their black students or don't care about them or never have their interests in mind. But what we're saying is that black athletes have choices.

"Think outside the box. And know that whatever choice is made, there's a consequence. Sometimes the consequences are positive, sometimes they're negative, and sometimes they're both. I'm thankful that Chance Knight, Dink Johnson, Maximus Miller, Mike Jones, and Jason Jacks decided that their community, people who look like them, their well-being as a whole, is greater than each of their individual aspirations.

"They came here, to Howard, willing to potentially sacrifice the full potential of their basketball futures for a greater purpose. And a special shout out to Bobby Banks, who is in this with us. I'm thankful. Our basketball program is thankful. Our entire university is thankful. In just this one year, through games with top schools and growing media attention, we've already increased, significantly, the revenue coming into our school over what has come in during past years. And guess what, their futures haven't suffered. You *can* go outside the box and prosper. So with all due respect, I say to those schools, this time it isn't about you. It's about us."

Coach Mac and Chance look at Deon, and then at each other and smile. Back at home, next day local headlines read:

"Bison Upset Mountaineers to Advance to March Madness 2nd Round"
"Number 14 Seed Howard Bison Face #9 Seed Virginia Cavaliers"

"Howard Bison Basketball Office Receives Death
   Threats"
"Howard University Basketball Star Calls Out Black
   Players at UVA, Their Next Opponent"

The second round matchup between the Howard Bison and the Virginia Cavaliers is set to begin. Both teams are on the court warming up.

"Greetings, folks," says the sportscaster. "We're coming to you live from Lexington, Kentucky, for an unexpected second round matchup between the number fourteen seed Howard Bison and the number nine seed Virginia Cavaliers."

"Howard's obviously the surprise of the tournament. They're playing with house money at this point. No one, except them apparently, expected them to make it this far. They've looked impressive all year and they're making people believers. Love them or hate them, since they've definitely stirred up some controversy, you can't deny their shockingly impressive performance and achievements.

"As far as the Cavaliers, this isn't the same team that won the national championship last year. They lost three key players to the NBA and have had some struggles ever since, especially in the first half of the season. But I have to admit, they did finish the season pretty strong. They've only lost seven games and that's rather impressive considering the change to their starting five and the toughness of their ACC conference.

"Howard and controversy have been pretty synonymous this season. It isn't surprising that there's been some additional controversy leading up to this game as a result of comments that Bison star Chance Knight made about African American players at UVA, Florida, and Old Miss. The first round postgame press conference is where it all went down.

"As a matter of fact, I'm sure you heard it, when Howard came out onto the floor tonight they were greeted with some boos. Typically, the underdog Cinderella team gets a lot of love and support from the crowds during March Madness. But after some of the things that were said in the press conference, it seems that Howard has ruffled a few more feathers. The fact that we're in the South probably doesn't help their cause either. This makes tonight's matchup all that more interesting. This game just might get personal. We'll continue in just a moment. Let's pause briefly for the singing of "The Star Spangled Banner.""

Everyone takes their positions. Fans have their hats off and their hands on hearts. The Virginia Cavaliers are all standing. The Howard contingent takes a knee. In sudden movements, two of the African American players on Virginia's team drop to one knee. Chance notices. Chance looks over to Coach Mac who also notices. Coach and player take in the moment. Game action begins. The final scoreboard reflects a thriller: *"Howard 77; Virginia 72."*

"Wow, what a game!" the sportscaster screams. "These Bison are for real. I did *not* expect to be saying this, but the Howard University Bison have put on a stellar performance and are moving on to the Sweet Sixteen! The Bison are going to the Sweet Sixteen! This is absolutely incredible! There's never been a MEAC team to make it out of the second round. In the past, Coppin State, Hampton, and Norfolk State each won a first round game only to lose in the second. Howard has made history tonight!

"The other thing that came out of tonight that I'm sure is trending right now is the fact that two of the Virginia Cavaliers' African American players kneeled during the anthem. Virginia has eight African American players. The fact that any kneeled is major. Especially coming off the heels of what Chance Knight said in his postgame press conference. As I said at the start of the game, I thought it might get personal. I'm sure tonight's postgame press conferences are going to be must see TV. That's all from here for now, folks. Congratulations to the Howard Bison who are moving on to the Sweet Sixteen!"

The cameraman cuts away from the sportscaster and back to the court. The Howard Bison are approaching the tunnel that leads out of the gymnasium to the locker room. As they approach, they are jumping and chanting, "Sweet Sixteen! Sweet Sixteen! Sweet Sixteen!"

"We goin' to the Sweet Sixteen y'all!" shouts Chance as they disappear from view.

35 STAY WOKE

The Howard Bison arrive on campus. They are welcomed by a swarming crowd of students, fans, and media. The players high-five admirers as they make their way through the thousands of supporters. They're glad to be home.

The next day, the team stands outside of Walt's hospital room peering through the glass window for a glimpse of their friend. He is still in a coma. Chance walks inside the room and hands Mrs. Williams Walt's Sweet Sixteen shirt. They share a tender embrace.

"Congratulations, Chance. I'm really proud of you. Walt will love this shirt. I know he'll wake up soon and want to wear it as soon as he sees it. He'll wake up soon. He will. I know it."

Chance rests his hand on Mrs. Williams' shoulder as she sits in the mint green recliner. He walks over to Walt's bed and holds his hand. He breaks down. He does not care who sees him. One by one, the teammates file in and out of Walt's room to wish him well in hopes that he can hear them and it will make a difference.

Five days later the Bison are playing Villanova during their Sweet Sixteen matchup. The Bison are on fire. The final score reads, *"Howard 90; Villanova 86."*

Howard's confidence is growing with every victory. Two days later, in the Elite Eight game against University of Tennessee, the Bison continue to put on a convincing performance. They close the game out with eighty-eight points to Tennessee's seventy-five. Chance finishes with thirty-seven points and thirteen rebounds. He shows game after game why he was the number one recruit. The teammates are presented ceremonially with Final Four tee shirts. They joke that they will never take them off.

The next day, college basketball sports fans can't believe the headlines and big schools take note:

"UVA Shocker: Two Players Announce Intent to Transfer to HBCUs"

"The Nation's #3-Ranked High School Point Guard Picks Florida A&M"

"Top Recruit Chooses Hampton University over University of Virginia"

"#14 Seed Howard Bison to Play #1 Seed Michigan State in NCAA Final Four"

Chance and Big Dink return home for a brief trip. Although coming home for them is usually welcomed, this trip is different. They are anxious. They are scared. They do not feel ready or that they could ever be. Mrs. Knight drives them to the courthouse in Upper Marlboro, Maryland, in the early morning. Their mood is sullen as they silently review the events of the afternoon when Coach Knight was slain. The prosecutor had advised them that Chance will testify first.

They arrive at the courthouse and park. They clear through the metal detectors and the prosecutor is waiting for them. They follow her to a waiting room.

"The trial is set to resume today in thirty minutes, but I don't know how long it will be until you're called to the stand," says the prosecutor. "We need to finish direct examination of a witness—carryover from yesterday. Chance, Dink, you'll stay here until you're called. Chance, again, you'll be called first, and then Dink. April, you can come with me into the courtroom."

Chance, Big Dink, and Mrs. Knight acknowledge the instructions. The prosecutor makes her way to the courtroom with Mrs. Knight by her side.

Sixty-four quiet minutes pass by. A bailiff enters the room and lets Chance know that it is time. Chance follows him down a long corridor, around a corner, and down another long corridor until they reach two oversized doors. They stand there. A few minutes pass by and then the doors open. Chance feels sick to his stomach. He takes a deep breath and enters the courtroom. The doors close behind him.

On the way home, both boys are filled with self-doubt as to how they answered the defense attorney's rapid fire questions on cross-examination. Mrs. Knight assures them that they rose to the occasion.

Meanwhile at the hospital, Walt's eyes finally open. His mother is crying out and thanking God. Repeatedly. She is smothering him with gentle kisses as the nurses run in. The weight that has been holding her down and keeping her stuck is instantly lifted. Her baby is awake.

36 REDEMPTION

The night Coach Mac has dared to dream of is finally here. He peers out of the window of the team's bus and sees Mercedes Benz Arena in Atlanta for the first time. Both its structural beauty and its significance for these young men overwhelm him. A billboard sized sign greets all who arrive, *"Welcome to The Final Four."* Coach Mac thinks of Chance and his great talent, and he knows, as his coach, he has not failed him. He is the proudest he has ever been of anyone.

Walt, wearing his Final Four shirt, is alert in his hospital room while watching the pregame coverage on the small screen television. His brother and mother sit with him. He sees his team wearing their all black HBCUs Matter shirts with "WaltStrong" printed on the back.

"You see, Son, you *are* there after all." Walt's mom squeezes his hand.

Howard and Michigan State players are wrapping up their warmups. After a display of crowd-arousing dunks by Michigan State, warmups conclude. The players line up for the national anthem. The Howard players and coaching staff kneel. The cheerleaders and band members kneel. Many of the Howard fans in the crowd kneel. Once the anthem is over, the teams come together at half court for the jump ball. The ball goes up and the action starts.

The final buzzer of the game sounds. It is over. Chance drops to his knees and then lies on the basketball court crying hard, more emotional and vulnerable than ever. He played his heart out and has nothing left to give. He desperately wants his father. Big Dink bends down, picks him up, and lifts him in an embrace. Everyone around him is celebrating and screaming his name. The scoreboard reflects a hard fought battle, *"Howard 95; Michigan State 92."* Howard, having lost to Michigan State earlier in the regular season, feels redeemed. But more importantly, they will play for the national title on Monday night.

Walt, Teddy, and their mother are celebrating in Walt's hospital room.

"They did it!" shouts Walt. "They actually did it! This is absolutely incredible!"

Walt pumps his fists in the air as Teddy jumps up and down. Their revelry is interrupted when the phone rings.

"Who in the world is calling at this time of night?"

"Mom, you act like I'm ten years old or something."

"Whatever."

Walt picks up his phone and realizes it is a video call. His eyes light up. Chance and the rest of the team are calling Walt from center court mid-celebration.

"Oh, snap, it's Chance and the fellas," says Walt as he presses "Accept."

"I told you, boy!" Chance screams over the shoutouts to Walt from his teammates in the background. "We made it to the championship and we did it all for you, bro!"

"Hell yeah, bro."

An on-air reporter and her cameraman approach Chance. He raises his phone to show Walt in his hospital bed with his Final Four shirt on.

"Chance, who are you chatting with in the middle of celebrating this monumental win?"

"Our team leader, Walt Williams. I wanna make sure he's a part of this celebration, but our biggest celebration is that he's outta his coma. We can't enjoy this without him. Say hi, Walt."

The cameraman zooms in on Chance's phone.

"We did it! Howard's here to stay! Come here, Teddy, Mom."

Mrs. Williams hurriedly scrambles to fix her hair.

"Look, Mom. We're on TV," says Teddy.

When they see themselves, they giggle. The reporter senses that Walt's heartwarming story will resonate with her viewers.

"Well, hello to you and your lovely family," she says. "So glad you all are able to join us. Walt, the entire network wishes you a speedy recovery. Will you be able to attend the championship game Monday night?"

"Thank you so much. I truly appreciate that. Unfortunately, I won't be leaving the hospital by then, but I'll be watching front and center from here."

"Damn, man. Well, hell, we'll just video call you again then," says Chance.

"Now that sounds like a plan," says the reporter. "Congratulations to both of you and good luck on Monday."

Chance returns his full attention to Walt.

"We did it, boy. I told you. We got a chance to be national champions, bro."

"Hell, yeah. We did it, man. Promise you'll bring that trophy home to me?"

"Man, you know I got you."

Walt smiles.

"Man, get off the phone and go celebrate right, bro. I love you."

"Love you, too, man. Get well."

Chance ends the call, looks over to where everyone is celebrating, and takes it all in. He looks up to the ceiling with a big smile and nods.

"Thanks, Pops."

The Howard Bison are at Mercedes Benz Arena for practice the day before the championship game. The team huddles around Coach Mac at center court.

"This is it, fellas. We've accomplished just about every goal we set out to accomplish this year. You put Howard basketball on the national map. You put HBCUs on the national map. You worked hard and believed in yourselves. We've knocked off the best teams in the nation. And you did it while protesting injustice. You weren't afraid to take a stand.

"Chance, you and your teammates are living your father's vision. He had faith that this was achievable. We still have one game left. We still have one more goal to achieve.

"Y'all are about to play the undefeated number one ranked team in the land. The Kentucky Wildcats. Be aware, they're gonna come after Chance. They're gonna come after him because he's our leading scorer. But more than that, this game is gonna be personal for them. They had a verbal commitment before he changed his mind—albeit for good reason, that's not gonna matter to them. They're using that as bulletin board material, fellas. But remember, they're ranked number one only until they're beaten by the real number one. I know we can beat this team. We know we can beat this team. But we're gonna have to play the best ball we've ever played.

"I need y'all extremely focused as we go through practice today. Let's go out here and get our reps in and then get back to the hotel and rest up for tomorrow. Everybody—every one of you—bring it in. National Champs on three. One, two, three. National Champs!"

Chance wakes the next morning and stares out of his window. He is buoyed by the spectacular sunrise over the Atlanta skyline. He turns his head and thinks the view next to him is even more spectacular.

"Morning, Chance," says Kia.

"Morning, Mo County."

"You gonna get in trouble for sneaking me in here last night after curfew?"

"Seriously? What they gonna do? Suspend me for the championship game?"

They laugh.

"I don't think so. But you know they do say sex the night before or the day of a game is bad for you," he adds.

"Well shoot, if that was the case, you would've had a terrible season."

"That's a great point."

Chance laughs.

"But this is the national championship. Maybe we should play this one safe," he says.

"We had sex last night, though."

"Yeah, can't do nuthin' 'bout that. But we can be smart today. At least until after the game."

Kia starts to kiss Chance's chest.

"Yeah, you're probably right," she says. She then aims her kisses a little bit lower on Chance's stomach.

"See now you playin', girl."

"Do they say anything about . . ."

Kia's head dips under the covers as she slides down below Chance's belly button.

"Naw, there ain't never no restrictions on some good mornin' head. That's okay 24/7 no matter what."

Kia sticks her head out the covers. "Of course you would say that."

They share a laugh as Kia's head disappears again.

"Damn, baby girl," Chance moans as he closes his eyes.

Coach Mac sits on the couch in his hotel room and punches in the correct channel number on the remote. His favorite host is speaking.

"Welcome to *Sports Highlight Center*, folks," says the host. "Today is Championship Monday. We have the number fourteen seed underdog, the *Cinderella* team, Howard Bison, facing off against the mighty undefeated number one seed, and overall number one ranked team in the country, Kentucky Wildcats. Vegas has Kentucky as a seventeen-point favorite. That's the highest spread in history for a national championship game. Not too many people are giving the Bison any chance of winning. Howard has had an historic season. But most think it ends tonight. Some people consider this Kentucky Wildcat team to arguably be one of the greatest college basketball teams ever assembled. I don't know folks. Maybe those predictions are right, and they probably are, but the Bison have proven you just can't ever count them out."

He pauses and Coach Mac predicts what is coming next.

"Something else that will be a hot topic tonight is the national anthem. Howard's received a lot of backlash this year for kneeling in support of Colin Kaepernick and raising awareness for perceived social injustice. Specifically, police killing unarmed African

Americans. The Howard Bison's star player, Chance Knight, as many of you know by now, lost his father at the hands of police. Coincidently, the verdict for the police officer who killed his father may actually come today. The jury's been out for several days. No matter what the outcome, this has to be rough on Chance, who, by the way, many are comparing to LeBron James. He's going to have to bring his LeBron game tonight for this team to have a shot at beating Kentucky."

37 JUDGEMENT DAY

The Howard Bison are eating brunch at an Atlanta soul food restaurant frequented by locals. Bird gets a lot of teasing as he samples cheese grits for the first time.

"Chance, call Walt so we can get some encouragement from him before the big game tonight," says Coach Mac.

"Bet."

Chance pulls out his phone and tries to reach Walt on a video call. The phone rings and rings.

"He isn't answering, Coach."

"Okay, message him to hit us back when he can."

"All right, I'll text him now."

The players are diving into the food in front of them with abandon. Piles of thick, crispy bacon, bowls of cheesy grits, platters of moist scrambled eggs mixed with cheddar cheese, plates of crunchy on the outside and soft on the inside scrapple, are devoured in short order. They are all enjoying every moment and every bite as they try to divert their focus from the nerves dancing deep within the pit of their stomachs. The volume of the wall-mounted television facing their table competes with the restaurant chatter. A banner appears on the screen and reads, *"Breaking News."* The restaurant owner turns up the volume as a reporter with microphone in hand appears.

"A verdict has been reached in the trial of Officer Sean Parker who is charged with killing Craig Knight, father and former AAU basketball coach of star collegiate athlete Chance Knight," says the reporter, sounding breathless. Heads turn quickly to the screen and conversations cease. The table goes eerily silent for a moment.

"Give that mutha fucka life," Big Dink yells out.

"Fuck that. Give that bastard the death penalty," shouts Mad Max.

Chance places his hands in the prayer position as he holds his breath. With the microphone in her right hand, the reporter holds her left hand to her earbud as she listens to the verdict. She winces and looks into the camera.

"The jury has found Officer Sean Parker *not* guilty in the death of Craig Knight. Again, Officer Sean

Parker has been found *not* guilty. He'll walk free on *all* charges. This news will come as quite a surprise to many pundits who were confident that he would be found *guilty*. The only question in their minds was the length of his sentence.

"Officer Parker's defense team argued that preexisting conditions caused Craig Knight to go into cardiac arrest, leading to his death; and that it was not caused by the neck restraint, *their* term, which they insisted adhered to police policy. They claimed the officer, therefore, could not be held accountable. On the other hand, the prosecutor argued that had it not been for excessive force, and a deadly chokehold, Coach Knight would still be alive. The jury apparently agreed with the defense. A not guilty verdict is bound to be, quite frankly, shocking to the many people following this case."

Chance scoots his chair back from the table, drops his head down in his lap, and starts rocking back and forth in anger and disbelief.

"Are you fuckin' kiddin' me?" yells Big Dink. "That officer is a murderer! I saw the chokehold with my own eyes. Coach Knight couldn't breathe!"

Video of Officer Parker hugging his lawyers and family seem to jump off of the screen. Members of Chance's extended family are pictured solemnly exiting the courthouse. Mrs. Knight elected to come to the championship game to support her son instead of staying in town waiting for a possible verdict. While she hoped the verdict would not be delivered until their return, she could not miss this moment for her son. Coach Mac stands up, walks over, and sits next to Chance in a futile attempt to console him.

That night, the team quietly stares out of the bus window en route to the biggest game of their young lives. The not guilty verdict has sparked immediate outrage in cities across the country. Riots have broken out in Washington, DC, and Capitol Heights, Maryland, where the killing occurred. The unrest has swiftly spread to Los Angeles, New York, Chicago, and Atlanta. Many of the protestors are loyal fans of Chance, who has become a rising hero in the black community.

Chance sees smoke in the distance. A CNN update alerts on his phone. Stores are on fire in Atlanta and police are in riot gear. The Mayor considers cancelling tonight's game but decides against it. The police heavily secure a five-mile perimeter around the stadium. The bus is waived through the security checkpoint.

Inside the locker room, the players are sitting down trying to get their heads right for the game.

"Chance, did Walt ever call or text back?" asks Coach Mac.

"No, sir."

"Okay. We'll make sure to call him after the game."

Coach Mac looks around the room at the players' faces and has his first pangs of doubt. Maybe it is not even fair to have Chance play tonight. He sits with this thought for a moment. It passes.

"All right, fellas. Today's been extremely rough. We all received terrible news we weren't expecting. Our community is as outraged as we are. There's nothing we can do about the verdict now. I know the timing couldn't be worse, but we gotta focus on what's in front of us. For this moment right now, we're doing what Coach Knight would want us to do. I know many of y'all didn't know him, but you know his story. This was his dream and now it's ours. As hard as it is, we have to stay focused and remember our final goal. We've worked too hard and come too far to not see it through." Coach Knight is speaking as much to himself as he is to them.

"We probably won't all be together next year," he says. "Some of y'all will be playing in the NBA. Chance, you figured you'd be here tonight if you went to Kentucky. You walked away from that and did what you knew was right and you got here anyway. Think about that. We're your family. And all that anger that's inside you right now needs to be gathered up and used as fuel. Take that shit out on Kentucky tonight. Let's turn that negative energy into fuel to accomplish something positive. For Howard. For our HBCUs. For us. One game left, fellas. This is it. No one outside this room is givin' you a chance. We've got nothing to lose so play like it. Go out here and play like you know how to play. Bring all you've got and leave it all on the court. Everybody bring it in. Let's go with champions on three. One, two, three. Champions!"

The locker room door opens and the Bison walk out into the hallway. The Kentucky Wildcats, clapping and chanting, walk by with well-earned swag. The Bison recognize Montae Mills, a six-foot, nine-inch sophomore shooting guard from Oakland, California. Montae, averaging thirty points per game, is the second leading scorer in the nation. Following Mills is the Shaquille O'Neal-sized Pat Perry, a seven-foot, two-inch sophomore center from Detroit, Michigan. He is the leading rebounder and shot blocker in the NCAA, just ahead of Mike Jones. Pat is walking beside Lamont Jackson, a six-foot, six-inch freshman point guard from Baltimore, Maryland. Lamont was the number two ranked player coming out of high school behind Chance.

The Kentucky Wildcats gradually disappear around the corner. The Howard Bison, trying not to be in awe of the Kentucky team, or intimidated by the power of their presence, remain standing in the hallway.

Coach Mac surveys the faces of his team. He gives them his final words of encouragement before they take to the court.

"One final goal, one final game, and one final victory. Let's go!" he says.

They run out onto the court with hearts still heavy, but are soon swept up in the echo chambers of screams and clapping reverberating from every corner of the stadium. For the Howard community in the building tonight, the entire scenario is surreal. Chance's black warm up shirt features a picture of Coach Knight's face on the front, under "RIP" in white lettering. The back of the shirt again reads, *"Walt/Strong."* Every Howard player wears the same.

The television sportscaster welcomes the viewing audience to the national championship game.

"We have a dandy tonight," says the sportscaster, voice brimming with excitement. "On one end, we have the undefeated Kentucky Wildcats. They've held on to their number one ranking the entire season. They have Montae Mills, the nation's second leading scorer, averaging thirty points per game. Montae was also just named Southeastern Conference Player of the Year.

"On the other side of the court, we have the Cinderella story of the tournament. The number fourteen seed Howard Bison have been on a magical run all season long. This is Howard's first ever appearance in the national championship, and their first appearance in March Madness in over seventeen years. Howard has Chance Knight. Chance is averaging thirty-three points and eight rebounds per game. He is MEAC Player of the Year and the favorite to win the Naismith Trophy for national player of the year. This young man is a beast and leads the Super Seven for Howard.

"Most of you have heard that Chance's father, Craig Knight, but referred to by those closest to him as Coach Knight, was killed at the hands of police," says the sportscaster. His voice takes on a more somber tone. "That killing is what led Chance and several other top recruits to come to Howard. Coincidentally, today the jury found the police officer on trial for his killing not guilty. As I am sure you all know, riots have broken out in major cities, including here in Atlanta. I'm not making any judgements, but many people are outraged. I can only imagine what Chance is going through. And to get the news hours before playing the biggest game of your life . . . you have to feel for the kid. He witnessed his father's death and now he has to deal with the verdict and fallout happening not far from this very arena. Our thoughts and prayers are with him and his family.

"Kentucky's going to come after Chance hard though," says the sportscaster returning to his normal cadence. "There's some bad blood here on their end. As we keep reporting, Chance verbally committed to Kentucky but then signed with Howard, his father's alma mater. Kentucky's Lamont Jackson was ranked the number two rated high school recruit behind Chance. Lamont still to this day feels that he was the best player and his ranking should've reflected that. He wants to go out here tonight and prove it.

"Let's hope for a battle, folks. Kentucky's unbeaten and Howard's only lost twice all year, although they played mostly very different opponents. Kentucky is clearly the favorite, but this still has the potential to be a nail-biter. You just can't put anything past the Bison.

"Ya know, besides the anticipated revenge by Kentucky on Howard, specifically Chance, another big topic of this tournament has been the anthem protest. There have been a frenzy of headlines all tournament long about Howard kneeling during the anthem. Some say it's a peaceful protest, but others see it as a hateful action. The Bison have fielded a lot of criticism and taunts, but have stayed true to their cause. One would think that everyone will understand Chance kneeling tonight. Speaking of the anthem, let's listen to the announcer introduce the singer of the "Star Spangled Banner."

"Now to sing the national anthem . . . " Predictably, the Howard basketball team and coaches take a knee. " . . . please welcome Howard University basketball player Walt Williams!"

To everyone's shock, Walt, with assistance, walks slowly out onto the court wearing the same Coach Knight tee shirt as the players. Chance looks like he has just seen a ghost. Although it is not immediately apparent, he is beyond elated.

"You knew about this?" Chance asks, looking over at Coach Mac.

Coach Mac smiles and nods. Walt takes a knee and serenades a captivated audience with the "Star Spangled Banner." Chance and Coach Mac, transfixed by the power and beauty of his performance, are frozen in place. Walt finishes to roaring applause, although some in the audience are confused as to how they feel. They love the rendition but do not appreciate it being performed on one knee. The NCAA officials, knowing Walt takes a knee, have made a statement by allowing him to sing the anthem. The Howard players rise to their feet and join the majority of the crowd in their ovation.

Chance runs to Walt and gives him an emotional embrace before helping him to the bench. They are both overwhelmed with mutual admiration and the magic of the moment.

"All right, man," Walt says. "Enough of this mushy shit. Look, bro," he says as he puts a hand on each of Chance's shoulders. I'm so sorry about the verdict, and the fact that it happened today. But Kentucky's the last obstacle. That team over there is the only thing stoppin' you from fulfillin' his dream. His vision. Now what you gonna do about it? The time is right now, Chance. Now! Right now, bro! You gotta push the heartache away for the next forty minutes of game time."

Walt daps up Chance but knows full well the burden and sadness he is carrying tonight of all nights. The irony is not lost on Walt.

Chance stares at the Kentucky players. He focuses first on Montae Mills and then on Lamont Jackson. He looks over to where he knows his mom, sister, and Kia are sitting. Mrs. Williams and Teddy are next to them. Chance closes his eyes and at that very moment everything goes black.

The game begins. Four seconds later, the crowd hears a thunderous bang from a dunk by Chance. On the very next play, Chance drains a three-pointer. Walt is cheering from the bench. He will not be playing but wears his uniform and warmups.

Later in the first half, Montae dribbles down the court as Chance guards him. Montae executes a crossover move, takes a step back, and releases a three-pointer. He drains it. Coach Mac calls a timeout. Montae and Lamont chest bump each other and then run back to the Kentucky bench celebrating. The scoreboard reads, *"Kentucky 18; Howard 12."*

"All right, fellas. Let's settle down. We don't want them building momentum going into halftime. Let's get back out there and do what we do best."

The crowd's heads swivel with the fast back and forth play. Lamont brings the ball up the court. The clock winds down to twelve seconds, eleven, ten. Lamont, with basketball under hand, drives right. He spins off of a defender and finds the open lane. He drives and then soars over Big Dink's head, slamming down a powerful dunk. Lamont posturizes Big Dink and the stadium is going crazy. The Kentucky players are celebrating. Coach Mac puts his hands over his face in disbelief. The scoreboard reads, *"Kentucky 45; Howard 35."*

The Bison sit quietly in the locker room during halftime as they wait for Coach Mac, who is making a quick pit stop. Walt is caught off guard by their dejected looks and downtrodden vibes.

"Come on, fellas. Don't look so down," he says.

Coach Mac walks in unnoticed as Walt is talking.

"You're only down by ten points to an undefeated team. I see that as a cup half full. This team ran through their opponents all tournament. But we're only down by ten. We're right there. Now lift your fuckin' chins up and get some swag in your game for this second half. I didn't get out of my sick bed and come all the way up here to see my boys give in."

"Now y'all mutha fuckas wanted me here," he says. "Well I'm here. I showed up for you. Now go show up for me! Lord knows all the trials and tribulations I've been through this year. I could've given up plenty of times. But I picked my chin up and fought through it all. Just what y'all told me to do. I'm out of my coma and am now finally out of the hospital, early, just to come all this way to be here with y'all. My team. My fam. You can understand after all that why I'm ready to fuckin' celebrate. I want to celebrate with y'all and I want to celebrate tonight, dammit! Don't tell me y'all gonna deny me that? Huh? I can't hear you. Y'all gonna deny me that?"

"Fuck no!" Chance shouts.

"Hell naw, we got you, son," says Big Dink.

"But, Walt?" asks Chance.

"Yeah?"

"You said you came all the way up here. You meant all the way down here. We're in Georgia."

"Man, shut up Einstein. Not everybody has a 4.0 G.P.A. like you. You knew what da fuck I meant, fool."

Walt and Chance laugh.

Coach Mac shows himself.

"Well, Walt said it perfectly," he says. "I don't have much to add except if you're gonna do it, then you gotta do it now! There *is* no tomorrow! One more half of basketball to determine it all! Y'all waited your entire life for this one shining moment. This very moment is what y'all dreamed about. It's right here for the fuckin' takin'. Success is when opportunity meets preparation. You guys are prepared and the opportunity is right out there on that court for you. Now what you gonna do?

"Let's go!" screams Chance. The excitement in his voice, clenched fist, and repeated jumps up and down evidence how pumped up he is.

"Don't tell me. Show me."

Over the next few minutes, the crowd witnesses what will certainly become the top highlight plays of

404

the entire tournament, sure to be played repeatedly on every sports recap show.

The Kentucky players have lost their swagger. The Howard players, on the other hand, have found a momentum that cannot be tamed. The jumbotron above the center of the court reflects the score, *"Howard 72; Kentucky 71"* with 22 seconds left in the game. Mrs. Knight, Amaia, and Kia are on the edge of their seats. Amaia can barely look.

The Kentucky coach is screaming at his players and calls time out.

"Are you fuckin' kidding me? You let this team come all the way back and take the fuckin' lead?"

Howard is in their team huddle.

"All right, fellas, we're all out of timeouts," says Coach Mac. "We're up by one and they have the ball. If they score here, then this is the play that I want us to run." He draws the play on his dry erase clipboard. "Chance, the entire stadium thinks you'll be getting the ball for the last shot."

Meanwhile, back in Kentucky's huddle, Montae confidently assures his teammates.

"Man I got this y'all," he says. "This shot goin' down for the ball game. Game over."

"If possible, try not to leave them time to get another shot up after you drain yours," says the Kentucky Coach.

"Done."

"All right. Everyone bring it in. Undefeated on three. One, two, three. Undefeated!"

A Kentucky fan in the first row behind the team bench hears the team shout, "Undefeated," and begins chanting it. The chant quickly grows louder as nearby fans join in and spreads throughout the stadium.

"You hear that?" Coach Mac asks rhetorically. "Let that be your fuel. Them going undefeated isn't an option. Go out there and bring this home. Bring it home on three. One, two, three. Bring it home!"

Both teams get up and head back onto the court for the final twenty-two seconds. The inbound pass comes in to Montae. He dribbles the ball across half court. Chance is guarding him.

"Sorry, freshman, but I'm 'bout to end all your dreams right here," says Montae.

"Not today, playa."

The clock counts down—eleven, ten—and then Montae takes two dribbles right. He surprises Chance with a crossover move. Chance slips and falls. Montae drives toward the basket and Deon slides over to guard him. Montae is beginning a spin move on Deon as Chance gets back on his feet. Montae completes the spin. He is now free for a short distance pull up jumper. Chance runs toward him. Montae goes up for the shot and releases the ball. Chance flies out of nowhere—at least it seems that way to Montae—and swats the ball into the stands right as the game buzzer sounds.

"Game over! Game over! Game over!" screams the sportscaster. "Chance blocked the shot to win the game for Howard! I can't believe I'm saying this but Howard University has just won the national title!"

Howard fans storm the court. The team tackles Chance and piles on top of him. Confetti falls from the rafters. The assistant coaches embrace Coach Mac. Mrs. Knight, Amaia, and Kia are jumping up and down. Mrs. Williams, Tasha, and Teddy are doing the same. The mothers embrace and both families make their way onto the court.

"You heard me correctly, folks." says the sportscaster. "Howard University, an HBCU, is the National Collegiate Athletic Association National Champion. This is the first time ever that an HBCU has competed in or won a national title. You're witnessing history. Chance Knight has been named tournament MVP. He finished tonight's game with thirty-four points and twelve rebounds to go along with ten assists. A triple double. Looks like the powerhouse schools might be in for a rude awakening."

After the awarding of the trophies, Chance and Coach Mac embrace. Walt, with his broad smile, watches. Chance spots him. They both stand there for a moment, about twenty feet apart, staring at each other. Chance points at Walt and then Walt points back. They both simultaneously walk over to each other and hug.

"You did it, bro," says Walt. "You fuckin' did it."

"Naw, man. We did it. We did it, bro!"

Chance puts his arm around Walt and then the rest of the team comes over, lifts Walt, and carefully positions him on a couple of teammates' shoulders. Bird hands Walt the trophy. Walt smiles and raises it in the air with both hands as the crowd goes berserk. The next day, that picture graces the cover of newspapers across the nation.

PAST, PRESENT, FUTURE

Chance and Coach Mac are in Suitland, Maryland, driving into Lincoln Cemetery where Coach Knight was laid to rest. They pull over on the side of the long narrow driveway, exit Coach Mac's 2014, unscratched, freshly washed Mercedes Benz ML350 SUV. They both came dressed especially for this occasion. Coach Mac, outfitted in professionally pressed navy blue slacks, a white button up shirt, and red silk tie tucked into his navy cashmere sweater, is wearing his old Howard Bison jersey on top. Chance, wearing a fitted sweat suit, also wears his jersey on top. In Chance's hand is the future jersey of the high school class of 2020's number two ranked basketball player who has verbally committed to Howard University.

"To have you be the one to bring his vision to life, man, I tell ya, God sure is good," Coach Mac says as they approach the gravesite.

"All the time."

Coach Mac pulls out the NCAA and MEAC Championship rings. He places them both on top of the headstone and leans over to touch it, scrolling his fingers across the engraving, *"Craig Martin Knight. Beloved Husband, Father, Coach, and Friend."*

"You were right all along, my dear friend. Chance and your AAU guys took the team straight to the top. Others are coming to HBCUs left and right. I feel your presence so strongly, my brother, and know you can see our jerseys—past, present, and future."

Coach Mac chuckles.

"The power schools are running scared, Craig, that they may be losing their golden eggs or rather their black gold," he adds.

Chance silently reflects on the months following his father's death. He thinks about how stoic he has appeared to be, but how overwhelming the pressure to fulfill his father's dream has actually been. He has never confided the enormity of it to anyone. He not only had to carry the future of the other recruits on his shoulders but, in his mind, the future of HBCUs. He had to right a wrong—the draining of black talent from black schools that needed the resources they could bring. He reflects on how much was at stake. If he had failed, then he would have been thought very foolish—a joke. He had carried the weight of the burden for far too long. He takes this moment to release those pent up emotions in a heartfelt conversation with Coach Mac.

"I know, Chance. I know, son. That's a lot to ask of anyone."

"I miss him so much, Coach." The pain is as raw as that dark Sunday when his father stopped to help, as he always did—but that time for the last time.

"Just know that he's looking down on you and he's thinking you're not only a champion on the court, but a hero to our community."

The coach and his player pick up the rings and head back to their cars. Check. All five goals are complete.

39 DRAFT NIGHT

The excitement is palpable on NBA draft night at Madison Square Garden in New York. The NBA Commissioner is standing on stage in front of the podium.

"With the number one pick in the 2020 NBA Draft, the New York Knicks select Chance Knight from Howard University."

The crowd erupts.

Chance, dressed in a new navy blue with black lapel tailored slim fit tuxedo, smiles. He hugs and kisses his mother, Amaia, and Kia. Kia is wearing a sparkling half karat diamond engagement ring she loves, but that Chance has promised to upgrade. Coach Mac and Walt step in for their embrace. Tasha, clad in a very becoming spicy red flowy maternity dress, stands beside Walt. Chance leans in and kisses her on the cheek.

"What up, little Walt Jr.?" asks Chance while staring at and gently touching Tasha's protruding belly.

Walt smiles.

Chance rubs the top of Teddy's head. He then walks up to the podium and shakes the Commissioner's hand. The Commissioner gives Chance a New York Knicks basketball cap and Chance places it on his head. They shake hands again as they turn and smile for the cameras. Chance steps down from the podium and a *Sports Highlight Center* reporter requests a live interview. Chance obliges.

"Congratulations, Chance," she says. "Wow. First you lead Howard as a freshman to its first ever national championship and tonight you have the high honor of being the first pick in the NBA draft. How does this moment feel?"

Chance puts his head down and places his hands over his face as he is bested by his emotions.

"I'm so sorry," he says.

"You don't need to apologize for anything. We all know what you've gone through to get here. Take your time."

"Thank you. It just feels so amazing, you know? I feel so blessed and grateful. I just wish my pops could be here with me. We had conversations about what this very moment was gonna feel like."

Chance drops his head and pauses for a second to compose himself.

"I just want to thank my pops because none of this would be possible without him. I also want to shout out Coach Mac who was a close friend of his when they played basketball together at Howard. He's the one who emphasized how important my dad's vision was and how important it would be for me to carry it out."

"Most people by now have heard about your father's vision. His vision was to have top rated black athletes go to HBCUs so that the HBCUs could benefit financially from showcasing their talent. You initiated that. You initiated making that dream a reality for HBCU basketball programs. And guess what? It's now crossing over sports. Top rated football and baseball players are coming as pairs and triples to HBCU programs. They want to ensure an immediate impact. A force multiplier like your Super Seven. At the pace this movement is growing, we can see major changes sooner rather than later. You know, as in epic. You have certainly passed the torch to the next group of athletes and the networks are paying very close attention to what their audience wants to see. What do you have to say about that?"

"It's thrilling. But, honestly, it saddens me that so many of our assets never make it back into our communities. Maybe if athletes can show what black empowerment can mean, we'll start supporting black businesses in a way that circulates money within our communities for more than six hours. We used to have thriving self-sustaining communities. After the civil rights movement, as it has been said, we gained political power but lost economic power. Somehow we lost our way. This isn't just about sports, but maybe our athletes can show us the way home."

The reporter is taken aback and wonders if Chance might not have a political life after basketball. She brings the conversation back to the moment.

"Chance, can you tell me what it was like to be at Howard?"

"Coach Mac had promised me that there is magic at an HBCU. I thought he was just talking about girls," Chance laughs at the memory and quickly adds, "I did find my fiancé there so that was definitely part of it. But the entire experience was magical . . . the pride in the black doctors, lawyers, executives, scientists who had once walked The Yard as students. The pride in knowing we are among the best and the brightest. Knowing that we are graded on merit and not skin color. Knowing we can fall asleep in the library and nobody is going to call the police on us, thinking we don't belong. Knowing friends made will have our backs over our lifetime. A place where anything is possible. And part of it is something you can only feel. It's indescribable.

I'm going to miss that magic, but Howard will forever be in my heart. It's the MECCA, baby! Like my pops always said, H-UUUUU!"

Chance pauses and looks up toward the ceiling.

"Thank you for everything, Pops. We did it! We really did it!"

EPILOGUE

five years later

Officer Sean Parker moved to West Virginia where he resides peacefully with his family. He still "protects and serves" on a small town police force.

Mike Jones and **Jason "J.J." Jacks** both entered the draft after one year at Howard University. Mike was the ninth pick in the first round. He was drafted by the Philadelphia 76ers and averages seventeen points a game and twelve rebounds. Jason was the fifteenth pick in the first round. He was drafted by the Brooklyn Nets and averages fourteen points and seven assists per game.

Deon played for Howard University all four years. He entered the draft following his senior season. He was the third pick of the second round. He is eighth man off of the bench for the Toronto Raptors.

Dink "Big Dink" Johnson entered the draft after his sophomore season but went undrafted. He was picked up as an undrafted free agent by the Golden State Warriors and later traded to the Washington Wizards.

He played one season for the Wizards before being cut and taking the position of Head Coach of the varsity boys basketball team at Capital Heights High School where he led the team to the State championship his first year coaching.

Maximus "Mad Max" Miller opted not to enter the draft. During his senior year of college, he was awarded a grant to fund a prototype for a bulletproof baseball cap that looks and feels like a regular cap. He sold the prototype to a successful tech startup company and now lives in Silicon Valley working as a product advisor earning a multi-million-dollar salary.

Bobby "Bird" Banks entered the draft after four years of playing for Howard. He was the last draft pick of the first round. Although he does not average a lot of court time for the Boston Celtics, he has proven himself to be a contributing role player. Bird and his long-term girlfriend, Shannon, just welcomed a baby boy named Bobby Craig Banks.

Charlie "Make America Great Again" was convicted on three counts of second degree murder in the deaths of the three locals. He was sentenced to sixty years in prison, eligible for parole after serving thirty-three. In a separate trial, Charlie was convicted and sentenced to life without the possibility of parole in the attempted murder of Walt Williams. He will spend the rest of his life behind bars in a state penitentiary. Surprisingly, all four shootings were deemed not to be hate crimes. Charlie proudly joined the Aryan Nation and quickly became a respected member in the prison system.

Billy reached out to Walt a year after the shooting. They have developed a special friendship.

Walt Williams played for one year at Howard University before becoming team manager. He was still able to maintain his college scholarship. After graduation, Walt joined Coach Mac's coaching staff. He and Tasha are happily married and rearing their daughter. Everyone predicted they would have a boy, but Victory Miracle Williams was born seven pounds, eleven ounces.

Tasha graduated from Howard University with a major in social work. She plans to eventually attend law school. She has remained faithful and in love. She and Walt are expecting their second child. They have confirmed that it is a boy.

"Two Ton Tina" continued to pine for Walt the remainder of his freshman year until she joined a running club. She lost an insane amount of weight and became Howard's Homecoming Queen her senior year. She is now a fitness model and married to a well-known actor. She still thinks of Walt and can often be found snooping through his pictures on social media.

Coach Mac led Howard to a second MEAC win. They swept through the NCAA tournament until finally narrowly falling to Duke University in the Final Four. Duke went on to win the NCAA championship. Howard University lost the MEAC the next year to Florida A&M, who made it to the NCAA Sweet Sixteen. In the years since, the MEAC has become an unpredictable free for all; most teams having at least three top-rated players.

Teddy remains cancer free. He now goes to Walt Disney World every year, courtesy of Chance. When riding roller coasters, he loves to feel the wind in his thick black hair.

Mrs. Williams remains blessed with two healthy sons. Although she wasn't thrilled that at eighteen years old Walt was expecting a child, she is affectionately known as Nana to her favorite little one. She cannot wait for the arrival of her grandson, although she cannot imagine loving someone as much as her granddaughter.

April Knight now lives in Potomac, Maryland. She has taken up golf and is a member of an elite golf club.

Amaia attends Howard University on a full academic scholarship and has an "awesome" wardrobe.

Kia is now Kia Knight. She and Chance live

more than comfortably in New York City. She is carrying their first child, a son, perfectly timed with Walt and Tasha's. She transferred to Columbia University and received her degree in business. She graduated with high honors.

Chance was the NBA Rookie of the Year. He averaged twenty-two points, five rebounds, and three assists. He has since gone on to easily make the All-Star team each year. He is touted as one of the best players in the league. Every year he provides Howard University with a sizeable donation.

Coach Craig Knight's vision is a work in progress. The increasing number of top level athletes at HBCUs has generated excitement among HBCU alumni and students, and forced "powerhouse" schools to reevaluate their commitment to and respect for the needs of minority athletes. Revenue from HBCU sports paraphernalia has increased significantly. NBA scouts regularly visit HBCUs with ranked basketball players, and the players are repeatedly showcased on national television. Self-empowerment, awareness, and pride dominate the HBCU campuses because premier athletes are *choosing* them and "coming home."

Made in the USA
Middletown, DE
30 June 2022